Trying to Make the World a Better Place

Becky Bexley
The Child Genius
1

Diana Holbourn

Becky passes on advice on bullying, mental health problems, psychic frauds and more

Windy
Seaside
Publishing

Cover design, book design and formatting by Gareth Southwell
art.garethsouthwell.com

First edition June 2023

ISBN (paperback): 978-1-7391809-2-8
ISBN (ebook): 978-1-7391809-3-5

First published 2022 by Windy Seaside Publishing

Contents

Chapter 1

Becky Helps a Boy Stop Other Kids Teasing Him

Becky Bexley was allegedly a child genius who could talk quite well as soon as she was born, owing to her mum being so talkative she managed to pick up a lot of words in the womb. Equally as improbably, she was supposedly such a genius she managed to go to junior school at the age of one, and to senior school at the age of three.

She was a legend. Or at least this story could be said to be one ... because you know what legends are like: they tend to be rather far-fetched ...

But a lot of what Becky did wasn't so legendary.

When she first went to senior school, which was just a couple of years after the start of this millennium, her mum stayed with her for a while in case she got bullied, thinking that since all the other kids were so much bigger than her, if any of them did decide to bully her physically, she probably wouldn't stand much of a chance against them, since after all, she was only three, allegedly. But when it seemed that her class was quite friendly, her mum let Becky stay there on her own.

A few kids treated Becky like a strange monster at first, just staring anxiously from a distance at what they thought was the oddity, too nervous to go nearer, since they'd never even dreamed that it could be possible that a three-year-old could know as much as they did and be in lessons with them. But they got used to her, and eventually thought of her as a heroic figure whose wisdom exceeded that of some of the teachers.

There were just a few kids who could be unpleasant, not just to Becky, but also to others in the class. For instance, there was one boy who'd broken his leg a couple of months earlier, and had come back to school, but walked with a limp. A couple of other boys made fun of the way he walked, and laughed at him. Also, they made fun of the packed lunches he brought to school, till he became ashamed of them.

Becky first discovered they were doing that after she spotted a packed lunch in the bin. She wondered what could have been wrong with it. But when she spotted another one there the next day, and another the day after, she began to ask questions.

The first people she asked didn't know who they belonged to. But then a boy said they were his. At first, Becky felt annoyed that he was wasting good food, and told him crossly that it wasn't a nice thing to do, and that if he didn't like his lunch, he should give it to someone else, or ask his mum to make him different things to bring to school.

But he said it wasn't that he didn't like it. He said he'd become too embarrassed to eat it, and worried about what people would think, since one boy had told him his egg sandwiches looked like vomit. He said he felt as if he couldn't tell his mum that's what they'd said. And the same boy who'd told him that and a friend of his would laugh at him and call him a goodie-goodie, because his mum would give him snack packs of nuts and fruit to eat instead of the salty snacks and chocolate bars others were given. So he'd just come to think his lunch wasn't as good as theirs and was ashamed to eat it, because he thought he'd never be cool enough to fit in with his friends and the others if he ate food they looked down on, and thought eating it would just make them pick on him.

Becky felt sorry for him, and said, "It sounds as if they're just being mean because they think it's fun. Did you think your sandwiches looked like vomit?"

The boy said no. So Becky said, "Then how do you know anyone else thinks they do, besides those boys – if they even really do? What if everyone in the class was asked whether they do, and no one said they thought so except those two boys? Would you take their word over the word of nearly thirty other people? When someone says something nasty, it doesn't mean it's the truth; it often just means it's their opinion, and a lot of opinions are just plain wrong. A lot of opinions aren't even sensible. But loads of people can believe them anyway. So even if quite a few kids in the class made fun of your sandwiches, it still wouldn't mean those kids were right, or talking sense. Lots of people believe stupid things. I mean, take the millions and millions of people who thought Hitler's opinions were great, when really they were not only wrong, but they were a pile of nonsense! People believe silly things sometimes."

(Unfortunately, the school curriculum didn't take account of the fact that not just Becky, but the normal-aged children in her class might be at too sensitive an age to be able to take in the gruesomeness of such topics as what the Nazis did without being at risk of being disturbed, and they'd been taught them regardless.)

Becky continued, "And people often laugh at things that don't deserve to be laughed at at all. Imagine if a few hundred years ago, someone had said they reckoned that one day people would walk on the moon. A lot of people might have laughed at them and told them not to be so stupid, and given reasons why they were sure it was impossible. And yet, today we know people have walked on the moon. Even if those boys laugh at you and sound as if they're sure what they're saying's true, you don't have to believe them. Those opinions certainly sound like nonsense to me."

The boy looked thoughtful, and said he could see the sense in what Becky was saying.

She continued, "And being made fun of makes you think your lunch isn't good enough and throw it away, but how do you know those boys aren't laughing at you just as much for throwing it away as they would if you ate it? You could be going hungry every day of the school year, only to discover they didn't think throwing your lunch away was better than eating it, but in fact they laughed at you even more for it, just behind your back. It's not worth trying to please them. Besides, it might just make them feel all powerful and want to bully you more and more for fun, to see what else they can make you do. It's not fair, but that's the way some people think. They get their kicks from trying to make people do what they want – I've been reading about it. So it's better to stand up to them."

The boy didn't look hopeful, and asked how he could do that.

4

Becky said, "If you seem confident and they don't think they're bothering you, they might get bored and go away. I mean, if you start eating your sandwiches in full view of everyone and they come up and laugh and say they look like vomit, maybe you could say something like, 'Well they're obviously not vomit, are they, otherwise I'd be ill and have to spend time off school. Besides, I don't think they look like vomit, and they certainly don't taste like it, and that's the important thing. Besides, it's my opinion that counts, since I'm the one eating them.' It won't be any fun for them teasing someone who just doesn't take what they're saying seriously, but just thinks it doesn't make much sense, and isn't bothered by it."

The boy thought that sounded like a good idea, but wasn't sure he had the confidence to stand up to the boys, since being laughed at made him feel so bad. And he said that wasn't the only thing they made fun of; he didn't like it when they laughed and called him a goodie-goodie for having fruit and nuts in his packed lunches instead of chocolate and crisps.

Becky said that sounded like a silly accusation, and suggested that next time they called him that, he could ask them just what was wrong with wanting to be healthy; and if he enjoyed eating the fruit and nuts, he could tell them so, and say he didn't see why he shouldn't eat them if he liked them. She advised him to speak in quite a serious tone of voice, calm but determined if he could, since if he sounded as if he was sneering at them, they might get offended and say worse things; and if they thought he was getting hot-and-bothered, they'd think they were about to witness some fun, because they probably thought of riling people up till they got into a temper as fun, so they might say worse things to get more.

Becky said they might not even believe anything they said; they might just be saying it because bullying could be a kind of addiction in a way, where the challenge of thinking about how to react to whatever the person being teased said when they became agitated and offended by it in a way that meant the bullies would come out looking good would bring some excitement into their lives, so they'd want to tease them some more for the adrenaline buzz that gave them. She said the boys doing the teasing might not be saying what they were saying because they thought it somehow needed to be said, but just because they knew it would get them the reaction that would mean they'd start to have the fun and the adrenaline buzz. So the boy could be thinking the bullying was about his food, when all along, it was just about the bullies thinking they were going to get a bit of fun by teasing him.

But Becky told the boy that even if they did believe what they were saying, it shouldn't matter to him; if they made unkind comments, he could remember that even if they meant them, the fact that they believed them didn't mean they were right, and that even most of the rest of the people in the world might think differently. And if they told him that didn't matter because all the sensible people would think the same way as they did, he could ask them where the evidence for that was. Becky suggested he could ask the teasers whether they thought they would really think some of their opinions were sensible if they had a good think about them.

The boy said he liked the sound of what Becky was saying, but that he'd still feel nervous around them, and that another reason he didn't feel good about himself was that they made fun of the way he walked, and imitated his limp, and laughed at it.

Becky suggested he try asking them questions and saying things like, "Why is it funny that I have to walk with a limp? It's just because I broke my leg and it hasn't healed up properly yet. If you broke your leg, you'd have to walk like me too. You wouldn't want anyone to laugh at you, would you. It wouldn't be fair if anyone did, since you wouldn't be able to help it. Imagine how you'd feel if you were recovering from a broken leg and had to walk with a limp, and you got teased."

Becky also said that if he didn't feel confident, he could try pretending to be confident, holding his head up and just imagining he was full of confidence; and if he found that talking back to the bullies worked, then he'd likely develop confidence for real after a while.

The boy said he'd try.

Then Becky said, "Another way you could try responding is by saying things that make it sound as if you're agreeing with the teasers, or at least understanding why they think what they do. I know you won't feel like doing that, especially if you know full well they're trying to be mean and it's upsetting you. But they might stop feeling like teasing you if you talk about what they're saying as if it's just an ordinary point of view that's not worth getting agitated about, like whether baked potatoes taste better if they're cooked in the oven or in the microwave.

"This is the kind of thing I mean: Next time they tell you they think your egg sandwiches look like vomit, you could maybe say something matter-of-factly like, 'Yeah, I suppose they might look a bit like that; but they're not really vomit, and they taste nice, and they're quite healthy as well, so I like them.'

"Or when they accuse you of being a goodie-goodie for eating fruit and nuts instead of crisps, maybe you could say something like, 'I can understand how you might think that, I suppose, but they're nice, so I like eating them.'

"And next time they say you walk funny, maybe you could say something like, 'Yes, perhaps my walk does look a bit funny; but it's just the way people have to walk when they're recovering from a broken leg'.

"And if they accuse you of other things, you could try saying the same kinds of things, like, 'Yes, I can understand why you might feel that way, but I like them anyway', or, 'Yes, I can understand you thinking it looks that way, but it's just the way I'll be doing things for now'.

"They might actually respect you more for standing up for yourself than they would for changing your behaviour because of what they think. Or they might decide you're not so easy and fun to tease any more because they realise they haven't got any influence over you any more, so they might stop bothering to.

"They might try saying worse things at first to try and get a flustered reaction from you again so they can have fun; but if you respond to everything they say in a way that sounds boring, like by just saying things like, 'Well, we all have our opinions', then maybe they'll decide you're no fun to tease any more, so they'll stop. It might be worth a try anyway.

"Or you could make it sound as if you're well aware of what they think, but that they're making a big deal out of nothing, by saying things in a bored-sounding voice like,

'Yeah yeah, my egg sandwiches look like vomit; I know; I know', or, 'Yeah yeah, my walk looks funny; I know; I know. Yeah, it looks weird; I know.'

"Or you could try making a joke of things. If they're just teasing you because they think it's fun, then if you can make them laugh, they might get as much fun by being entertained by you as they do by teasing you, so they won't feel the need to tease you any more; or they'll like you better so they won't want to. You might even get to be friends.

"I know it sounds as if it would be a hard thing to do; and it's possible they might just mock you if they don't think your jokes are funny, so that'll make it worse. I know how that feels a little bit, since something like that happened to me a while ago; you know that girl Cindy who calls people cowbags sometimes? She's called me a cowbag a few times, and once when she did, I thought that sounded like a funny insult and said, 'How many cows have I got in me?' She got scornful and said that was a silly thing to say. She was probably so used to using the word she didn't get the joke. But oddly enough, I haven't heard her using the word since. Maybe she thought about it afterwards and realised it sounded like a funny insult. I don't know.

"But here's the kind of thing I'm thinking you could try: When you're about to eat your egg sandwiches, if you see the teasers looking as if they're about to tease you for it again, you could maybe declare to them, 'I'm about to eat my vomity egg sandwiches now. I could be in the circus. Imagine an announcer with a microphone loudly proclaiming to the audience, 'And now, watch the boy who's not scared to eat vomit! This must be the bravest boy in the world, a boy who's not afraid of gobbling down vomit sandwiches! Yum yum!'"

The boy said he'd think about giving those things a go. But then he said, "Sometimes, people aren't just expressing opinions though, or at least, I wouldn't like to say, 'Oh well, that's just your opinion', or make a joke of things, or sound as if they aren't bothering me. I've been bullied online as well as by people in school. I thought it would be nice to play a game with people online, who I didn't know; but I've been put off it a bit, because whenever I started winning, I got people saying horrible things. I even got one saying he'd like to come and kill me!"

Becky said, "That's horrible! Maybe there are moderators you could report people like that to on the websites where you want to play games; or maybe you could block them, so you don't have to put up with them any more. But anyway, try not to take the bullying personally if you can; it says more about what kind of people they are than it says about you. I know it must come as a bit of a shock when people say that kind of thing to you when you aren't expecting it, so it must be hard not to take it personally; but try and remember it's probably just some troll getting carried away. Maybe you could think of things you can plan to say back to them whenever they say things like that to you, like, 'Wow, you must be a terrible loser if you would even like to kill me because I'm beating you in the game! Wow, how did you get to be such a terrible loser? Did you learn to be such a bad loser from your parents? Are they terrible losers too?'

"If they tell you to leave their parents out of it, maybe you could say things like, 'But I'm curious to know how you got to be the kind of person who wants to talk to people like that. Do your parents talk to you like that? Is that where you learned to talk to other people like that? I feel sorry for you if your parents do talk to you like that. Would you prefer it if you'd been taken away at birth and given to nicer parents? Or are they not all that bad really?'

". . . Well, I don't suppose you'll be able to say all that at once, or you'll end up not having time to play the game any more; but you know the kind of thing I mean. Some of the bullies might really have come from families who say horrible things to them a lot; so sometimes, they might really deserve to have people feeling sorry for them. You never know, there might be some who even tell you they have come from homes where their parents talk to them like that, and you might end up feeling sorry for them for real. Mind you, nothing they say will be an excuse for them carrying on bullying you."

The boy grew thoughtful, and said, "That's an interesting way of looking at things."

But then Becky said, "Mind you, I suppose you'd have to be careful what you said to them, since they might have friends who might start being horrible to you too if they think you're not being very nice to their friend, so you'd have a worse problem. Maybe it would be best to mostly just talk back to them in your mind, thinking of what you'd like to say to them, but just ignoring what they've said and not really responding to it, or writing it down afterwards if it's still bothering you, and then writing things to make fun of it that'll cheer you up, or writing something to tell yourself why you shouldn't let it bother you, or writing about it to report it to a moderator on the website or something."

The boy said he'd have a think about that.

Lastly, Becky said, "You've been feeling bad about yourself and the things you've been doing here because of what the teasers in the class say and the way they make fun of you, but don't ever forget that They're the ones in the wrong, not you! They've been making you feel bad about yourself all this time, when really, they've been the ones doing the bad things, just because it makes them feel important when they know they can have that effect on people, or it gives them a laugh or something! You've been wasting nice food, just because a few boys in the class like to have a laugh by bullying someone!"

The boy became a bit angry, thinking about them wanting to just have a laugh at his expense, and all the nice food he'd wasted. Suddenly he felt full of confidence, when only a minute before he'd felt as if he didn't have any, because the anger gave him new energy and determination; and he made up his mind to absolutely stand up to those boys next time!

He felt a lot better for his talk with Becky. And though he felt nervous again the next time he saw the boys, because his anger and determination had died down, he tried talking back to them in the way she'd advised him to. To his surprise, it worked. Not straightaway, but after a little while. When the boys finally realised he wasn't going to get upset by what they said any more and that he had answers that made them feel silly, even though he didn't seem to be trying to make them feel silly, they left him alone.

The boy felt especially comforted because Becky had asked him if he'd be willing for her and him to tell other friendly children in the class what had happened and ask for their support, and he'd agreed. When they did, several said they'd back the boy up; and the next time the bullies laughed at his packed lunch and told him his egg sandwiches looked like vomit, they were standing nearby, and told the teasers they didn't think they looked like it. That reassured the boy that he didn't have to feel inferior to everyone else as he'd started to before, because it wasn't really as if everyone else in the class thought he was uncool for eating what he did. And the bullies didn't fancy standing up to several children at once, so that was another reason why they stopped pestering the boy after a while. They were embarrassed when they found out that a girl who was years younger than them had inspired the changes they were seeing around them.

Chapter 2

Becky Helps Make her School's Anti-Bullying Strategy Better

Not long after Becky joined the senior school, allegedly at the unlikely age of three, or thereabouts, she found herself sorting out problems the grown-ups should really have dealt with, but they didn't seem to know how to.

When she was four – or at least some age or other – there was a small boy in her class who was being bullied by three other boys, one of whom was the ringleader. They would ambush him in the toilets and push his head into one, calling him a boffin for being good at maths, as if that was somehow an insult. Becky asked the maths teacher, who was also their form teacher, why she didn't do anything about it. The teacher said she didn't know what to do. She said she had heard reports that it was going on for a while, but would feel awkward going into the boys' toilets to find out if it was true or to catch the boys at it.

Becky told her she was sure there must be other ways of dealing with it. She said it seemed from some things she'd heard that the ringleader felt inadequate because he was sure he was no good at maths, and he was jealous of the boy who was, and that was why he was bullying him and had convinced the others to as well. She suggested that if the teacher tried to build up his confidence at doing maths and he realised he was better at it than he'd thought, he might not see the point in bullying the smaller boy any more, since he wouldn't be envious of him any more, and there would be no point in bullying someone for doing something well that you could do well yourself.

She suggested the teacher give him easier work than the rest of the class for a while, not telling him it was easier, but making sure it would be something she knew he could do; and when he'd done it right, she should praise him a lot for it, so he'd become more enthusiastic about doing it and more confident he could; and the work he was given could slowly become more difficult at his pace, so he would stay confident, and wouldn't feel as if he couldn't cope any more.

The teacher thought it was a good idea and tried it. It seems it worked, because to her surprise, within a few weeks, he and the other boys had stopped bullying the smaller boy. The teacher thanked Becky for coming up with the idea.

There was a boy in the class who took inspiration from the idea after Becky privately mentioned it to him, and managed to stop another boy bullying him, a boy who'd started making spiteful remarks to him just after he'd got some expensive new shoes. He couldn't understand why the boy was being mean at first, but then he started wondering if he might just be jealous of his nice-looking shoes. He thought that would be silly, since the boy's own shoes looked quite nice. But he decided to compliment him on them and see if it made him feel better about them, or more friendly towards him, so it would help. So he did. He didn't have a high expectation that it would work, but to his surprise, the boy didn't make spiteful remarks to him any more.

Some bullies weren't so easy to deal with though. Some seemed to be cruel by nature. It seemed to Becky that they weren't being disciplined for it well at all, and she went to the headmaster and told him the school ought to have a better anti-bullying strategy. The headmaster said she was probably right, but that he didn't really know what to do for the best. Becky said she had some ideas, partly based on one or two books she'd read about good ways for schools to deal with bullying, and that she'd help him devise a good policy. He said that might be helpful, and thanked her.

She said that for a start, the common punishment of sending the bullies all out together litter picking in the school grounds after lessons didn't work, because she'd seen them all having a laugh together, enjoying the opportunity to be with each other. The headmaster looked thoughtful, and then agreed that something different would be better, saying that for a start, each one would be sent out on their own from then on.

Becky said she was pleased about that. Then she suggested other things too:

She said she thought it might help to change some kids' behaviour if with every bullying incident they were told off for, if they admitted to it – either at first or after persuasion – they were instructed to phone their parents and own up to it. She said,

"It seems that a lot of bullies lie to their parents and say they were wrongfully punished by teachers, and their parents automatically side with them and get angry with the teachers.

If the bullies could be persuaded to actually phone their parents up and admit to what they'd done, that would stop happening.

"If that policy's introduced, then a teacher, or whoever's given the job of doing it, can speak to the bullies' parents on the phone as well as them, or instead of them if they absolutely refuse to speak to them themselves; and before they phone them up, they can give the bullies an incentive to be honest if they don't want to own up to their bullying, by giving them a little bit of time to think, saying something like, 'I'm just going to do something in another part of the room for a few minutes; and when I've finished, I'll ask you what you did again. If you own up to it, then when I phone your parents, I'll be able to tell them you told the truth about it. But if you still deny the bullying, I'm going to ask everyone who witnessed it what happened; and if I decide you did do it, I'll tell your parents you didn't tell the truth about it.'

"Chances are they will own up to it after that. If some of them don't, they can be asked again after the investigation into their behaviour's done, and told that the teacher will still be able to tell their parents something nice about them by letting them know they told the truth if they own up to it. More of the pupils might do it then.

"When the parents are phoned up, the bully can tell them what kind of discipline they got for their bullying, so their parents will know they weren't just allowed to get away with it, so they might be less likely to think they ought to punish them at home.

"If the bullies feel awkward about thinking up just what to say when they phone their parents, they can be given the opportunity to practise first."

Becky said that another part of the anti-bullying strategy could be to separate bullies from the others under staff supervision for a while, either for a lunch hour or for longer, depending on how severe the bullying had been.

She suggested there could be a detailed list of consequences for various kinds of typical bad behaviour printed out and put up in each classroom, so pupils would know what they'd get for each thing they did wrong if they were found out, so they might have more of a think about whether to do those things before they did. It would also mean teachers would know what to do, and wouldn't have to make punishments up on the spur of the moment, and then possibly face the anger of bullies who were being punished worse than someone who'd done the same thing the week before but didn't get punished as badly.

She said all the children could be asked to read the rules at the start of each year, and confirm they thought they were fair, perhaps signing them, or else raise objections to them that could be discussed if they were sensible, with the possibility of the rules being slightly altered if children made good points.

Becky said, "If a bully who gets challenged about their behaviour starts claiming that the person they bullied did something to them first, they might just be trying to get out of being disciplined for it. If the teacher they say that to doesn't really believe them, or doesn't know whether to, it's best if they don't get into an argument with them about whether they're telling the truth right there and then, because it could end up being a distraction from the procedure of questioning them about their own behaviour and disciplining them for it, which might be exactly what a bully's bringing it up to try to achieve.

"So if a bully claims they were bullied first, a teacher can say to them something like, 'You can tell me about that later. First I want to hear about what you did.' They can also tell them that even if the other person did do something first, there are ways they could have dealt with it other than by bullying them. That'll help them learn that even if someone did do something to them they didn't like, they still have responsibility for their actions.

"Then after the bully's been disciplined, they can be asked what the other person did. If the person they bullied didn't really do anything first, or nothing that was that important, the bully might well drop their accusation, since there won't be any point in it any more if it was only a way to try to get out of being disciplined."

Becky also said she thought bullies needed to be made to have a serious think about what they were doing and how it was affecting their victims. She suggested that in their detention or time spent separated from other students under staff supervision, they could be made to fill in a form about what they did and why it was wrong, what effect they thought it might have had on their victims, the reasons they wanted to bully, and harmless ways they could achieve the same kind of satisfaction they got from it.

She said there could be several options they could choose from as part of some of the questions on the form, as well as boxes where they could write any reasons that weren't included in the options. For instance, with the question about why they bullied, there could be several suggestions, such as whether the issue they had was boredom, a desire for amusement, the wish to get to feel good by experiencing any sense of power over others they got from tormenting or attacking them, a desire to get anger out of their systems, or whatever. They could tick more than one option. Then there could be an option for them to write other reasons. Then there could be space for them to go into detail about the reasons they'd given.

The headmaster said, "Hang on, let me write this down, before I forget it all! This is beginning to sound like too much detail for me to remember!"

Becky patiently waited for him to get something to write on and start making notes.

Then she suggested that the question on the bullying form after the one that asked the bullies why they liked to bully other kids could ask them what harmless ways they could think of to get whatever it was they got out of bullying. She said the teacher supervising them could give them guidance if they couldn't think of much.

For instance, if they said they bullied for fun, they could be asked to think up other ways of having fun that would be just as enjoyable for them but wouldn't harm anyone; or if they said they bullied out of boredom, they could be helped to think of ways of making their lives more interesting so they wouldn't feel the need to try to make them more lively by bullying people. Or if they said they were bullying someone because that person kept doing things deliberately that provoked them, and the teacher thought they might well be telling the truth rather than just making excuses, they could be helped to think of other ways of dealing with the problem, and a teacher could offer to look into the behaviour of the other person and see if they themselves needed disciplining. And they could offer to investigate any other problem the bullies said someone else was causing them, where help from a wiser person would be useful.

As the headmaster alternately jotted down notes and thoughtfully scratched his head, Becky said, "The teacher supervising a bully when they're filling out the bullying form could ask them questions about the answers they've put on it, to find out more about them. And actually, whenever they see or find out about pupils bullying other pupils, they could ask the bullies privately right there and then about the real in-depth reasons why they're bullying, if they've got time then. If the bullies give silly reasons, like saying, 'I bully them because they're stupid', the teacher could say to them, 'Even if they really are stupid, which they're probably not, why does it make them deserving of being bullied?' and ask them more and more questions till they find out the real reason why they're bullying, if the bullies even know themselves!

"Having said that, it might be best to wait till they've had a cooling-off period before they're spoken to, in the hope that they're not feeling so aggressive and argumentative as they were right after the bullying happened by that time, so they're less likely to just argue with the teacher. There's also some benefit to waiting till after they've been disciplined before having that conversation with them, so they don't use it to pretend to be sorry for what they did just to try and get out of being punished, and so they're less likely to deny what they did to try to get out of it.

"If there's a group of bullies having a go at someone, it'll probably be best if they're interviewed about it one by one, not all together, because sometimes some of them might admit to reasons why they do it when they're on their own that they'd be too embarrassed to admit to in front of their friends. And it might be easier to reason with a lot of them on their own than it will be when they're all together, because they might want to look tough in front of their friends, so they might be less likely to admit to being in the wrong, and less open to persuasion to change then."

The headmaster said thoughtfully, "That's a good point."

Encouraged, Becky continued, "From a few things I've read, it seems that not all bullies bully because they want to be nasty. I think there might be all kinds of reasons for it. One seems to be that some of them feel kind of insecure sometimes, and they try to put people they feel uncomfortable around down as a way of getting to feel better in some way.

"I'm not really sure what might be going on in their minds, but maybe if their subconscious motives could talk to the person they're bullying – somehow managing it without being shushed by the bully to stop them revealing the truth about how they were acting tough but full of weaknesses like insecurities really, they'd say something like, 'There's something about you, or the way I feel about something about you, because of a prejudice I've picked up or something else, that's making me feel a bit nervous and uncomfortable or inferior or ignorant around you, because I'm not sure why things are the way they are, so it seems a bit strange to me, and I don't like that; or I know you're much better at something than I am, so I feel as if I could be shown up as being much less skilled than you are at it; and I know that if I tease you and get the better of you, I'll stop feeling so uncomfortable around you, because I'll know the thing that worries me won't bother me so much, because I'll know I can so easily get the better of you in one way at least.'

"Well, that's the way the bullying might sometimes start anyway, and then some bullies might realise they enjoy bullying so much they don't want to stop."

The headmaster asked, "Do you really think that kind of thing might be going on around here?"

Becky said, "I bet it's possible. And a psychology book or article I read says that if what's bothering the bullies makes them feel uncomfortable, it doesn't necessarily have to be something strange; it could be, say, that someone's hair's all fallen out because they've had cancer and their chemotherapy made it fall out, and the bullies don't understand why it did that, and that makes them feel ignorant, or spooked that such a thing could happen, so it makes them want to get their confidence back by doing something that'll make them feel as if they've got one up on the person. I know that sounds a bit strange, but I think that's the way some people's minds work, for some reason. Well, it's probably because it's just instinct to try to get rid of an uncomfortable feeling as quickly as possible, instead of taking the time to decide what would be the most sensible way of getting rid of it and then doing that, which would mean it would hang around for longer before it was got rid of.

"I think it's common for people to try to get rid of bad feelings in quick ways instead of the best ways in all kinds of situations really. You probably do it yourself in some ways. I mean, how many times have you, say, felt a bit depressed and immediately reached for a chocolate bar to make yourself feel better, instead of working out what's really wrong, and only then trying to get rid of the feeling? . . . Well alright, you don't have to answer that one if you don't want to.

"Mind you, sometimes that's not a bad idea, actually, like if someone's just starting to feel a bit down because they're brooding on things someone said to them that were a bit mean, and just brooding on them more will make them feel worse, but they'll feel better if they soothe themselves with some chocolate or something and then move on to doing something else.

"But what I'm saying is that if bullies know that bullying gets rid of an uncomfortable feeling quickly, their instinct will naturally be to do that, instead of to think of better ways to get rid of the feeling, which might take longer, if they can even think of any at all. So it'll be good if teachers help them think of some that they can use in the future, if they find out after some questioning that that's the reason they're bullying.

"Another thing is that because some people might bully others because something's making them feel uncomfortable around them, even though it doesn't have to, sometimes, if someone's got something a bit unusual about them, I think it can put some people who have an instinct to bully them at ease if they're given encouragement and the time to stand up in front of the class and explain all about it, so everyone understands it better, if they feel alright doing that. Or some bullies could just be encouraged to read about people's personal experiences of it on the Internet, if it's bothering them.

"It might not always work; the teasers might sometimes just carry on teasing the person with the unusual character-istic anyway because they think it's fun; but it might often be worth a try.

"But as for trying to understand bullies better in general, so you can know more about what they can be asked about when they're being interviewed by the teachers at a time such as during their detention when they're filling out the bullying form, I think another reason some bullies bully is because they know it gets them advantages. For instance, if they want extra money, they'll know yelling and threatening or attacking will intimidate a lot of people into giving them theirs. Their yelling might make them look bad-tempered or crazy; but really they're doing it deliberately because they know it intimidates people into giving them what they want. Some of them might have learned to behave that way because they've picked up the habit from one or both of their parents who behave like it.

"And something related is that I think another reason people can bully is if they've been badly treated by other people, such as where they get bullied themselves at home; or it can sometimes be that they've witnessed or been involved in things that have made them angry, like big family arguments; and they want to get their anger about those things out of their systems, or being bullied themselves makes them feel a bit powerless, and they feel like compensating for that by doing things to make themselves feel as if they're the ones in the positions of power over other people, because that feels especially satisfying after they've been made to feel a bit powerless, so they do that by fighting people and intimidating them, and things like that.

"If you come across what seem to be serious cases of bullies actually being bullied themselves by their families, it might sometimes be appropriate to get social services involved.

"Teachers could maybe ask bullies all kinds of questions about whether things like that are happening in their lives, and whether those things are some of the reasons why they're being bullies. Not that the bullies should be automatically believed, because some of them might just be making up stories as excuses for bullying, in the hope of getting sympathy so they're treated more leniently for it in future. Still, if that kind of conversation's taking place after they've been given their main form of discipline, and if they know the consequences for different types of bullying are always the same no matter what, to teach pupils that they still have responsibility for their actions, that'll probably be less likely to happen.

"And you could tell teachers that if they're interviewing a bully and they give them one reason why they've been bullying, it'll be best if they don't assume that's the only one; the bully might just be telling them about the one they're least ashamed to admit to, or the one they think will be the least unacceptable to them, or just using the first excuse that comes into their head. So teachers should always ask them what other reasons they've got for bullying too, and ask for more and more reasons till the bully says there aren't any more."

The headmaster said he thought what Becky said was interesting, promising to give it some thought.

Becky also suggested that the younger classes could have lessons where the pupils were split up into groups where they did such things as role plays, where all the kids in turn could play the role of a victim being bullied, which would mean the bullies would do that as well, and it would hopefully give them more insight into how it felt to be bullied, if they didn't already have some, at least if they put some imagination into it or it stirred up some feelings in them, so they might start caring more about the feelings of victims, since they might understand them better and realise they were worse than they'd thought, so they might not want to bully anyone any more, although it was possible that the most sadistic ones might enjoy bullying even more if they realised they were having more of an effect than they thought. Becky said it was something a lot of thought would have to go into before it was tried.

Just then the bell went for lessons to start again, and Becky said she had to go; but the headmaster asked her to come back as soon as possible after school to suggest and discuss more ideas with him. Becky agreed to, and rushed back at the end of school to tell him about other things she'd thought of, including recommending he find a way to have the teachers trained to advise teasing victims about ways of standing up to teasing that wasn't that serious, in a similar way to the way she'd advised the boy who was being teased about his packed lunches and the way he walked.

Then she said, "I read about a thing one teacher did that stopped a whole class from wanting to bully a girl who'd been bullied a lot by some of them before. I don't know how often the kind of thing the teacher did would work; the children in her class were only about seven or eight, I think, and maybe a lot of older ones wouldn't care about what the teacher said and the girl's feelings so much; I don't know. But it might be worth teachers being told about what she did, to give them the idea to try something like it if they think it might help:

"What happened was that there was a girl in the class this teacher taught who she said looked and behaved and talked a bit differently from the other kids. The teacher didn't say just what the differences were. But she said she heard that the girl was often being called names like spastic and moron. She'd tried to stop the bullying before, but nothing had changed. Then one day, a friend of the girl told her about names the girl was being called that she hadn't heard before, and she spoke to the girl who was being bullied, who told her about even more names she was being called; so she realised the bullying was worse than she'd thought. She decided something just had to be done straightaway.

"She had an idea. She spoke to another teacher about it, and asked if she would take part in her plan, and the teacher said she would. Then she asked the bullied girl and her friend if they'd like to go and help that teacher with her younger students for the afternoon. They loved the idea, and went off to her class.

"While they were away, the teacher announced to the other students that she had something very serious to tell them about one of the children in the class, and that she was very sad about it. She told them who it was, and said that she'd heard that the girl who'd been bullied had been called a lot of unkind names, and that she was going to write on the board every bad name she'd heard people call her or been told that she'd been called. She wrote names like cow, stupid and moron. Then she asked them to tell her what names they'd heard the girl being called, and she wrote those on the board too; and soon the board was packed with unkind words, things like slow, mental and crazy. She wanted the class to know just how bad the bullying was.

"She said the kids looked shocked to see all the unkind names and other words, and they started whispering to each other about how horrible it was.

"The teacher was upset about the nasty words too, and said they made her feel like crying, and asked any of the children who felt the same way to put their hands up. They all did. I don't know if some only did because they thought they'd look mean if they didn't, since it would have to have meant the bullies put their hands up too; but still.

"Then the teacher asked them how they thought those names must be making the girl feel. They came up with words like sad, hurt and depressed, and phrases like 'not wanting to come to school'. She wrote those on the board too.

"Then she asked them what the bad words must make the bullied girl think about herself. They didn't know, so she asked whether they thought she'd believe the words were true. They all didn't think she would. But the teacher told them that actually, the girl would believe they were true, since if a person gets told they're a certain way enough times, like that they're ugly or stupid, they'll start to believe it.

"The kids were surprised. They hadn't realised that. The teacher told them their words had so much power they could even change the way people felt about themselves.

"Then she said, 'How can we fix this?'

"The class asked her if they could write cards and letters to the girl saying nice things. She said they could. She had some nice-looking paper in different colours that she said they could choose from, and they were all enthusiastic to make the cards, and they all made the girl really nice ones. She told the pupils who'd actually called her unkind names to apologise in their cards, and they did. She said it would be nice if the children could say lots of nice things about the girl, so she would have those to think about instead of the nasty words.

"They all wanted to start encouraging the girl instead of being unkind, and said they'd stand up for her on the playground if they heard other people bullying her from then on.

"Near the end of the afternoon, the teacher called the teacher whose class the girl and her friend had been in and said they could come back. She told her class not to say much to the girl right then, saying she'd give her all the cards in a big envelope when it was time for them to go home.

"When the time came, she took the girl aside and said she'd had a talk to the class about how she'd been bullied, and that they were all sorry and had said it would stop from then on, and they'd made her some nice cards. She could see the girl felt like crying. She gave her the envelope and told her she could read all the cards when she got home. The girl went away happily.

"Maybe that kind of technique wouldn't work with everyone. I suppose it could have easily gone the other way, with the kids sniggering at all the bad names and saying the girl deserved them, and arguing with the teacher if she tried to defend her. A teacher who wondered whether to use a technique like that would probably have to think about how likely it was that the kids in their class would be sympathetic, or if it was more likely that they wouldn't care. But still, it might be worth some teachers thinking about it, to decide if something like that might work with the children in their class. And even if some of the kids didn't care and just sneered at the bad names, it's possible that the weight of all the other kids' caring opinions might make them think they ought to stop bullying if they wanted other kids to like them."

Then Becky said that for very serious bullying, the school should get the police involved, since after all, if the same thing happened to an adult, it would be considered a crime. For instance, if a man was walking down the road and someone even just tripped him up, the aggressor could be reported to the police for assault, and yet there were a few people who did much worse things at school, but hardly got punished for it at all.

The headmaster thoughtfully agreed, and said not dealing with serious bullying harshly enough was something that should probably be changed, and that he'd look into it.

When Becky's mum came to pick her up from school, Becky and the headmaster were deep in conversation. Her mum couldn't find her, and asked if anyone knew where she was. Someone told her she was in the headmaster's office, and her mum thought, "Oh no, what's she done?" She went there anxiously, thinking Becky was being punished for something. She was surprised when the headmaster said that actually, she was helping him work out a new anti-bullying strategy. Becky's mum was pleased, so she and Becky went home feeling happy.

Chapter 3

Becky Has Ideas For Inventions, and Gets the Teachers to Let the Kids Eat All Day in Class

Becky's mum had never been shy of letting her stay in the bathroom with her when she was using it; when Becky was little, she thought it was best to take her in with her a lot of the time so she could supervise her while she was there, so Becky didn't get into any trouble while having to be left alone.

Becky would sometimes play with toys and games on the floor while her mum was in the shower. But she wasn't always completely distracted by them; she would look to see what her mum was doing quite a bit. She noticed she would sometimes spend time in the shower just soaking after she'd had a wash, and one day she asked her why.

Her mum said she loved the feeling of hot water running over her – she found it soothing.

When Becky was at senior school, she heard news stories about water shortages, and warnings that people really ought to reduce the amount of water they use because water shortages would never really go away. She remembered what her mum had said about enjoying the feeling of hot water flowing over her, and the thought came to her:

"I'm sure it's not the water itself that she enjoys, but the heat of it! I bet it's the same with lots of other people too, since I've heard that a lot of people like a good soak in a hot shower."

She decided it would be great if a shower could be invented that had a knob that could be pressed – with the elbow or something, so people wouldn't have to put soap down or anything to press it – and it would switch the shower between water, and hot air that could flow all around the person in the shower, giving them the same nice soothing sensation her mum said the hot water gave her. She thought one use for it could be that people could put the hot air on while they were rubbing soap over themselves, since they often wouldn't need water then, and then they could switch the shower to water to rinse it off, and then back to just heat if they wanted to spend longer in the shower just enjoying themselves. And it could have a half heat, half water setting, for when people just had a little bit of soap on them so it wouldn't take much water to rinse it off. And there could be a knob to change the temperature of the hot air, just as there would be with the water.

She had once asked her mum why she didn't turn the shower off while she was putting soap on, and her mum had said that whenever she'd done that in the past, she'd felt cold standing there with no hot water warming her up. Becky thought it was probably the same for a lot of people, so she felt sure they'd enjoy gentle heat blowing all around them while they were doing that.

Then it occurred to her that it wasn't even necessary to have a proper shower; just a bucket of water with a scoop would do for people who were especially concerned about saving water; the bucket could be attached to the wall at a height where it was easy to reach, and a mini shower could just deposit a few litres of water into it for them to use, and then stop. People wouldn't get cold or feel the need for the lovely sensation of water flowing over them if they had hot air blowing gently all over them instead, and they would only really need the same amount of water they'd use if they were washing at a sink, or not much more.

"As for hot air drying people before they're ready," she thought, "everybody knows from using some of the hand dryers out there that hot air isn't necessarily all that quick and efficient at drying, so it probably wouldn't dry people too soon. Plus the hot air would only be blowing around gently, so it wouldn't blast water droplets away like a powerful hand dryer might. And anyway, it would only take a few seconds for people to get wet again once they'd changed the setting back to having water flowing. And just think about the amount of water that could be saved!"

Becky told her mum about her ideas, but was disappointed when her mum looked skeptical and said, "I'm not sure it would be that appealing, really. It's not just the heat that makes a shower enjoyable; it's the combination of the heat and the pressure of the weight of lots of water; somehow a more powerful shower gives you a bit of a feel-good buzz, but one that isn't very powerful can seem a bit boring. Well, I think so anyway. So if having just a bit of water's boring, maybe no water at all would be even more boring! And I can't imagine anyone wanting to keep faffing around pressing buttons with their elbows!"

Becky protested indignantly, "Mum, it won't take much effort for people to press the button! And I could always recommend that the shower gets made so the air can come out quite powerfully, so it feels just as good as a power shower! I could recommend that there could be a knob on it to adjust the air pressure, so people can get it just how they like it."

So she modified her design ideas a bit.

She looked up the addresses of shower manufacturers and sent her ideas to them. She suggested they could launch the new showers with an enthusiastic advertising campaign about how much water a person who cared about the environment and water shortages could save by using them.

Unfortunately, the manufacturers didn't seem that interested. Perhaps it was partly to do with the fact that after months of drought, a few days after Becky sent them her ideas, there were severe storms with torrential rain and flooding, making people wish there was less water around for a while.

But she had more ideas for inventions. She did a couple of science subjects at senior school, and from the time she first went there, she would sometimes go to the library after school and read more and more complex things, learning what the long words in the books meant by finding out their definitions in the books' glossaries or on the Internet as she went along. Sometimes there were so many long words the process could seem a bit laborious; but still, by the time she was five years old – or so the story has it – she was reading the most complex books they had in the school. Not that they had many, and the ones they did have weren't as complex as all that.

Still, she managed to work out that a certain chemical combination could help people lose weight very quickly. She designed a drink she called "fat absorber", which would clear lots of the fat out of the system, not just out of the food people had just eaten, but even some of the old fat that had been around for a while. It looked as if it would be so effective that people could lose pounds and pounds in days.

She couldn't make much of the drink herself because she couldn't get hold of enough of the chemicals. So she told the press she'd designed it and what it could do, hoping to interest scientists who could make it.

She got some encouraging letters from some therapists who were in the business of helping people overcome problems related to being overweight, and from other people, who told her they were glad she wanted to do something to help.

But unfortunately, the bosses of some dodgy companies that sold expensive diet programs and weight loss coaching got to hear about it, and they were worried that if it came onto the market, it would be so effective it would put them out of business. So they wrote to Becky and threatened that if the fat absorber was ever made, they'd send scary warnings to the press about how the long-term effects of the drink hadn't been studied, so it might harm people for all anyone knew; and they'd warn that it simply had to be an unhealthy drink, because it would encourage people to eat junk food instead of healthy things like fruit and vegetables, because they would know the fat that resulted from doing that could be got rid of easily. But then they'd get health problems because they weren't eating healthy food.

There were some scientists who were genuinely worried about whether drinking the drink might lead to unhealthy behaviour too, such as if people with anorexia drank pints and pints of the stuff at once to try to get thin quickly and lost more fat than was healthy. They were also concerned that the drink might have some dangerous side effects.

Becky wrote back to the scientists suggesting it could be a drink people could only get on prescription, and that there could be clinical trials of it first to find out if it was safe. She wrote to the company bosses, saying she was glad they'd pointed out that people might start eating more unhealthily, promising to make sure big warnings were put on cartons of the drink that told people not to do that because they'd suffer later in life if they did. She also asked if there was any evidence that the particular chemical combination in the drink could harm anyone, saying she'd be happy if they would help her design an even better product, and they could make all the money from it, because she wasn't interested in the money.

A few of them suddenly lost interest in any harmful long-term effects the drink might theoretically have at the thought of sharing in the profits from it, and wrote back enthusiastically asking to be allowed to sell it so they could get some, without a mention of helping to redesign it. But others thought it would be too difficult to change their own line of business, and wrote back just repeating their threat to try and discredit the drink if it ever went into competition with their products.

Becky was still only about five years old, and was scared off trying to get the drink made. She decided she'd put off trying to invent anything else till later in life. So lots of people who might now be thin if it had been invented are still fat.

She was disheartened to get such a hostile response to her invention idea when all she had wanted to do was help people. She resorted to comfort eating to console herself, and put on quite a lot of weight, which she realised she'd have to try to get rid of the normal way, since no one wanted to make her invention.

Then she discovered something she was amazed by – that some small things have got a lot more calories in them than some much bigger things, so some little things are a lot more fattening than some big things. She found out that vegetables often don't have many calories, but that something like a small innocent-looking pasty a person might have for a snack could be over 400 calories. She discovered it was possible to eat about eight times the weight of such a pasty in broccoli and get about the same number of calories! A massive bowl full of it would last for much of the day, and be quite a bit less fattening!

She discovered she loved the taste of raw vegetables. She hadn't realised before, because she'd almost never had them, only cooked ones, which she'd never been keen on. She realised that was probably because almost all the flavour seemed to disappear then, and she thought that what flavour they did have left wasn't that nice. But she discovered she really liked some raw ones. Her auntie Diana really got her into them, saying she'd always really liked them, and that munching on lots of them instead of eating fattening foods had helped her lose quite a bit of weight a few years before.

Some of the children in Becky's class were concerned about their weight, especially since everyone except her was a teenager by then, and some had begun to worry about the way they looked; so she decided to try and convince them to chomp their way through big bowls of raw vegetables all day instead of munching on chocolate and junk food during their break times.

When she told them about the calorie difference, they were impressed, and decided to try it. They didn't ask the teachers if they'd mind; they just started bringing huge bowls of mixed raw vegetables into class and munching on them all day, sometimes getting their families to help prepare them the night before, and keeping them in the fridge till school time.

The teachers were surprised. When there was no talking in the class because the children were all busy working, they could hear the sound of thirty people biting into and crunching up vegetables; and it sounded remarkably loud when they were eating them all at once. Some teachers asked the kids to stop, not knowing if they'd be heard over the sound of all the crunching. But when Becky explained that it was their new way to try to stay healthy and get slim, and reassured the teachers that they could still be heard, and that the vegetables weren't so yummy and absorbing they were stopping them from concentrating on their work, most of the teachers stopped minding and let them carry on.

Chapter 4

Becky Gives Advice to Her Class About Losing Weight, and Helps a Girl With Bulimia

Becky Gives her Class Tips on Cutting Calories Easily

After the children in Becky's class discovered they could munch on big bowls of raw vegetables all the way through lessons without being told off, they became more enthusiastic about getting healthy and slim, and asked Becky if she had more ideas about how they could.

She gave them more suggestions they thought they'd try, such as replacing high-calorie foods with lower or low-calorie alternatives that could turn out to be just as satisfying or even more so, for instance replacing chocolate and other sweet sugary things with sugar-free chewing gum, which might mean having a sweet taste in the mouth for half an hour or more, as opposed to the mere seconds they'd have one in the mouth for if they ate some chocolate. Another idea of hers was that they could have bowls of fruit they could keep beside them and nibble on all day in class, some of which they could buy sliced or cut into chunks and all ready to eat from supermarkets, like melon, which some of them thought tasted quite like sweets.

She said they could also sometimes replace crisps and other salty snacks with a bit of cracker bread or something similar, which could have about seven or eight times fewer calories, and yet would still sometimes have a salty flavour and always a nice savoury taste; and they could sometimes replace high-calorie snacks like chips with soups – making sure to check they were low in salt so they were healthier than a lot of soups – at least when they fancied some chips just for the nice taste and the warm comforting feeling they were hoping to get from them, or just from habit, rather than because they were hungry.

Also, Becky discovered and told the class that sometimes hunger pangs come on and can make people assume they need something big to satisfy them, but that actually, sometimes something very small, like just a small handful of nuts, or even a cup of tea, could make them go away. She said they don't always come on because the body needs a big meal. She did advise them not to go over the top with that idea though, saying the body does need decent-sized nourishing meals every day to be healthy.

She also told them she'd discovered there's a mere one single calorie in a whole hundred grams of tea, as opposed to a small can of a lot of soft drinks having as many calories as a couple of cookies or more, about 140. But before there was any chance of them all rushing to the vending machines to buy tea, she told them that adding milk to tea tends to add about 20 calories to it, though that's still loads less than a lot of soft drinks have, although naturally if they put sugar in it, the calorie level would begin to zoom up pretty quickly, depending on how much they put in, of course.

Several of Becky's classmates enthusiastically decided to try the ideas, and thanked Becky for suggesting them. Some did lose weight after that, and became healthier; so even though some hadn't really needed to be concerned about their weight, it was worth them changing the way they ate.

Becky Gives a Bit of Advice to a Girl Called Teresa With Bulimia

Unfortunately, a few girls in the school were way too concerned about their weight and had eating disorders. One day Becky met a girl from another class called Teresa who had bulimia, binge eating massive amounts of food and then making herself sick to get rid of it. She'd seen a psychologist several times over the past year, but her condition hadn't improved. She met Becky one day, and during the conversation they had, told her she had bulimia. She said she'd heard Becky had managed to persuade the teachers to let her and the rest of her class eat all day in lessons, and was interested. She confided that she felt miserable sometimes because she felt fat and ugly, and sometimes about other things, and that whenever she did, she would eat lots and lots of food in one go for comfort, and then feel so disgusted with herself for having done it, and so concerned that she'd soon be fatter and uglier than ever before, that she'd vomit it up.

Becky had an idea and said to her:

"Tell you what: Take the attitude that you're allowed to eat as much food as you like; but chew every mouthful you take very very slowly, at least seventy times before you swallow it, with several seconds between each chew, when you just let your taste buds capture more of its flavour. While you're eating it, really concentrate on counting to seventy before swallowing each mouthful, and also concentrate on how nice it tastes; really allow yourself to enjoy the flavour of it. It'll take you so long to eat what you're eating, you probably won't eat nearly as much as you usually do, so you won't feel the need to sick it up afterwards; and you'll enjoy it a whole lot more than you have in the past when you've just piled it in and swallowed it without really thinking about what it tastes like or even what it is, so it'll probably be far more comforting, even though you're eating a lot less.

"All the concentration you're doing on counting and enjoying it will take your mind off what was making you want to binge too, so chances are that those thoughts and feelings will fade, so you'll stop wanting to eat so much."

Teresa tried Becky's suggestion. It might not have worked for everyone, but it worked for her. Everyone was surprised at how effective it was, and she never binged on food and vomited it up again. It seemed that what the psychologist she'd seen had failed to do in a whole year, Becky had achieved with one simple suggestion.

Becky also told Teresa that it's possible to lose weight by eating more than ever before. It would just depend on what she ate: chomping her way through big bowls of mixtures of raw broccoli, carrots, chopped celery and other things all the way through class would not only make lessons more enjoyable, but if she started eating that kind of thing sometimes instead of chocolates and other high-calorie foods too, she'd lose weight even if she ate more vegetables than she ever had eaten chocolate. Becky spoke to some of the other kids from Teresa's class, and soon they started trying to get away with noisily crunching their way through big bowls and lunch boxes of raw vegetables all through lessons, just as Becky's class did. After a bit of dismay at the noise, the teachers let them.

Some of the pupils started adding healthy things for extra flavour, such as mixing a can of sardines with every big bowl of vegetables they ate. And even some of the teachers began to join in.

Becky was pleased at having helped so many people eat more healthily.

Becky Gives Some Parents Advice About Dieting

Word got around, and the parents of some of the pupils who'd become more enthusiastic about eating more healthily came up to Becky after school sometimes when they came to collect their children, and told her they themselves had tried dieting for years, but had never kept weight off for long, so they wondered if she could give them some advice. She'd read a bit about losing weight, and some tips had stuck in her mind. She told the parents that though the tips probably wouldn't work for everyone, they were worth a try:

Apart from making sure they knew the good news that they could feel free to gnaw on most raw vegetables all day if they felt like it and not get fatter, and that if they did that, they might be a lot less likely to get cravings for high-calorie foods, because they wouldn't be going for hours eating nothing, so they wouldn't get hungry, she suggested the parents do their shopping just after a meal, so they wouldn't be hungry then, saying they might not buy so much then, since high-calorie snacks might look more enticing if they were hungry, so they might be more tempted to buy them if they went shopping before a meal. And she said they could go shopping with a shopping list they'd made in advance, and stick to getting only what was on it, rather than browsing around the shelves, so they wouldn't be so tempted to buy enticing-looking high-calorie foods on impulse.

She said that buying foods that were labelled as 'low fat' wasn't necessarily better than buying the ordinary versions of them, since they weren't always lower in calories, because sometimes they were higher in sugar or other carbohydrates than the ordinary versions. So she said it was worth looking at the labels to see how many calories they said were in the food, even if it did say it was low-fat. She said that also, low-fat versions of foods could be higher in salt, so they could be more unhealthy, so it would be worth them checking the salt content of the food on the labels too.

Another thing Becky suggested was that if the parents were hungry between meals, they could see if a cup of tea quenched the hunger pangs instead of food; or if they thought they had to have a snack, they could promise themselves they could have it, and go to the kitchen to get it . . . via the end of the road or a circuit of the block. She said sometimes they might not want it after that, or if they did, at least they'd have done a bit of exercise first, though chances were that the snack would contain far more calories than they'd lost through the exercise. Still, she said the exercise would probably be good for them in any case. And she said there were at least low-calorie tasty snacks they could have, such as a handful of grapes or a bit of cracker bread.

She said that another thing they could try if they fancied a snack was cleaning their teeth first and then seeing if they still wanted it afterwards; they might decide they'd prefer not to spoil the cleanness of their teeth by eating, or else the minty flavour of the toothpaste might be just as satisfying as eating something.

She said, "Another thing you can do if you fancy a snack is not to just take something out of a packet and stand in front of it eating it, but to put what you've taken out on a plate, if it's the kind of snack you might do that with, and put the packet away and take the plate into another room, so the packet or the food cupboard won't be right there in front of you, making you feel tempted to take more food out of it after you've eaten the bit you've got. Or else if it's just a little snack, you could try walking out the room while you're eating the last mouthful of it. Maybe by the time you've finished the snack in the other room, where you might have started giving your attention to other things, you'll be absorbed in thinking about or doing those, so you won't be thinking much about food any more, so you won't feel as if you want some more so much, whereas if you were just standing in front of a load of food, thinking about food, you'd be more tempted to have it."

She suggested that smaller portions at mealtimes might help them lose weight too, if their portions were currently bigger than they needed to be.

She made the parents cringe with another suggestion, that they look on the Internet for information about the health problems that being overweight increases the risk of, write a list of them, and stick it on their fridge or food cupboard, so they'd always see it when they were thinking of eating something.

Still, the parents thanked her, and some said they'd try the ideas, or at least some of them.

Becky and Other Children Have a Laugh Talking About Food

Becky's conversations with other people about food weren't all serious though. Sometimes they had a laugh.

One day one of her fellow pupils said, "The other day I was walking down the road, and I smelled this really nice omelette smell that must have been coming from a house, and it made me start craving omelette, and I thought, 'Ooh, I wish I could have some of that! It smells as if someone's cooking's a lot better than the school dinner I ate today!'

"Just about a minute after that, I smelled roast chicken coming from somewhere, and I started craving that, thinking, 'That smells yummy! I fancy some roast chicken!'

"Thankfully, the cravings went away a few seconds after they came on. But then I started imagining what it would be like if someone kept craving different things, and started cooking something new every time they craved it, till they had this massive meal! Just imagine if they smelled omelette first, and they decided they really wanted one, so they started making one, but just a minute later they smelled a waft of fresh roast chicken, and they fancied some themselves, and they had some in the fridge so they got it out to heat up; and then a waft of burgers and fries came in the window, and they fancied some of those, and they were with someone, so

48

they asked them to go out and buy some; and then a waft of paella came in the window from a neighbour's cooking, and they really fancied some of that, so they started cooking some, and it went on and on like that, till they ended up with this massive meal, and they ate it all at once, and then felt uncomfortably full for ages!"

Becky grinned and said, "It would be even worse if they kept craving sweet things as well as savoury ones, because they kept smelling those as well, like hot cross buns, and home-made cakes, and strawberry jam, and they had all those things, so they put them all in the big meal, all mixed up with the savoury things, because they were craving them so much they thought they just couldn't wait to eat them; and then they ate them all at once; and there was so much on their plate it was piled as high as their head! They'd probably feel sick afterwards! That's if they didn't decide the mixture was so disgusting as soon as they started eating it that they wished they hadn't craved so many things at once, and just threw it all away!"

They laughed.

Then one of them said, "I was on an Internet forum that sometimes used to get cluttered with spam threads, advertising things like penis enlargements and probably dodgy pills, or just talking gibberish. It's a good thing the moderators were there to delete the spam. I think a lot of it might have been posted by spambots rather than real humans.

"Anyway, I made a couple of jokes about it. One day I said, 'So many spammers sign up here that I think we ought to have a special punishment as a fierce deterrent to stop them. It should be such an unusual punishment that its fame gets spread far and wide, so they get put off coming here before they've even set one of their dirty bot-feet in the place! What we need to do is to track them down. And then . . . What? Here's one idea:

" 'We could force the bots or human spammers to wear clothes made of spam, complete with silly hats that they have to make from spam all by themselves every morning. When they sit on part of their spam-clothing and it squelches underneath them and gets squashed, they'll have to cover themselves with more spam. So they'll have to carry pounds and pounds of spam around with them in a rucksack to replace the squashed bits every day.

" 'Then again, they'd make everywhere they went dirty if they were covered in spam all the time . . . unless – and this could be a good plan: Once they've put their spam-clothing on, they'll have to cover themselves in plastic bags to stop it getting everywhere. There will be special spam inspectors who will make them take the bags off every now and then to make sure they are wearing spam underneath.

" 'They'll be allowed extra thick layers of spam in winter to keep out the cold. If they get hungry during the day, they'll be made to eat part of their spam hats. They can nibble at them all day till they only have mostly-eaten bits of spam on the tops of their heads.

" 'They can only go back to wearing ordinary clothes and eating non-spammy food when they've kept away from spamming forums for a month.'

"Then I said, 'What alternative ways are there of punishing them?' No one came up with any though."

The kids giggled.

Becky met some pupils in her school who were always worried about their weight and whether other people were judging them as too fat. Becky didn't think they were that much fatter than anyone else. They started becoming less anxious about their weight though after they started regularly joining in with the group of pupils who often had a laugh about food-related topics.

Becky Gives More Serious Advice About Losing Weight and Eating Healthily

Sometimes, Becky's conversations were serious though. Or at least parts of them were.

One day, she said to the other pupils who were with her, "My Auntie Diana told me she put on quite a lot of weight over a few years a while ago. She thinks it was mostly because she ate lots of baked potatoes with lots of cheese on them ... Not all at once, of course. I mean over time ... Well, she says that was apart from all the chocolate she ate, and crisps.

"But then she decided she needed to get slim, and she managed to lose an average of a pound a week for almost an entire year, just by making a few adjustments she thought were easy, such as spending some days when the weather was warm not eating any big meals, but nibbling on raw vegetables all day from a big bowl that she'd filled up with them in the morning, so she didn't get hungry, so she wasn't so tempted to eat chocolate and other fattening things. And she swapped some high-calorie foods like crisps with foods that tasted quite similar but didn't have nearly so many calories, like cracker bread – she'd eat just one slice or half a slice of cracker bread at the times when she'd eaten a packet of crisps before, and she thought that was a decent substitute.

Her telling me about those things is partly where I got the idea to recommend that people here do things like that. And she did more exercise than she had before.

"There were a few things she gave up for a while, like cheese and crisps. But instead of thinking she needed to give them up altogether, she decided to treat herself to them on special occasions, like at Christmas and Easter, and at around the start of the summer, so she didn't feel as if she was depriving herself of them altogether.

"I know someone who says she tried doing more exercise, but as soon as she started, her muscles started hurting, so she gave up, and never tried it again. But my auntie Diana said her own muscles started hurting when she started trying some new exercise, but she carried on trying, not doing much in one go, but just building up gradually to doing more, and she said that more quickly than she expected, her muscles stopped hurting a lot of the time, and it got easier. So maybe the same thing would happen to most people. She said that sometimes when she starts, her muscles hurt again, but if she stops for about thirty seconds and then starts again, they don't hurt any more, as if they're just protesting at having to move at first, but once they're warmed up a bit, they don't mind. It sounds a bit like the way I feel when I have to get out of bed in the morning!

"I suppose a person who gets teased about their weight or criticised by a doctor for it or something might want to lose weight a lot quicker than my auntie Diana did. If a doctor says you need to, then naturally I expect it's probably best to listen. But apart from that, if people can learn ways of standing up for themselves against people who are just teasing them, maybe they can stop some of them doing it. Or maybe they won't mind it so much if the teasers don't stop if they learn some good assertiveness techniques, because then they'll at least be able to express their point of view confidently and deal with it, instead of feeling helpless to cope with it and letting it get to them. And if they're confident they're doing something good about their weight, maybe they won't mind it taking longer to lose weight than they'd hoped it would.

"Mind you though, my auntie Diana said she lost about ten pounds in as many days once. She said she was surprised. She thinks some of the weight loss might have just been fluid that there might have been too much of in her system for a while though. I'm not sure, but I think everyone who loses weight starts off by losing a bit of fluid from the things they've been drinking that's been hanging around their systems, so people can lose a bit more weight than they expected to at first. But she reckons that some of the weight was fat . . . She doesn't mind me telling other people about this kind of thing.

"She said she didn't have to go anywhere much in that time, so she didn't need to eat foods that would give her quick energy first thing in the morning; so she just had a little handful of nuts for breakfast, and then spent all day just nibbling bits of melon and other fruit that she bought ready-prepared from a supermarket, that didn't have many calories at all. I think she ate a healthy amount of that, but not enough to put on weight. And she did more exercise than usual. So she'd have been burning off more calories than she ate, and that's why she lost weight.

"So it sounds as if that's worth doing for a bit of very short-term weight loss, although you'd need more of a variety of foods than that to stay healthy in the longer term, since you could eat a really really healthy food, but if that was all you were eating, you'd still end up really unhealthy, because it might not have anywhere near the number and variety of vitamins and minerals in it that your body needs.

"I heard that there are five categories of food that people should ideally eat – or drink – at least one thing from every day, or at least pretty often, because that way, you're more likely to get all the vitamins and minerals you need, or at least a lot of them, since all the foods in each one contain some of the nutrients you need, but none of them contain them all."

Becky grinned as she said, "... Sorry, I know it sounds a bit weird that I just said you should drink the foods. Well, I didn't mean all of them. Imagine trying to drink a peanut, or a slice of bread, or a lump of cheese or something! I just said drink because what I heard about these food categories said milk's classed as being in one of them – the dairy category, and you drink that; you don't eat it, of course ... Well, actually, I suppose if you put it on your cereal, then you'll be eating it.

"But anyway, actually, I think the five groups are split up by different organisations in slightly different ways, and some say it's four groups you need something from every day, because they class two kinds of food in the same category that other people split up ... Am I still making sense? Maybe not. Oh well, I might in a minute. Anyway, I'll tell you one way the five categories are split up if you like."

She grinned again as she joked, "Actually, how about if I tell you what they are whether you like it or not, instead of just, 'if you like'?"

Without waiting for an answer, she said, "OK, I will. One category is protein, which is found in its complete form in meat and cheese and eggs, but it's also possible to get some of the building blocks that make it up in different foods, and then it can be easy to eat combinations of foods that together contain all the building blocks that are necessary to make a complete protein ... Well, I don't mean literal blocks, obviously – you know, I'm not saying bits of protein are like microscopic stock cubes nestling in the middle of vegetables or something. As if you'd think I did mean that! Mind you, they could make the taste of some vegetables more interesting if they were like that! You know, you might be eating a tin of baked beans – well hopefully not the actual tin; hopefully just the baked beans – and they might taste of gravy or something! Then again, it would take a whole lot of microscopic stock cube things for it to be possible to notice the flavour.

"But anyway, what I was saying is that although only animal products contain complete proteins, things like nuts, beans, peas and lentils contain some of the ingredients that make up protein, and if people eat things like rice or pasta on the same day as they eat those, the ingredients of protein in those can mix with the ones in the beans or peas to make complete protein ... Actually, I think the body breaks all the bits of protein it gets down and makes different kinds of proteins anyway. But people still need enough of a variety of foods to get all the ingredients of complete protein in their systems. I don't suppose the technicalities of what the body does with it afterwards really matter to anyone other than food scientists, since the important thing is just that we eat enough of the stuff for it to do us good, since it helps the body grow, and repair itself from bits of wear and tear it gets when we exercise or do other things that damage it a little bit; and it helps the immune system function well, and quite a few other things.

"Anyway, another food category is carbohydrates, that people need for energy, that can be got from things like potatoes, or whole grains, or things that contain or consist of whole grains, like wholemeal bread, wholemeal pasta, or brown rice, and things like that; and they're especially useful if they're carbohydrates that are high in fibre, since that helps the digestion. Wholegrain foods are higher in fibre than processed grains, since there's fibre in the outsides of the grains that are in things like wholemeal bread, but the bits on the outsides of the grains are taken off when they're processed, and they aren't used in things like white bread.

"Foods high in carbohydrates like that also contain quite a few minerals and vitamins, especially some B vitamins, I think, and a bit of calcium, that people need to help keep their bones and teeth healthy.

"Scientists say it's best to get carbohydrates from wholemeal grains and other healthy things, instead of from cakes and biscuits . . . because all scientists are killjoys; . . . or it might really be because the carbohydrates in some unprocessed foods give people energy for longer, even though the energy they give them in the first place might not be as much as they'd get from more naughty foods. And they're not so fattening and unhealthy.

"Another food category scientists say we should eat at least one thing from every day is fruit, since it contains quite a lot of vitamins and minerals, besides other nutrients that plants make."

The Serious Conversation is Mixed With Humour

Someone listening to Becky grinned mischievously and said, "We should eat 'at least' one, but not necessarily more than one? So they reckon just one bit of fruit a day will do? Hang on! Aren't we supposed to be eating at least five portions of fruit and vegetables a day? I read that that's about four hundred grams. Imagine how big a fruit would have to be if you wanted to eat all four hundred grams' worth in fruit, but you only wanted to eat one a day! Imagine really massive apples growing on trees! It would hurt if one of those fell on a scientist's head ... or anyone's, actually! I mean, four hundred grams is about the weight of a tin of baked beans! Imagine if there were bananas that were as thick and heavy as one of those! Imagine if you tried to get your mouth round one of those, like you would with an ordinary banana!"

They laughed.

Becky said, "I think the words 'at least' one a day are the important ones here! Yes, they reckon people should ideally have quite a few more, although I think they say it's best if people have more vegetables than fruit. I think that's because fruit contains natural sugars that'll get you fat if you eat loads and loads of it ... Mind you, who'd want to eat loads and loads of it! Well, I suppose you might do if you found a fruit you really liked, especially if it was already chopped up, so all you had to do was cram it in your mouth! Actually, I think some people here have said they think some fruits, like melons, can taste as nice as sweets! I've found that. So it would be nice to eat them all day!

"I don't know how healthy it would be to eat loads and loads of them in one go though! Hey imagine if someone ate so much fruit at once they died, like half a ton of it or something, and the tabloids had a headline that said, 'Eating Too Much Fruit is Bad for You!' and some people didn't read the article where it explained that someone had died because they ate way way too much in one go, but they just thought fruit must be bad because of what the headline said, so they thought they'd better stop eating it altogether.

"Actually, that reminds me: I heard about an April Fools' joke that was played by a news outlet in America, where they had a headline linking to an article that said nothing much at all, so anyone who read it would realise it was just a joke article, but they put it there with the headline just to see if people got upset and put comments in their comments section that were all annoyed about an article even though they hadn't read it. There were loads of comments! The headline said, 'Why Doesn't America Read Any More?'

"Loads of people either got offended or agreed that it was true! I think the people who played the joke took that to mean that there must be some truth in the headline about people not reading things, since they thought the people commenting can't have read the saying-nothing article and realised it was an April Fool!"

The others giggled.

Then Becky said, "Talking about food again though, I think another reason it's probably best to eat more vegetables than fruit is because certain fruits – not things like melons or bananas – but things like oranges and pineapples, are quite acidic, so over time, they can corrode your teeth a bit. Mind you, there are some foods that can protect the teeth against that kind of thing. I heard that nuts can, although I don't know how effective they are. But I know that if you drink mouthfuls of milk while you're eating fruit that's quite acidic, maybe holding each mouthful of milk in your mouth for a little while before swallowing it, that can protect the teeth quite a bit."

One of the other kids said, "Wow, imagine how much milk you'd have to drink if you were eating fruit all day, drinking a mouthful of milk after every mouthful of fruit! Mind you, maybe you could just chop the fruit up and put it in a bowl and pour quite a lot of milk over it, like you would with cereal, and maybe that would be enough.

"Hey just imagine: Maybe if you ate a fruit that weighed over four hundred grams, it would last all day on its own! There actually are some fruits that must be over four hundred grams, aren't there; you know, like melons, and coconuts – I think those are probably way over four hundred grams, although I don't know how much of that comes from the weight of the coconut shells. Maybe not much. Mind you, I think coconuts are quite fattening, so you probably wouldn't want to eat a whole one in one day!"

Another one of the group talking grinned and said, "Has anyone ever told you your head may as well be a coconut, since it hasn't got any brains in it? I mean, I'm not saying that's what I think; I'm just thinking coconuts must be about the size of heads, and they've got hair on them as well. Imagine if scientists discovered they really were like heads, and the coconut inside was really the brains of the coconut tree! If you ate it, you'd be eating brains! Just imagine if they discovered that the only reason coconut trees can't work on computers, and do complicated mathematical calculations, and all kinds of things like that, is because they can't move, and they haven't got hands, and they can't talk, so they never get the chance to show what they can do!"

They giggled, and one said, "I should think most people would think a scientist who claimed that coconut trees could do all that was a nutter! Let's hope he wouldn't be one who was working on something really important, like the invention of a new medicine!"

Another one of the kids grinned and said, "If he thought coconut trees were that brilliant, he'd want everyone to take coconut medicine! Imagine the adverts: 'You've got a cold? Take this coconut medicine! Your brains are failing? Just eat some substitute brains by chomping down a whole coconut! Well, be careful to remove the shell first; but then you'll get to the yummy brains inside! I eat a coconut a day, and you can tell how good my brains are!'"

They giggled again, and one said, "I heard someone insulting someone else by asking them if their brains had fallen out. Well, if coconuts were really heads with brains in, they really would fall out! Imagine it! One week the coconut tree would be a powerhouse of brain power, and the next week, the coconuts would be ripe, and all its brains would have fallen out of the tree, as all its heads fell off!"

Another one of the kids said, "Imagine if coconuts could talk though! Maybe they'd swear when they fell out of the trees! And imagine if they could see out of those things people call their eyes, and they could hear too!

"Imagine if you were on holiday in some tropical country where there were coconut trees, and you were walking past some when you accidentally dropped your sun cream, or you started having some silly argument with someone else in your family, and all of a sudden you heard loads of high-pitched laughs, and then you realised the coconuts were all laughing at you! Or just imagine if they all started talking about you!"

One of the group said, "You wouldn't know what they were saying though, because they'd be speaking coconut language."

Becky said, "Imagine if you saw someone standing in front of a coconut tree, trying to teach all the coconuts English!"

They tittered, and one said, "Mind you, if everyone knew coconuts could talk, that wouldn't seem odd ... If you just saw someone doing it now though, you really would think they were odd!"

They chuckled.

Then the conversation turned serious again for a little while, as Becky said, "Anyway, what I was saying before was that basically, it's healthy to eat quite a bit of fruit. And vegetables are in another one of the food categories, or at least they are the way some people split them up, although other people put them in the same category as fruit. They've got a lot of vitamins in them that the body needs, as well as fibre, and antioxidants, that help protect the body against some kinds of chronic diseases like heart disease, that people are more likely to get as they get older, as well as maybe some cancers. It's best to have a variety of vegetables, since no single one contains all the nutrients people need, I don't think.

"And then the other food group is dairy products, like milk and cheese and yoghurt. Here's where scientists seem to talk about drinking food, where they say milk's in the category, although actually, they say vegetable and fruit juices can count as portions that can help make up a person's five portions of fruit and vegetables a day – although not too much fruit juice because of the unhealthy sugars in it – but that must mean those are more drinks that are classed as foods. Or maybe if you left them out on a table for about a year, they'd all go solid. Then maybe they'd be all crunchy, so they really would be more like food. Imagine crunchy milk! I don't suppose it would taste very nice if it had been sitting around for about a year!"

The kids giggled, and one said good-naturedly, "Don't be daft, Becky!"

Becky said, "If you insist. Really, it doesn't matter that there are drinks in the food categories, since I suppose the important thing is that they've got the minerals and vitamins and other stuff in them that people need.

"Anyway, one reason they say dairy products are good for you – in moderation – is that it's easy for the body to absorb calcium into the system from them, and I think they contain more of it than a lot of foods do.

"I think there are some vegetables that have got healthy minerals like iron and calcium in them, but for some reason, the body finds it hard to take them from them so it can digest them, so they can just come right out the other end, into the sewage system instead, which doesn't need them at all, obviously. The nutrients in food won't help the sewage system to grow or anything . . . which is probably just as well! I mean, imagine if the pipes under the road, or wherever they are, started expanding more and more the more protein and other nutrients they got flowing through them, till the roads burst open and they all had to be repaired! And imagine if the pipes under the floor and in the walls in people's bathrooms grew and grew till people's loos were as high off the ground as their heads, and they had to stand on a chair to reach them; or imagine if their houses started falling apart because the waste pipes in them were growing so big with all the protein and iron and things they were getting that was making them grow!"

The others giggled, and one said, "If engineers knew pipes did that, they'd have to invent special nutrient shields to stop the nutrients affecting them!"

They laughed again, and then Becky said, "Yeah! Anyway, another thing scientists say dairy products contain is protein, and also vitamin B12, which I think people can only get from animal products, so it's especially useful to eat things like cheese if you don't eat much meat, or at least to find some kind of substitute for a dairy product that'll give you enough vitamin B12 because it's been artificially fortified with it by the manufacturers, since if people don't get enough vitamins, they can get really unhealthy.

"I suppose even the healthiest things in the dairy food group will be quite fattening if you eat a lot of them though. Imagine eating something really really healthy, but you ate so much of it you ended up with a body that was absolutely packed with certain kinds of nutrients, but you were still dying, since you had some kind of horrible obesity-related illness! Maybe scientists could harvest your body for nutrients as soon as you died, and then feed someone who didn't have enough of them with your fat, to give them a big boost of them – maybe someone who didn't have enough because they'd been eating loads of food from the least fattening food group, but nothing from the others! . . . Actually, I'm sure there are much better ways they can give people boosts of minerals or vitamins – like giving them food supplements, or persuading them to change their diets!"

Becky grinned as she said that, and the others giggled again.

One of them grinned and joked, "You can be a bit yucky sometimes Becky. Actually, the words 'yucky' and 'Becky' sound quite similar. Maybe we could call you Yucky instead of Becky. Maybe that could become your official name, so it's on the teacher's register, and that could be what they always call you, and the name they put on your school reports. Imagine what they'd say: 'Yucky has been badly behaved this term!' "

They all laughed, and Becky grinned and said, "I think my mum might come storming into the school and have something to say about that!

"Anyway, we were talking about losing weight before, weren't we. If you eat foods from all those groups, I don't suppose there's any way you could lose weight as fast as you could if you just ate vegetables and nothing else or something. But apart from that not being healthy, even though vegetables are healthy, I've read that losing lots and lots of weight quickly means you're more likely to get loose skin hanging around your middle, and that wouldn't be nice at all. So it's best to lose weight slowly, unless a person's health's in danger of suffering soon if they don't.

"And I've read that going on a drastic diet for a little while to lose weight doesn't help people keep it off, because lots of them go back to eating the way they were before when they finish it, and even want to eat more than they used to, because they think it's so nice to be able to eat the food they like again after they made themselves go without it for a while that they don't want to stop any time they start; so people often put most of the weight back on again when they finish their diet. So it's best for a person to change their eating habits for good really, not doing anything drastic, but limiting their favourite fatty foods to special occasions and when they really feel like eating them, and eating low-calorie substitutes for fatty foods the rest of the time. That's what lots of people who know about these things advise people to do anyway, I think.

"But you lot don't actually look as if you need to worry about this stuff; you're not all that fat. You know, it wouldn't be worth forcing your parents to start giving you different things to eat . . . if that would even be possible."

One of the kids giggled and said, "Yeah, just imagine going home and saying, 'Right, Mum and Dad, from now on, I'm going to decide what we eat. I've decided I need to take over the running of the house and be the parent, to make sure we eat the right things; so you're going to be like the children . . . So you can be the ones to go to school from now on, and I'll be the one to decide what we're going to eat every evening when you come home and at weekends."

The kids chuckled. Then another one said, "I laughed the other day when I went past my sister's room. She had the radio on, and there was an advert on, and I don't know what it was for, but just as I went past, I heard someone on it say, 'Download and dine!' At first, I thought it said, 'Download and die!' Who'd want to do that?"

Becky grinned, and said in an imitation of the kind of voice that might be heard on an advert trying to make something sound impressive, "Download and die! This computer virus is so powerful that not only will it kill your computer, but it will also kill you! But it will do it in such an exciting way that you definitely don't want to miss out on it!"

The other kids laughed.

Then Becky said, "Hey imagine if everyone had things like little doorways into their bodies in certain places, and it was possible for them to open them and reach in, and pull lumps of fat out, and then they would often spread them on toast, and they would taste just like margarine. Imagine if people thought of it as a really enjoyable treat, that they wanted to have every morning for breakfast!"

The kids Becky was talking to made faces and giggled, and one said, "I really don't think I'd fancy that, somehow!"

Becky said, "Ah, but you might if you were used to it, if you'd just grown up thinking it was natural to do that. People might especially like it if it was possible to pull bits of fat out of themselves and mix them with sugar and eat them as treats, or mix them with other ingredients too and then cook them and make little cakes. Hey imagine if it was normal for mums to make cakes with fat from members of the family in them instead of butter or margarine, so they'd say things to their children like, 'Do you want to help me make a cake? It's going to be a nice big family cake, for Dad's birthday. And just so it feels like a nice special sharing time, we're going to ask everyone in the family to contribute some of their fat, and then mix it all together, weigh out the amount we need, and then mix it with sugar and eggs and flour to make some nice cake mix. And when it's cooked, you can help me put icing on it if you like.'

"Maybe if people were used to eating fat from everyone in the family in cakes, they'd enjoy it!"

The kids Becky was with screwed up their faces, and then giggled, and one said, "Somehow, I think it would take quite some getting used to!"

They all laughed.

Becky said, "Actually, we probably all think of fat as yucky stuff, just causing a nuisance, bulging around our bellies and things . . . alright, I'm speaking for myself here! But I heard that fat's really the body's way of storing unused energy. So we could really think of fat as just fuel that's being stored up, waiting to be used up. I know it doesn't make people feel energetic, so it's a funny kind of energy really! But once people start exercising, or if they eat less, so the body has to start using a bit of the fat in its fat stores as the fuel it needs to keep all its processes going, like the process of sending the blood whizzing around our systems . . . well, actually, I don't think it really goes anywhere near as fast as that; but still, if the body starts using it as fuel to help it with that kind of thing, then it's serving a good purpose.

"So a lot of people might have way way more stored-up fuel than they need; but at least they can think of it as something that can serve a good purpose . . . in the process of being ruthlessly destroyed, once they get determined to start really putting it to good use . . . That's if it doesn't accidentally kill them first, with some kind of obesity-related illness!

"So you know, you've got to get ruthless with flab, by doing things like, I dunno, jogging, or trampolining, or weight lifting with big lemonade bottles, or whatever.

"Just imagine if someone said to someone else, 'I'm just going out for a ruthless jog around the park.' The other person might say, 'Why is your jog going to be ruthless? Are you planning to jog right into the duck pond and try to tread on the heads of all the ducks or something?'

"Or maybe they'd think the person was being daft, and say, 'What's so ruthless about jogging? Maybe next, you'll be telling me you're going to terrorise the neighbourhood by having a little paddle in the sea!'

"Mind you, the person who said they were going out might have a joke and say, 'Actually, if I put my swimming costume on so my flab was on full display for everyone to see, maybe it really would terrorise the neighbourhood!'

"Then they could tell the other person what they'd really meant when they said it would be a ruthless jog – that they were just hoping to get rid of a little bit of flab!

"Or just imagine if when they said they were going to go for a ruthless jog around the park, the other person didn't hear them properly, and thought they must have said they were going to go with a ruthless dog around the park, or that they were going to take a ruthless jug around the park! If they thought the person was talking about ruthless jugs, they would think they were being even more daft!"

The kids laughed.

Becky said, "One thing, though, is that it wouldn't be good for anyone to try to ruthlessly destroy flab by starving them-selves, so the body had to use its fat stores to give it fuel to do all the things it needed to do during the day, since then you wouldn't be getting all the nutrients you needed to stay healthy. People start to feel weak if they haven't eaten for a while. Imagine if the body felt so weak, it didn't even have the energy to turn its fat stores into energy to use up!"

The other kids smiled.

Then Becky grinned and said, "Hey, imagine if some writers of books that teach French grammar wrote new ones, and advertised them as being updated for the modern day, and schools thought that sounded really good, and they bought them. But imagine if the people who wrote them didn't explain that what they meant when they said they'd updated them for the modern day was that the sentences they would tell people to recite in class to practise French were all about bad habits a lot more people get into nowadays than they used to.

"I'll tell you what I mean: You know when you learn French grammar, you have to learn the differences in the ways some words end, since they end differently depending on who you're talking about – you know, it's not like in English, where you just change words a bit by using plurals some-times, but some words in a sentence can have different letters on the end, depending on who the sentence is about, like it'll be O N S if it's 'we', E Z if it's 'you', and E N T if it's 'they'? So some French teachers make you recite boring things in French, like, 'I am going to the park. You are going to the park. We are going to the park. They are going to the park.' And that kind of stuff, till you get the hang of using the different word endings.

"Well just imagine if instead of sentences like that, the new books told people to recite sentences out loud in French in front of the teacher and the class like, 'I am obese. You are obese. He is obese. We are obese. They are obese. I am a fat pig. You are a fat pig. He is a fat pig. We are fat pigs. They are fat pigs.'

"But imagine if there was a mistake in a book, so we all learned to say things like, 'I am a lazy slob who can't be bothered to exercise', and so on, till we were saying, 'We are a lazy slob who can't be bothered to exercise. They are a lazy slob who can't be bothered to exercise.'

"And when the teacher told us we were wrong, we'd argue and say we must be right because the book told us to say it."

One of the others grinned and said, "Maybe when the teacher told the class they were wrong, she'd really mean it was unfair of them to say she was a lazy slob along with the rest of them. Imagine if one of them said, 'We can't be wrong about that; the book says it's true!' "

The others giggled.

They enjoyed their chats with Becky.

Becky Talks to Teresa About Bulimia Again, and Teresa Tells her About a Bad Experience She Had With Mean Remarks and Diet Pills

Becky sometimes found herself being called upon to give advice when she wasn't expecting it, though she didn't mind. The girl she'd helped to overcome bulimia, Teresa, came to her one day and confessed that though Becky's advice had worked at first, recently she'd been tempted quite a few times to buy a load of cake and chocolate and stuff it all in her mouth without thinking about it as she had before. She felt bad about that; but Becky said it seemed really impressive that although she'd been tempted, she'd never once done it since they spoke last. She complimented her on her strength of willpower, saying she'd read that those temptations could be strong, so to resist them all was quite something. Teresa hadn't thought of it like that, and it cheered her up.

A few days later, Teresa told Becky that a couple of years earlier, she'd been bullied about being a bit overweight, and some other girls hadn't wanted to be her friends unless she was willing to really make an effort to eat less and make herself look fanciable to attract boys. She wasn't really into attracting boys, but they thought that was part of being cool, and she had wanted to be like them so they'd be more friendly towards her, and because they seemed sure that their way was the best way to be. They were only thirteen! But besides wanting to look attractive, they didn't eat much at school, and looked down on her when she did. She'd felt bad about herself, and under pressure to lose weight quickly. She'd really wanted them to like her. She'd felt left out without friends. One day she'd found a company she'd never heard of on a website with a strange name, selling some diet pills, and thought they might be a quick fix, so she'd bought some with her pocket money. But they'd made her seriously ill, and she'd ended up in hospital.

Becky said, "I think it must be risky to buy things from companies you just happen to find on the Internet, when you've never heard much or anything about them before – you've got no idea who they really are, or whether what they're selling really is what they say it is! I think criminals sell some of the stuff people can buy on the Internet. And spammers. I get lots of spam emails for pills and other things – even emails that insist they can help me increase my penis size!"

(Teresa didn't feel uneasy about discussing such things as dodgy emails that advertise things like penis enhancement with Becky, since after all, Becky was learning what the rest of the pupils in her class were learning, including sex education, and it wasn't her fault if she got emails that must have been intended for adults.) Teresa just laughed and said, "Now if they could even get you a penis in the first place, that would be a miracle!"

Becky chuckled and said, "Yes. They even call me Mr Becky, and sir."

Then she said seriously, "The thing is, though, if companies disrespect their customers enough to bombard them with spam, then in my opinion anyway, there's no reason to think they respect them enough to make sure what they're selling is safe!"

Teresa said, "That's a good point! I'd never buy anything from some random company I came across on the Internet now. I'm lucky to be alive! I reckon that if dodgy companies just think of these things as a way to make money, which it wouldn't surprise me if they do, they'll probably have no interest in telling customers what side effects the ingredients have, in case it puts some of them off buying them. So a lot of them probably won't mention them. And if their products are being sold from another country, they'll be outside the laws of this country. I've since learned that some ingredients some of these rogue companies sell in diet pills over the Internet have been banned in a lot of countries! One I've since heard about was banned as far back as the 1930s, because it was found to have dangerous side effects! But if they're sold from countries where they're not banned, no one here can close those companies down, I don't think.

"I've learned that they sell them as diet pills because they can boost your metabolism, which means they make your body burn fat more quickly, because metabolism's a process that converts fat and the things people eat and drink into energy they can use, so some of the things that would otherwise be turned into fat won't be, because they'll be turned into energy before they can be, and some of your fat that's already there will be turned into energy to be used; or the pills suppress your appetite; but when they do those things, it causes them to do nasty things to you at the same time, that you're just not told about, such as the ones that boost metabolism a lot making the body burn fat off so intensely that the body itself feels as if it's burning! That sounds as if it defeats the object of having the fat turned into energy in a way, because you're not going to want to use the energy if you feel way too hot to exercise! Mind you, maybe turning fat into energy really quickly takes up a lot of energy itself or something.

"Anyway, I also found out on the Internet that some drugs sold online have got things in them that aren't even anything to do with any chemical that could help anyone diet, like cement powder, which might be put in there to make people think there's more of the drug in there than there really is! I don't know. But it seems the companies that sell them just want to make money, and they don't care how.

"I've found out since that it's possible to buy diet pills that don't do you nearly as much harm as the ones I bought, from ordinary chemist shops or respectable companies on the Internet, or on prescription from a doctor, although I don't think they're as powerful as the banned ones, and I think the only thing that truly helps people lose weight is eating more sensibly. But when I bought the diet pills that turned out to be dangerous off the Internet, I don't think I'd have been interested in pills or anything else that didn't seem to be fast-acting and powerful."

Becky and Teresa Have a Laugh

Becky asked Teresa if she was still being bullied, and she said she wasn't much, but that the very people who'd bullied her for being overweight had cruelly ridiculed her for being 'stupid' enough – as they put it – to buy diet pills from some unknown company on the Internet to try to fix the problem so she'd fit in with them better.

She told Becky that she still got told by the popular girls that she didn't look 'cool'. Becky asked what girls had to look like to be supposedly cool, and Teresa said they had to be tall and slim.

Becky joked with a grin, "Well that's me out then! I'd have to grow about another half a metre to be cool! I suppose I'd have to be stretched. Maybe if I dangled from the top of a tree, one of the really tall cool girls could grab my feet and pull them till they reached the ground. Then I'd be tall!"

Teresa laughed and said, "I expect the branch you were holding onto would break long before you'd stretched enough to reach the ground! But just imagine if it worked! You'd be stretched out so much you'd probably be as thin as a tree branch by then!"

Becky grinned and joked, "Ah, then I'd be really really really cool, according to them, wouldn't I!"

Teresa laughed again and said, "I think you might be too thin and tall even for the cool ones then."

Becky smiled and said, "Probably. And just imagine if I was as tall as the tree I'd been stretched on! I'd have to bend double when I came in here so I could fit under the ceiling! I'd have to get down on my hands and knees just so I could get through the door!"

Teresa said, "Gosh! Imagine if you were walking around in the shape of a massive tree branch, with really really thin long arms and legs, like little branches branching off the main branch! That would be so spooky! You're spooky enough as it is, knowing so many things at your age, and being years above where someone your age would normally be at school!"

Becky smiled and said, "Oh, I'm spooky am I? Well, in that case, maybe I should go all the way and become a ghost. That could be fun. Then I could haunt all the 'cool' girls and the teachers! Maybe I could be invisible – that would be good! Imagine if I crept up behind one of the 'cool' girls and ruffled her hair, and whispered in her ear that I'd come to haunt her. When she saw there was no one there, she might suddenly lose that cool of hers and jump up and run out the door! And everyone would wonder why.

"And maybe I could start moving all the teachers' things around in the middle of lessons, till they got scared and ran out the door too."

Teresa burst out laughing and said, "Yay! That would be great! We might get to have lots of half-lessons without teachers, free to do what we wanted!"

Becky said, "Yes, that would be fun! Well, for some of us anyway. Maybe the 'cool' girls would spend the extra free time doing keep fit exercises to try to get even slimmer than they already are instead or something!"

Teresa chuckled.

Then Becky said, "I wonder if it's possible to do so much exercise you end up looking a bit like a skeleton! People need to have a bit of fat on them. For one thing, it helps people keep warmer in winter. You wouldn't have any insulation from the cold on you if you didn't have any fat on you at all.

Imagine the 'cool' girls being like skeletons, with no fat on them whatsoever! They wouldn't just be cool; if they didn't put a lot of clothes on, they'd be freezing!"

Teresa grinned.

Becky said, "And just imagine what it would be like to cuddle someone who didn't have any fat on them; it would be like cuddling a tree or something – all hard, with bits sticking out! Just imagine how uncomfortable that would be!

"Imagine if you wanted to impress the cool girls . . . or make fun of what they say about people having to be skinny to be cool, so you went into the science lab and found a skeleton, and you sneaked it out, and dressed it up, and put a wig and gloves on it, and put some kind of mask on its face to disguise the fact that it was just a skeleton face, and you took it to a dance with you at Halloween, and they were all there, and you told them it was your new boyfriend, who was wearing a fancy dress mask for Halloween, and you said he'd just been on a really strict diet so he was feeling weak, so you had to hold him up to stop him collapsing, and you danced around with him, telling them you hoped they were impressed with the amount of weight he'd lost. You could say he'd been on such a strict diet though that he'd got too weak even to talk to them. But you could ask them if they'd like to dance with him, saying you wouldn't get jealous of them if it was just one or two dances, and that they'd look really good dancing with such a slim person."

Teresa laughed.

Becky Encourages Teresa to Think of the Critical Bullying Remarks She's Been Receiving in a New Way

Then Becky got serious again and said, "Anyway, whenever any of the 'cool' girls criticises you scornfully, like if they say things that make you think they must think there's something wrong with you because you don't make an effort to look as attractive as they think girls ought to look, or that you're not slim enough, or that you're not going out with boys yet or whatever, one idea I've got is that you might not feel so bad if you think about whether you'd expect a grown-up who you'd expect to tell people to be kind and caring to each other, like a vicar, to say those things ... Actually, if a vicar did say things like that, you'd probably think he was an old perv!

"But you know what I mean: If you couldn't imagine someone who was supposed to be sensible and who would normally be supposed to teach people to be more kind and caring saying stuff like that, and being scornful like those girls are, and they're giving you the opposite of the good advice that you'd hope someone like that would give to try to encourage people to live better, then you'll know you don't have to just walk away from the girls feeling as if there must be something wrong with you; you'll know there must be something wrong with their attitude if they talk to you like that. And that might give you some comfort, since you'll know the problem isn't really that you're inadequate and they're so much more sophisticated than you are, or something else that's just to do with you.

"And even if they criticise you for something you know you ought to change for the better, maybe you could try saying things to them like, 'If you think there's something wrong with me, instead of just telling me what you think I'm doing wrong, how about telling me about little things you think I could do to try to improve things – you know, so you're trying to help me, instead of just criticising?"

"Mind you, then they might just tell you to do things you shouldn't really be made to feel under pressure to do. They might sound as if they're really confident that they're right about things and that anyone who disagrees with them is wrong; but chances are they only got to have their opinions because of things they read in some fashion magazine they like or something, that's just spouting the opinions of the people who want to sell it, who might just be promoting those opinions because then they'll make more money from people selling fashion products who'll be more likely to pay for their adverts to be put in the magazines if their articles say those products are fashionable or something. You know, not everything those girls say will deserve to be taken seriously, even if they do think there's something wrong with you if you don't behave like them."

Teresa said she felt reassured by that.

The Subject of Cosmetic Surgery Comes Up

Then Becky said, "Talking of looking fashionable, I heard something on the radio about how more people nowadays are going for cosmetic surgery, and how it can be a shame, because it can be risky, especially some procedures. I didn't understand why anyone would want to have cosmetic surgery, when in the worst cases, they might even be risking their lives to look better, especially if they travel to some places abroad where the safety record isn't as good as it is here, because they can get the procedures cheaper there.

"But there were young women on the radio saying they'd started feeling like having the procedures done partly because they wanted to look more like glamour models on the Internet, but also because all their lives, people in their families, like sisters and aunts and other people, had made comments about how they thought there were things wrong with their looks, so they got to be really self-conscious. It seems like a shame to me. If things went wrong, they might really regret having the surgery done, and all the people who'd criticised their looks might feel guilty. I hope you'd never think about getting something drastic done."

Becky then grinned as she said, "Anyway though, I started wondering why criticising someone a lot about their looks would make them want to change them, when criticising doesn't work like that for everything. I mean, I've never heard of someone who got criticised about not helping enough with the house-work getting obsessive about doing the washing-up, or someone who gets nagged to do more homework a lot getting really enthusiastic to do it from then on! Mind you, I suppose some people might. But I've never known it to work. It wouldn't with me! And my uncle Steven got criticised a lot for not bothering to do his homework; he even got lots of detentions for it, and there was one teacher who used to tell him things like that he'd never achieve anything in life if he carried on the way he was going. But he just got depressed about it, and stayed the same. There was one day when he met a new teacher, and when he said who he was, the teacher looked as if he was thinking, 'Uh-oh, you're the one I've heard so much about in the staffroom!'

"But when I thought about the radio programme, I realised that maybe the reason why people are more likely to go for cosmetic surgery than turn into obsessive homework-doing enthusiasts and that kind of thing when they're criticised is maybe because cosmetic surgery seems like a quick fix, and they probably dream of being admired for it afterwards, whereas doing more homework or housework would take years of boring slog, so it wouldn't be so appealing. And being criticised about looks might make people feel self-conscious and awkward in public where lots of people could see them too, so that would affect them more.

"Anyway, there was this young woman on the programme who was thinking of having cosmetic surgery, and they followed her for a while to see what she'd do, arranging for her to speak to a doctor about the risks, and things like that. She decided not to go for surgery in the end, saying that after she spoke to the doctor, she was more aware of the risks than she had been before, since on the Internet, she'd seen people parading their good looks when they'd had cosmetic surgery, but they hadn't mentioned the risks. The doctor said the woman didn't need to improve her looks at all, and that her friends might even be jealous of the way she looked already. But she said she was still interested in changing the way she looked, but she'd decided to try doing that by exercising and eating more healthily instead."

Teresa said she thought that was interesting. She told Becky she didn't need to worry about her trying any kind of cosmetic surgery, because she thought she was way too much of a coward to want to try it herself!

They chuckled.

Becky Gives Teresa More Advice About Overcoming Bulimia

Just a few weeks after they had that conversation, Becky read a bit about bulimia in some notes she came across in a classroom after someone had visited the sixth formers to talk about eating disorders. She told Teresa about that when she next met her, saying they'd given her some new ideas: She suggested to her that if she wanted extra help overcoming the temptations to binge eat and then vomit up what she'd eaten – although she seemed to be doing a very good job by herself – there were a few things she could try:

One thing was that she could think of the temptation – and in fact the eating disorder itself – as not just a set of feelings or a problem, but as a little monster on her shoulder, whispering things to her to try and draw her back into bad habits; but it was a monster she could talk back to and overpower, telling it she wasn't going to give in to it so it could just get lost, and things like that. She could have fun imagining what the monster looked like. Then she could think of herself as being in competition with it to see who was going to win – either the monster when she gave in to a temptation, or herself when she managed not to; and every time she defeated the monster by not giving in to it, she could feel triumphant, and congratulate herself.

Becky said another thing Teresa could do was to firmly say, "HALT!" to the temptation when it began to come on; she said she'd read that the word could be an acronym, standing for, 'hunger, anger, loneliness, tiredness', and that when Teresa said 'HALT', she could then think about which of those things was making her want to binge eat, or which one was the closest. Then she could try to think of alternative things to do about it:

If it was hunger, she could ask herself whether it was really a binge she wanted, or whether she'd be better off and satisfied enough eating something small and healthier; she could remind herself she had a choice, and didn't have to be ruled by the temptation or eating disorder monster, but could have a good go at the challenge of standing up to it and defeating it.

Becky said the notes said that it was worth bearing in mind that there's a difference between mindless and mindful eating: Mindless eating's where the body seems to take over and stuff food down while the mind might feel as if it's squashed up in a corner looking on, horrified, but feeling powerless to stop it, while mindful eating's making a deliberate choice to eat something good and sensible, bearing in mind how healthy it'll be, and what the consequences will be – for instance feeling good at having eaten a decent-sized amount, versus feeling guilty and disgusted at the amount binged on.

She also said the notes said that doing things mindfully could also involve thinking about what could be done with the time if it wasn't taken up with a binge; there might be nice enjoyable things Teresa could be doing instead, so it was worth her thinking of a list of fun things to do in advance, so when temptation came on, she'd easily be able to bring them to mind and could try choosing one. Or she could think about what tended to trigger off cravings to binge, such as heartless remarks from people, bad news, or whatever, and when one of those things happened, before the temptation even started, she could bring to mind the fun things, and do one of them to distract herself, if possible, so her mind would get absorbed in other things. Or if it wasn't possible to do one right then, she could plan to do one later, so she could at least have the pleasure of anticipating it.

Becky then told Teresa that if she realised the emotion making her want to binge was anger, instead of deciding to eat, she could try putting her mind to thinking of a way of resolving the problem making her angry if she could, or at least doing something else to let off steam, such as going for a run.

Teresa thought the ideas were interesting, and said she wondered why it had only been the top classes that had had the visit from the person talking about eating disorders.

Becky agreed that it would have been good if more classes had been given the lessons. Then she said the letter L in the word 'HALT' stood for loneliness, though the notes she'd read said the emotion might just as easily be boredom. She said to Teresa that if she realised that was what was making her want to binge eat, she could maybe try thinking of what would be a good way of overcoming the feeling, such as finding friends to chat with, getting on with something she enjoyed, trying to find humorous or interesting things or good or supportive discussions on the Internet, or whatever she knew she enjoyed doing or found soothing.

Then Becky said the T in the word HALT stood for Tiredness; she said the notes had said it's tempting for a lot of people to eat when tiredness comes over them, to try to replenish their energy, but eating things high in sugar like chocolate isn't the best idea, even though it feels like it, because although they give a brief burst of energy because the sugar will get into the bloodstream quickly, it will also leave quickly, so energy levels will slump again, and a craving for more chocolate or other high-sugar or high-fat food will come on, in the body's attempt to get the energy back. So it could be better to reach for a small amount of something not so rich in fat or carbohydrates, but that can still give an energy boost, like nuts, and then as soon as enough energy kicks in, to try doing other things, such as going to the window and breathing in several breaths of fresh air, in the hope it'll revive the body a bit. An alternative could be letting the body rest, putting the feet up and relaxing for a bit, or having a break for a sleep, and so on.

Teresa grinned and said, "I can just imagine what a teacher would say if I announced in the middle of a lesson that I was just going to have to take a nap!"

Becky chuckled and joked, "Yes, it would be far better if you just put your head down on the desk and dropped off to sleep without saying a word, hoping the teacher didn't notice."

They giggled. Then Becky said, "Hopefully you don't need to take many naps at your age though! But yeah, I do mean you could only have one when it was practical."

Then she told Teresa that if the worst came to the worst and she did start bingeing again like she had before, she didn't have to get too downhearted about it; she could still congratulate herself about the amount of time she'd managed to control the temptations for before the day she gave in, and start thinking about how effectively she'd managed to stop bingeing before, knowing that if she'd done it once, she could probably do it again if she just thought about what had worked for her before and tried the same things again, plus any new ideas she could think of.

She told Teresa that if she felt really discouraged after bingeing and started thinking the whole day was ruined, and the miserable thoughts risked making her want to binge again, she could try thinking about things differently: She could split the day up in her mind into three parts, morning, afternoon and evening, or even more parts if she liked; so whatever time of day she'd had a binge, she could think it was merely that part that had gone bad, and that as soon as the next part started, if not before, it would be her chance to have a fresh new start at improving things.

Also it would mean she didn't have to be daunted by thinking she had to get better all at once, which might seem a discouragingly huge task; but instead, she could think of herself as just having the challenge of not bingeing for the coming third of a day, and when that was finished, she could start afresh with the new challenge of not bingeing for the next third, and so on, taking one third of a day at a time. If she gave into temptation any time, she would know a chance to do better would soon come along. She might still feel discouraged, but she could remind herself she was strong enough to beat the bingeing urge, by thinking about all the time before that she'd spent not bingeing.

But Becky said Teresa had got better so impressively quickly that she might not need any of those techniques at all.

Teresa thanked Becky, and the advice came in useful, both for her when she was tempted, and for others she met with eating problems later in life.

Chapter 5

Becky Warns a Teacher Not to Be Too Quick to Trust Alternative Medicines and Therapies, and Helps Some Teachers Give Up Smoking

A Teacher Says She's Planning to Go for a New Smoking Therapy, and Becky Wonders if It's a Con or Ineffective and Warns That Not All Therapies Work

In Becky's last year at school, allegedly the winter before her tenth birthday, a new rule was brought in that said there was to be no smoking inside the school building. A few teachers smoked, but before then, they'd always done it in the staffroom. Now they had to go outside. Becky would see them standing in the snow, going out in the rain, braving the wind, the cold, hail and thunder storms, just so they could have a smoke in their break times.

Becky asked one of them one day, "Why is smoking so important to you that you're willing to go out in the freezing cold in nasty weather just so you can have a cigarette?"

The teacher told her that she wished she didn't have to, but that she'd tried to give up smoking several times but never managed to for long, so she couldn't help it. But she said she was thinking of going to a therapist who claimed to cure people of smoking addiction, by giving them a combination of ancient herbs, and by doing what she called 'energy therapy', where she would run her hands over clients' bodies without touching them, claiming that the transfer of healing energy from therapist to client through the hands could cure them. The therapist was charging a lot of money, but the teacher was sure the therapy was going to work, because she had a friend who'd tried it and praised it highly, saying it had helped her give up smoking.

Becky thought the therapy sounded a bit strange for smoking, and thought it would be a shame if the teacher spent a lot of money only for it not to work. She wondered about the teacher's friend's claim to have been cured by it, so she asked, "Was your friend trying anything else to give up smoking at the time when she went to see the therapist?"

The teacher said yes, she'd also been avoiding the places where she got the most temptations to smoke, trying nicotine patches, and often reminding herself of the reason she wanted to give up smoking – that she had a young child and she was scared he'd get breathing problems.

Becky said, "Then before you spend a lot of money on that therapy, you ought to wonder how much of your friend's cure had to do with the therapy, and how much was to do with the other things she was doing at the time."

The teacher had to agree that was a good idea.

Becky said, "It's the same with some products and gadgets that get sold for health problems; sometimes there isn't any real evidence they work, just praise from people who say their problems cleared up when they started using them. But those problems might have been about to clear up anyway, or they might be ones that often get better for a while and then worse again, such as cold sores that tend to be at their worst every winter, and then go away when the weather gets warmer, so some people who haven't had them for long probably think they've gone for good in the spring, only for them to return when the next winter comes. Sometimes the phase of a disease where it seems to be getting better might coincide with the time when a person who's got it starts using something they think will help them, and they think what made it go away was what they've just started using, when it wasn't really."

Becky then asked how long the therapy had taken, and the teacher told her that her friend had gone to seven sessions, one a fortnight, which she said didn't sound like very many, but that by the end, her friend's cravings to smoke had almost completely gone.

Becky said, "How do you know they wouldn't have pretty much gone anyway by that time, even if she hadn't had any therapy at all, and if she hadn't even been using nicotine patches to try to help herself?"

The teacher had to admit she didn't know, and that Becky had made a good point. But she felt sure the therapy could improve people's chances of giving up smoking, saying, "The therapist told my friend she's got a great success rate – almost nine in ten people who complete her course of treatment say it's working."

Becky pointed out, "Well apart from the fact that a lot of them might have been thinking the therapy was helping when they were trying other things at the same time and didn't realise how much those things were making a difference, just because a lot of people who finished the course praised it, it doesn't mean she's got a high success rate. Just how many people completed the course compared with the number who left before they finished, perhaps because they decided it wasn't working? You have to include everyone when you calculate your success rate, not just the people who stay to the end and so are probably the most enthusiastic ones. Also, did she contact the ones who praised the therapy some time afterwards, say, six months later, and ask them if they still weren't smoking? The course will hardly have been successful if it turns out that most of them relapsed a few weeks after they finished. Did she say anything about whether it works long-term?"

The teacher, going a little red with embarrassment, had to admit that she probably hadn't; all her friend had told her was that the therapist had claimed that most people praised her technique at the end of the course.

She wouldn't normally like feeling embarrassed because of what a young child had said, but now she was glad of the warmth it was causing on her face, because the weather was freezing. She even half-hoped she'd become more embarrassed by what Becky said so she could get warmer. She decided to start jogging on the spot and rubbing her hands together vigorously to help the process of heating up along. She was still concentrating on what Becky said though.

Some of the other kids thought the teacher looked funny doing what she was doing, and chuckled. But she didn't have time to tell them off, because Becky, taking hardly any notice, said,

"I wonder how many of those people really thought the therapy had helped, and how many were just people she asked to tell her whether the course had helped, and they said 'yes' out of politeness, or because they didn't want to cause a possible confrontation by saying no. You can't rely on the claims people make about their own success rates; to know a therapy's good, it has to be studied scientifically."

The teacher said, "But This therapist knows what she's doing. She says she's studied the subject for years!"

To her dismay, Becky said bluntly, "That doesn't mean a thing! It doesn't mean she's studied everything about it. What if she's just studied books by people who want to promote it, and they're not very scientific at all, even if they look as if they are because they use scientific-sounding language? They might have left out all the evidence that it doesn't work.

"Or what if she has looked at evidence that it doesn't work, but she didn't enjoy reading it so she didn't pay it much attention, and now she's long forgotten it? She might have even forgotten a lot of what she *did* enjoy learning! How much of what you learned on your teacher training course would you say you can remember? Maybe you've even forgotten over half of it! I'm sure I've forgotten a lot of what you and the other teachers have taught me just over the past few months! It's just human nature to forget a lot of things. Look it up. And saying you've studied something for years doesn't give anyone a clue as to how intensively you've studied it; you could say that and still be telling the truth if all you did was read a chapter of someone's book a week for a few years!"

The teacher really wasn't enjoying listening to Becky. She especially hadn't enjoyed the bit that made her realise she must have gone to all the trouble of teaching Becky and the others some things, only for them to have promptly forgotten them, and that she herself had probably forgotten a lot of what she learned about teaching. But she had to admit that Becky was making sense.

Then Becky said, "And even if this therapist uses scientific -sounding language with complicated words you find hard to understand to describe what she's doing, or if anyone else does, it still doesn't necessarily mean they really know what they're talking about; some scientific-sounding things people say or write are just rubbish, or worse, misleading and harmful. So don't be impressed or more likely to trust someone just because they seem to be talking about something in a more learned way than you can."

Then Becky was reminded of something she'd heard on a consumer programme on television about people buying expensive treatments for things that didn't work nearly as well as they'd thought they would, and said,

"And don't be fooled by any claims on this therapist's website about how people have been helped; she might not be one of the ones who do such things as these, but some companies or people trying to advertise things pay actors to pretend to be just ordinary members of the public raving about how good the things being sold are, and a lot of people assume they really are just ordinary people who are saying it, and not because they're being paid to say it either, but because they really think they're good.

"And I've heard about people advertising therapy and then offering people who start it a discount for future treatment if they give them a positive review on the Internet; and a lot of people who start the therapy think it seems promising at first, and like the idea of a discount, so they do give them a positive review, only to regret it later when it turns out that the therapy didn't help after all."

The teacher began to feel depressed, because her hope of an easy cure seemed to be slipping away. Too bad, the bell went for the end of break-time and she had to get on with teaching. But they agreed to meet again in the same place after lunch.

Becky and a Friend Have a Laugh Over Lunch

While Becky was having something to eat Before she spoke to the teacher again, A girl she knew well called Wendy sat down next to her, and asked her what she'd been doing at break-time, since she'd seen her talking to a teacher all the way through it.

Becky told her she'd been going to give the teacher advice about giving up smoking, since the teacher was hoping to, and she'd been warning her that not all therapies out there are actually helpful, and that some could even do harm, since the teacher had been thinking of going to an expensive therapist to help her give up smoking, but Becky had wondered whether the therapist really was any good at helping people do that.

Wendy said, "Wow! So you know quite a bit about stuff like this? You know, it's interesting to think about a pupil giving a teacher advice! It sounds like a fun idea actually. Hey just imagine if they introduced a new course into the school called life skills, and the curriculum included things like how to give up smoking, and how to do your best to make sure you don't end up going to a quack therapist; and since some teachers wouldn't know any more about things like that than us, imagine they had to go on the course too, and people would come in from outside to teach it. So there might be teachers in the same class as eleven-year-olds, who stayed with them on the course all the way up till when they left.

"Just imagine if the kids on the course went to a school reunion about twenty years later, and someone who was about ten years older than one of them, who'd been at the school before the course started so they didn't know about it, asked one of them they'd never met before who they'd been in the same class as, thinking they might know some of the people in it, and they said, 'Miss Fox, Miss Cobweb, Miss Pond, Miss Pudding, Miss Spectacle' . . . and the person who'd asked the question interrupted them and said, 'No, I mean what pupils were you with?' Or they might say, 'Wow, so that must mean all those teachers were pupils at this school when they were kids, and you were in the same class as them. Wow, you must be old! You don't look it! But some of those teachers had been there for well over a decade when I first went there; so if you were in their class, wow, you must be about seventy-five!' "

Becky chuckled and said, "I'm not sure how I'd like it if someone thought I was in my seventies when I was really only in my mid-thirties or something! Mind you, it would be funny if we really did have teachers with names like Miss Cobweb and Miss Pudding!"

Then Wendy said, "You know, it was my granny's birthday a couple of days ago. We had a little family get-together, where we had quite a few cakes. I didn't like most of them though, which was disappointing. I think home-made ones are often nicer than quite a few shop-bought ones. We didn't have any of those though. I remember making some with my gran when I was little. These cakes I had the other day though, they just tasted of . . . I dunno, baked additive mixed with half a tub of sweeteners or something!"

Becky grinned. Then she said, "Hey imagine if someone really liked the flavour of those cakes, and they thought they were nicer than home-made cakes, so they thought it must be the additives making them taste so nice, and they went to the shops and asked if they could just buy a packet of additives, saying they thought it would be nice to try making a cake at home, but they wanted some additives to make it taste as nice as the cakes they bought in the shops."

They both giggled. Wendy said, "Mind you, some of the cakes I've had from the shops have been really nice."

Becky agreed. Then she grinned and said, "Hey you know it's possible to buy boiled sweets called fruit drops? Well just imagine if it was possible to buy raindrops. Imagine if they were real rain, but each individual drop was packaged up in a little bubble-type thing, a bit like what you get in bubble wrap, and the idea was that people would bite them open and suck the raindrops out."

Wendy laughed and said, "Yeah, and just imagine if they were different flavours, so you'd get 'original rain' flavour, and carrot-flavoured rain, and strawberry-flavoured raindrops, and cabbage-flavoured ones, and beetroot ones, and all kinds of things like that, and they were advertised as tasting like rain that had landed on fruit and vegetables that were growing naturally outside."

Becky giggled again and said, "I wouldn't fancy beetroot ones! Mind you, it's a good job we don't really get beetroot rain! Imagine if it came down from the skies like that, and dyed everything it rained on red! What a mess!

"Do you know, I was lying in bed listening to the rain the other night, and it sounded louder than I expected it to, as if it was clattering down onto something, not just falling on the grass outside. Maybe it had turned into hail, and it was landing on the windows and things. But I started imagining what it might be like if some really big raindrops started coming down, so it sounded really really loud! You know you sometimes hear that in some parts of the world they've sometimes had hailstones as big as golf balls? Imagine if sometimes we got raindrops as big as golf balls!"

Wendy grinned and said, "Wow! I'd feel sorry for anyone who had to go out in that! They'd get soaked!"

Becky grinned and said, "Yes! And I was thinking, 'What if raindrops could sometimes be as big as footballs?' I bet no one would even dare go outside if you could get raindrops as big as that sploshing down all around you, and landing on your head!"

Wendy giggled and agreed.

Becky finished eating soon after that, and, realising she didn't have as much time as she'd have liked before the end of the lunch break, rushed off to meet the teacher she'd been talking to before.

Becky Gives the Teacher More Reasons Why Not All Therapies are Good, and Starts Suggesting Other Things She Could Try to Help Her Stop Smoking

When they met up, the teacher said to Becky, "I take on board what you said earlier, but I'm not convinced. After all, what harm could the therapy I'm thinking of having do? If there's a chance it'll help me give up smoking, it'll be much better than what I've tried up till now.

"And I suffer with insomnia, and the therapist said she'll help me with that too. So it sounds like better value for money than it would be if it was just to help me give up smoking."

Becky said, "The insomnia might go away naturally when you give up smoking. I heard that insomnia's a fair bit more common among smokers than it is among non-smokers, because nicotine makes people feel more alert, so it keeps people awake. When do you tend to have your last cigarette of the day?"

The teacher said, "I like to have one an hour or two before I go to bed."

Becky said, "Well you're waking yourself up when you do that, so it's going to be harder for you to get to sleep, because the nicotine will stay around in your system for a while, stimulating it. If you could only have your last cigarette earlier in the day, your sleep will likely improve by itself.

"A lot of people who give up smoking find they get insomnia for a few weeks or so afterwards. But there are things I can tell you about right now that can help with that.

"One thing is that it'll help if you don't drink any caffeinated drinks for a couple of hours before you go to bed, since caffeine's a stimulant as well as nicotine. There are some herbal teas that some people find soothing before bed, so it might be worth trying one or two if you think you might like them. Or warm milk might help. Some people find that soothing anyway. It'll help if you can drink fewer caffeinated drinks at other times of the day too.

"Another thing that could help is doing something soothing for an hour or so before you go to bed to relax you, such as having a warm scented bath, or getting your husband to give you a gentle massage.

"Avoiding alcohol near bedtime will help too, since although it can help people drift off to sleep, it can make them more likely to wake up during the night and find it hard to get to sleep again.

"Getting some exercise during the day can help too, although it's best not to do vigorous exercise in the few hours before you go to bed, since that can stimulate the system so it's harder to fall asleep.

"Another thing you can try is to avoid the places you typically used to smoke in or where other people smoke for a couple of hours before you go to bed, if that's possible, since things that remind you of smoking will likely make your cravings to smoke worse, and they might be agitating you when you're trying to get to sleep; and anything that causes you physical or mental discomfort will keep you awake. So, for instance, if you never normally smoke in your bedroom, you could perhaps try spending an hour or so in there getting absorbed in a good book or something before you go to bed."

The teacher said, "Thank you for the tips. I suppose you might be right that I could manage to cure my insomnia by myself. But I still don't really see the harm in this therapy. I mean, if it makes things easier, even if I could have done them myself with a struggle, I'd still prefer the easier option. And all those herbs they give you have got to be healthy, since they're natural."

The teacher couldn't help wondering whether it was healthy to stand around talking in the freezing weather, even though freezing weather's natural; but she thought she'd try not to worry about that till she'd at least finished her cigarette.

Becky said it isn't true that all herbs are healthy, and that she'd read that some herbs could even be poisonous, and some used in certain kinds of Chinese herbal medicine had given people serious medical problems, and a few had even led to death; and Indian herbal medicines had often contained toxic amounts of heavy metals like lead, mercury and arsenic that could make people ill.

She said that in ancient times, it wouldn't have been nearly so easy to find out that it was the medicine rather than a disease itself that was killing a patient or giving them certain symptoms – they didn't even know what caused diseases then – so a lot of herbal medicines would have been passed down the generations regardless of how good or bad they were, if some people in authority were convinced they were good; and some that hadn't been proven to be safe were still used.

She said, "I'm not saying that no medical treatments ever worked in the olden days; there are some treatments from even a thousand years ago that would have done a lot of good, some including things like honey and garlic and onions that even have antibiotic properties, and might even be useful for killing superbugs today, from what I've heard, when they're used in certain ways. And there were mixtures of herbs that could help with things like indigestion, and some other good cures.

"Some ancient and medieval remedies could still be worth people taking today if they're in circumstances where there are no better alternatives, for some reason. There's even a research project that was started when a doctor found that a recipe in a thousand-year-old book was for a combination of plant extracts like garlic, combined with some animal product that sounds a bit disgusting, that's actually as effective at killing some bacteria as modern antibiotics, and more effective at killing MRSA than some things that are used today.

"And there were some skilled surgeons and other doctors and herbalists around in medieval times who provided some good treatments for some things. But a lot of old-fashioned remedies were downright dangerous, or painful and ineffective. There was a whole lot of quackery around, and lots of people who were just taking advantage of people's illnesses to make money by selling them fake cures they'd made up."

Then she told the teacher to consider that although she seemed to assume plants are natural and good, she could tell they aren't all healthy for humans by just thinking about the poisonous berries she must have heard of. And she said even some herbs that are very healthy in the amounts people would normally eat them in could be toxic if taken in abnormally high doses. She said,

"You'd be much better off trying to get help from an organisation that's got a good reputation for healthcare like the National Health Service than going to some unknown private therapist who you might spend a lot of money on, only to discover the therapy doesn't work for you at all."

The teacher had to admit that was a good point. She was shocked to hear that some herbs could harm people, but now she was getting worried. Still, she couldn't quite believe that therapists would be allowed to give clients toxic medicines nowadays.

Becky said that herbal medicine wasn't regulated strictly like ordinary medicines were. She reassured the teacher that in all likelihood, the therapist she wanted to go to wasn't doing anything harmful at all and she was helping a lot of people, and that for all she knew, there might be herbs, and maybe spices too, that really helped people give up smoking, even if it was just by giving them a nice taste in the mouth that would take their minds right off their cigarette cravings; but she said it might be best to be on the safe side and use a treatment that was well-known to have a good reputation instead, or at least look at scientific evidence for whether a treatment that sounded appealing worked before trying it.

Then Becky reminded the teacher of a point she'd made at break-time, that after all, even if the therapy was safe, if it hadn't been scientifically proven to work, it was difficult to know if it really did work, or whether other things people were doing at the same time as getting it were having the most effect, possibly things they later forgot they'd even done.

She said that sometimes when people bought fringe health cures and thought they worked, but other things they were doing were what was helping really, those things might be things they didn't even realise were having an effect, such as if they had symptoms that were being caused by a food intolerance their body had, but they didn't realise they were being caused by that, and then the symptoms went away when they ate something different from usual, or when they stopped eating a certain thing they normally ate. They might not even have eaten it or had a break from eating it because they hoped that would help, but simply because they happened to fancy something different for a change at the same time as they were using the supposed health cure.

She said another thing that could happen was that people could attribute more significance to one thing they were doing than was warranted, and less to another thing they were doing at the same time than it deserved. She said an example was that someone might advertise an expensive health drink on the Internet, saying it could detoxify the body and help people become more energetic. At the same time, they might encourage people to give up junk food and eat healthily. A lot of people who bought the drink might follow that advice, and then start feeling better, and think it was the drink that mostly helped, and spend a lot of money on buying a lot more of it over time, when really it was their change of diet that helped.

Becky said, "Something a bit like that happened to me not long ago. I mean, someone thought one thing had helped with something when it was probably a different thing altogether. I choked on some food. I've choked on food a few times before, and I found out that if you breathe through your nose when it happens, it can be easier to breathe than if you try breathing through your mouth. Not always, but sometimes. And it helps if you put your head right down below your knees. It must be because the force of gravity means that if what's stuck in your throat moves, it'll fall towards your mouth, and hopefully unblock the blockage it caused if your top half's facing downwards, while it'll mean there's a risk that it'll fall further down your throat and get stuck further in and make things worse if you're sitting or standing upright.

"Actually, if I'm sitting down when I choke, I often stand up and then put my head right down near my knees, and I try to resist the urge to cough till my throat starts to unblock so it's easier to breathe, so I don't cough all my breath out before I can breathe some in again, and I just wait, and then I can actually sometimes feel the food tipping towards my mouth, and then it gets easier to breathe. Well, it seems to have worked for me so far anyway. Maybe it depends on how jammed-in the food is in your throat.

"I've heard that if that doesn't work, people can help stop choking if they clench a fist and put their other hand round it, and then shove themselves with it several times in an upwards direction just below the ribcage. But I've never tried that, and I think people probably need to get advice on how to do that properly from someone who's good at first aid, or from a good Internet site that goes into it in detail.

"But anyway, I was choking once, and I was trying to breathe through my nose, but it wasn't really working that time. I put my head right down, and I think the blockage must have tipped towards my mouth a little bit, because I slowly started to be able to breathe more easily. My mum was in the room at the time. She must have started worrying about me. She became a nurse not all that long ago. That's why my grandma and grandpa pick me up from school a lot instead of her. Maybe you know that already. But anyway, my mum told me once that she was being trained on a ward for old people one day when one of them started choking, and seemed to have stopped breathing. She lay her down and banged her really hard on the back. It was visiting time on the ward, and just then, the old woman's son walked in. It looked to him as if my mum was beating his mum up, and he got cross and threatened to take her to court for assault. He calmed down when he found out what she was really doing.

"But anyway, when I was choking, my mum came over to me and asked me if I was alright. I put my head up some of the way and tried to smile at her to let her know the problem was sorting itself out. But I still couldn't talk. So I couldn't let her know properly. It would have been good if she'd said something like, 'Put your hand up if you want me to try and help you', so I could have let her know I didn't want her to by not doing that, without even having to lift my head up. But anyway, I put my head down again and told my body to hurry up. I said to myself, 'Come on body you slow coach, hurry up or I'll be assaulted!' I still couldn't talk, and then my mum did bang me on the back. It was quite hard, but to my relief, it didn't hurt after all.

"Just after that, I found I could talk again. I bet my mum thought it was because she'd banged me on the back. But really it would have happened by then anyway.

"I'm not saying banging on the back doesn't work. I'm just saying I'm pretty sure it wasn't that that worked that time."

Then Becky started talking about what she'd heard about therapies again. She told the teacher she'd read about lots of ancient treatments that had been thought to work for hundreds of years, but when they'd been scientifically tested in the near past, they were found to be quack remedies; and one reason they were thought to work for as long as they were was probably because other things were happening to a lot of the people who tried them at the same time that helped.

For instance, if someone had scurvy, caused by lack of vitamin C, they wouldn't have known what the cause was in ancient times, and a witchdoctor or healer might have tried making the person eat worms or something. It might have sometimes seemed to work, so the supposed remedy of eating worms might have been passed down the generations and lots of unfortunate people might have been advised to try it; but the real reason it might have seemed to worked was that the scurvy was at its worst at the times of year when fresh fruit and vegetables were hardest to find and hadn't been around for a while, so most people who had it would seek treatment then, but that would have been the time of year when vegetables were just growing again and wild fruits were not far off beginning to ripen, and the person would likely soon start eating them again and get vitamin C from them, so in reality, it was that that made them better.

Snow began to fall just then, but ignoring it, even while the teacher shivered, Becky continued:

"Another example of a possible cure that might have seemed to work is that an ancient healer might have prescribed eating an apple with a maggot in it every day at sunset for a week to cure scurvy, and it might have seemed to help, so that cure would be passed down the generations, with no one testing out whether just apples on their own without maggots in them, and eaten at any time of day, worked, and no one realising that it was the vitamin C in the apples that was curing the person. A lot of what some modern therapists do and make people pay for might be unnecessary, although at least maggots have gone out of fashion a bit."

The teacher squirmed at the thought of maggots; or perhaps she was shivering with the cold, or doing a bit of both. She started to feel a bit upset with Becky for putting her off the therapy. She still had some hope though, and told Becky that even if the herbs that the therapist she wanted to go to gave her didn't really work, her friend had said the energy healing the therapist had given her had been lovely and soothing and relaxing, which was something you just wouldn't get from a doctor on the health service.

Becky said, "It sounds as if what was really making your friend feel good was being pampered and relaxed. I think some therapists who do this kind of thing think they have some kind of supernatural energy they're passing on; but I've read that scientists have done experiments where someone who doesn't believe that at all has done the techniques on people, and they've worked even better than they have when some of those therapists have done them. It's probably the relaxation and pampering that helps. You could get your husband to pamper you a bit and do relaxing things with you instead. Get him to massage you slowly and gently from head to toe a few times a week – then you'll get what the therapy probably really does for free; it'll probably de-stress you just as much, and give you nice feelings that make you feel more cheerful for a while. And it might help you get on better with him, which will make you feel better too. And the better you feel, the less you'll probably be tempted to smoke. That's probably how the therapy really works."

It was snowing harder than before, but although the teacher was visibly shivering now, Becky didn't seem to care in her enthusiasm to finish giving her advice. She continued:

"Also, think about things you enjoy, that you can get absorbed in, so temptations to smoke don't come on so much while you're doing them. Do more of them. You might realise they're a lot cheaper than that therapy, and maybe even safer."

The teacher thought that was a good idea. She wasn't really happy that a nine-year-old pupil was bossing her around, but she thought Becky seemed to have some decent suggestions. But she still wasn't confident about being able to give up smoking alone, since she'd tried and failed before.

More Teachers Become Interested in Listening to Becky, and she Gives Them Lots of Advice on Ways of Giving Up Smoking

Becky was planning to do a psychology degree after she left school in several months' time, along with one in media studies, and she had been reading some books on psychology, because she was interested in it, and also so she could be sure it was what she wanted to do, and also as part of a counselling course she'd done in her fourth form. She'd read a bit about giving up smoking. She told the teacher she was talking to that she'd tell her what she'd found out.

But then the bell went for the end of the lunch hour, so they agreed to meet up the next day at break-time.

The next day when they met up, Becky found three teachers, all hoping to give up smoking, and eagerly waiting for her to teach them what she'd read about how it could be done.

Becky wasn't surprised they wanted to give up smoking; since the smoking ban had been introduced in their school and they'd had to go outside to smoke, she'd seen one teacher desperately running after her pack of cigarettes after it blew away in the strong wind they'd had not long before, one coming in with snow on her coat, not wanting to teach at her desk but snuggling up to the radiator for a whole lesson and apologising to the class for it, and one of them coming in soaking wet from the rain, dripping water all over some homework one pupil had given her, till it was so wet she couldn't read it and the pupil had had to print it out again – it was a good job it hadn't been handwritten.

Becky started her talk by saying she expected the teachers were dreading giving up smoking, partly because they probably thought they'd feel more stressed afterwards. But she said they wouldn't necessarily; after all, they could always keep reminding themselves of the advantages of not smoking any more, such as not having to go out in nasty weather and get embarrassed by mishaps like their cigarettes blowing away in the wind. She said they could also look forward to feeling happier to attend social events, knowing they wouldn't have to keep excusing themselves and missing out on things because they needed to go out for a smoke, or smoking right there and facing some people's disapproval.

One teacher heartily agreed, saying, "Yes, only the other day I went to a friend's baby's christening, and I lit up a cigarette, and someone accidentally banged into the back of me, and I dropped it right in the font. The priest got a bit annoyed and said, 'Holy smoke! I can't baptise the baby in that!' We all had to wait while the water was changed, and quite a few people stared at me accusingly. It was so embarrassing!"

Becky suggested to the teacher that she could remind herself of that embarrassing incident often if it helped put her off cigarettes. Then she said to them all, "It'll help you not to give in to the temptation to smoke again after you've all given up if you think of as many advantages of giving up smoking as you can, as well as the disadvantages of smoking, and often remind yourselves of them."

One teacher said, "Yes, but it's the cravings that are the problem. It's difficult to stop when those come on."

Becky said, "Don't worry; I'm coming to those. That wasn't the only piece of advice I've got. Alright, I'll give you a quick tip before I get there. How about carrying a bottle of your favourite perfume or something else that smells nice with you, and whenever you get a craving to smoke, spray a bit on your wrist, and take a few long, slow sniffs of it. The craving might be for cigarettes, but your body might be reasonably satisfied with some kind of substitute for them. After all, some smokers who are trying to give up eat food instead, and that gets them through, even if it makes them fat."

One or two teachers blushed at the idea that they might be about to get fat, since they were a bit self-conscious about their size anyway.

Then Becky told them a story she'd read, saying:

"Anyway, when you're giving up smoking, you might think your cravings to smoke are bad, but you might realise they're not as bad as you think, just as a woman did who went to a therapist to help her give up smoking, and the next day she phoned him in a panic, saying she wanted to smoke so desperately she'd murder her children if she thought it would help her get relief from her cravings. She was so panicky at the thought that she'd even be willing to kill her kids, and that she shouldn't be having a smoke, that she wasn't in a state of mind where she could take in advice;

so the therapist calmed her down so she could think more clearly, by encouraging her to slow her breathing right down for a few minutes, which he said calms the body down. Then he asked her some questions:

"He asked her if she'd ever had a horribly painful toothache, and she said yes. Then he asked which was worse, the toothache or the craving. She said definitely the toothache.

Then he asked her if she'd ever had a mild, nagging toothache, and she said yes. He asked her to think about it and then say which was worse, the craving for cigarettes or that toothache. She paused, and then said that if she was honest, it had to be the toothache.

"Then the therapist asked how long her cravings usually lasted, and she said they lasted a good five minutes!

"Then the therapist said, 'So, let's get this clear, you are ready to murder your children for an amount of discomfort that's milder than a slight, nagging toothache, and which lasts for just five minutes?'

"The woman burst out laughing. Then she realised that her cravings were actually quite mild, and that it had been her panicky reaction to them that had made them seem so terrible. Once she realised that, she came off cigarettes with no problem.

"Part of what causes nicotine cravings is probably psychological, caused by the anxiety of wanting something and not being able to have it. I mean, if you think you need something to be happy, but you're not getting it, it's going to stress you out, isn't it, and it's probably going to be on your mind a lot, while you're worrying about how you're going to cope without it, and thinking about how nice it would be to have it again.

"So it might help to have a good clear image in your mind of how much nicer it'll be not to be risking getting breathing problems because of smoking, or seeming anti-social to non-smokers when you keep having to leave them to go for a smoke, and of all the other advantages you can think of that you'll get from not smoking, and of things you could do as a substitute that'll help relax you and make you feel better, because if you can often think of those things, it might help to soothe you a bit and give you some hope that'll cheer you up a bit, so it'll relieve some of the cigarette cravings."

The teachers were listening to Becky with interest. She continued:

"But according to what I've read, a lot of the time, cravings come on partly because the brain knows it's the time you'd normally have a smoke, and it feels the absence of it, because it's so used to having a smoke at those times that it signals that it thinks there's something wrong because you're not following your normal routine and taking in the substance it's used to getting at that time. It can help if at those times, you can change something about your routine so you're concentrating on doing something new, rather than your brain feeling as if you're doing the same thing as normal only something's missing. It can be as simple as eating a piece of fruit – perhaps something that occupies your hands and your mind for a little while in place of the cigarette – perhaps something like oranges that you have to concentrate on peeling before you can eat them, if you like them.

"Some people say one thing they miss about smoking is not having anything in their hands at those times. Eating fruit or raw vegetables – if you like them of course – gives you something to do with your hands and mouth at the same time. I say vegetables because they're low-calorie. I've heard about people who put on weight after they stopped smoking, because they started eating fattening foods instead. My grandpa did that. He ate loads of peanuts. They might be quite healthy, but they're fattening; but vegetables aren't.

"Some people say they can taste things better after they stop smoking, so maybe that'll happen to you, so that's one thing you can look forward to."

Just then the bell went for the end of break, and some teachers remembered they hadn't tasted the snacks they'd brought with them to eat before lessons started again, not to mention that they'd missed out on their cigarettes! They were a bit disappointed, and not really in the mood to go back into lessons; but though one slapped the back of her own hand as a punishment for not thinking to bring her snack with her and eat it while Becky was talking, they decided that missing out on them had been worth it, because they found what Becky was telling them interesting. They decided to come back the next day at break for some more advice.

The next day at break-time, even more teachers were there to listen to Becky. Word had got around that she had something interesting to tell them.

They'd decided to meet indoors, since meeting out in the cold again like they had before, only to not smoke because they'd feel guilty about smoking when they were discussing giving smoking up, which is what happened the day before, didn't seem to be a good idea. The ones who'd listened to Becky before wished they'd realised they'd feel that way before they went out the previous day and stayed indoors then. Still, they put it down to experience.

They stayed near the door that led out onto the playground though, so they could look out onto it from time to time in case anything dramatic started happening that they thought they might need to go and try to stop.

Becky started telling them things she'd learned about giving up smoking in an encouraging way – albeit a rather bossy one – by saying:

"It'll be easier to give up smoking if you don't think of yourselves as having to come to terms with missing out on something, and making sacrifices for your health when you give up, but as making a whole new start in life; so at the same time as you give up smoking, you might find it helpful if you start changing your lives in ways that'll make you feel better. Sit down later and think of a dozen ways your life could be improved – or as many as you can think of, and then plan ways you can work towards making those changes. Don't try to make too many at once, since if you're too ambitious and don't manage to achieve what you want, you might get discouraged and give up the whole attempt to make changes altogether, and want to smoke to comfort yourselves.

"What I'm saying is, just as an example, if you decide your life could be made better by not arguing with your kids, don't resolve to stop altogether right away, since that would be very difficult, so you might start thinking you've failed if you don't manage it. You'll probably have to experiment a bit to find out what helps you stop best. Plan to try things that have a realistic chance of improving things, rather than trying something you just hope will work well but might not work at all, such as your will power. Bear in mind you might have to find and try several techniques in combination before you manage to put together a strategy that really works. Just think of yourselves as working towards improvement. You could look on the Internet for advice about ways of improving things. Perhaps you could set a target, thinking to yourselves that in six weeks' time, your lives will likely be very noticeably better, and you'll be arguing with your kids a lot less, or doing whatever you're trying to improve on better.

"Then, instead of feeling more stressed because you're not smoking any more, you'll eventually feel less stressed, because several other things in your life will be improving."

Becky had developed quite a grown-up way of talking, using fairly big words, because she'd taken them in from all the books she'd read that were meant for grown-ups. And she'd got a lot of grown-up ideas from those books. But she'd begun to often carry some Farley's rusks that were made for babies with her to snack on, because she still enjoyed those. Nothing babyish about that really; she'd seen her grandma enjoy them too. She felt like eating one just then, and thought of asking the teachers if they'd like to share it; but then she decided it would be best not to, in case they stopped taking her seriously because they didn't share her grown-up grandma's view that eating rusks wasn't just for babies.

Just then, Becky had to stop talking, because they saw two boys run into the school carrying snowballs, probably planning some mischief that would result in a wet teacher's desk, or flying snowballs hurtling towards some unsuspecting pupil. One of the teachers ordered them to go and put them back outside. Instead, they threw them at the teachers, and ran back outside. Normally the teachers would have chased them, but they were keen to hear what Becky had to say, so they ran towards the door for several steps, and then decided not to and all turned around and ran back again.

Becky made no comment, just smiled. While snow dripped off them, she continued:

"The cravings you get to smoke will probably make you feel stressed, so you'll feel as if you need a cigarette to calm down. You might think it's smoking that's calming you down so you need it, but really it's at least partly the relief from the nicotine withdrawal symptoms you get when you smoke that'll be making you feel better. If you don't smoke again, the time will come when you're not getting those withdrawal symptoms, so you won't get stressed by not smoking, especially since you can have a go at finding new things instead that are just as good at calming you down.

"Maybe you think that one of the reasons it's worth smoking is because it stops you feeling so stressed; but can you be sure you'd be as stressed as you get when you don't smoke for a while if you'd never started smoking? Some people who've studied these things say that smoking doesn't make people calmer than they would be if they'd never smoked; what happens is that when they stop smoking for a while, they start to feel a bit stressed, because their body starts to feel the need for nicotine, and the relief of the craving when they have another cigarette calms them down. So they think smoking's doing them good, when it's really only calming the problem that it itself created in the first place.

"Well, I think there are some scientists who think nicotine can have a slightly calming effect on people for a little while when they start smoking a cigarette. But other things can have a calming effect too, without the harm of smoking.

"I think I've already mentioned that when you stop smoking, you might well get cravings to smoke at all the times of day when you're used to smoking, because something in your brain will be expecting it, and it'll feel sure something's missing if it doesn't happen. You could think of things you enjoy, that'll be quite quick to do and aren't that bad for your health, and plan to do them at every time of day when before you gave up smoking, you'd have had a smoke. You could at least do them for the next few weeks. Try to start them before the cigarette craving even starts, so you might be absorbed in them soon after you start them, so if you get the craving, you won't be fully concentrating on it so it won't seem so bad.

"Regularly doing new things at those times will help you develop new routines that don't involve smoking too, since your brain might well eventually prompt you to do one of the new things rather than making you feel like smoking at the times when you used to smoke, since it'll get used to you doing the new things then, and your subconscious mind will begin to expect you to do one instead of smoking. Now it probably makes you want to smoke at certain times because it's used to you doing that, so it automatically reminds you by giving you a craving to smoke then, because it thinks smoking's part of your natural routine.

"And if the new things you do aren't addictive, they'll be easier to give up if you want to when the cravings die down."

A few pupils walked past and heard what sounded like Becky ordering the teachers around, as if she was correcting bad behaviour. They thought it was a bit strange, but as they walked off into the distance, they had fun with the idea, pretending to order teachers about, imitating Becky's voice and saying things like:

"Mr Curtis, no, you don't eat your peas off a knife, especially in the middle of class when you're supposed to be teaching a history lesson!"

The teachers listening to Becky heard them, but thought it would be best to ignore them, since they thought listening to Becky was too important to get distracted from, even if they were being made fun of. She continued:

"Sometimes, you might have been used to smoking while you work on things, and you might think it helps you concentrate and relieves tension. But while the nicotine in the tobacco might help concentration at first, as soon as the levels in your blood begin to fall so the effect wears off, the craving for another smoke will distract you from concentrating. So there might be things that work better than smoking. And you could probably relieve tension just as much by doing some other things, including squeezing one of those little stress ball toys."

The teachers who'd had the snowballs thrown at them were shivering a bit, especially one who'd been hit on the neck by one, which had then partly fallen down the inside of his clothes and was now dripping out the bottom of his shirt. They thought it was a pity they were cold, since they'd stayed indoors to try to prevent themselves shivering. But they put up with it, because they wanted to hear what Becky said. Somehow it didn't occur to them to just move further away from the open doorway that led to the playground, or to shut it. Becky didn't seem to notice their discomfort, because she was so busy concentrating on what she was saying. She continued:

"According to a psychology book I've read, cravings to smoke are partly caused because part of the brain monitors how much of each substance in your body is in your blood all the time, and once it gets used to nicotine, it's as if it's been programmed to assume it's supposed to be there. So when supplies fall below normal levels, it sends out an alarm. That signals another part of the brain to investigate how important it is to have nicotine in the system, by getting information from the brain's memory stores about what taking it in by smoking's done for the person in the past. Lots of memories can then quickly flicker through the brain in response, about enjoyable and relaxing experiences that were had while smoking, going so fast they might barely register with the conscious mind; but the part of the brain that called for the information will conclude that smoking's so associated with good times that it must be important.

"The memory store of smoking scenes only has information to pass on about the past, naturally, so worries about future health problems won't be passed on.

"The part of the brain that called for the information can come to feel as if it's so important to smoke that it can flood the part of the brain where people make conscious decisions, that doesn't believe smoking's a good idea, with alarm signals about nicotine levels going down, and enticements about how smoking's caused an increased sense of well-being before so it'll do it again, that make it hard to resist the temptation to smoke. Those alarms and enticements are what you'll feel as cravings.

"I don't know how the authors of the book I read that in can know this stuff, but if it's to be believed, the cravings can be mild at the time when the part of the brain that monitors amounts of substances in the bloodstream first notices nicotine levels have fallen; but they increase a lot when the memories about how smoking's related to good times, and any thoughts about how bad it's been to try to live without it in the past, quickly pass through the brain.

Smoking might be easier to resist if you remember that's what's going on. That's especially if you think about the fact that those memories about how good smoking's been won't really be all to do with enjoying smoking, but about enjoying doing other things while you were smoking, like socialising, that have come to be strongly associated with smoking in your brain because you've smoked so often when you were doing them. In reality you could come to enjoy them just as much without smoking at the same time."

Some pupils had stopped to listen to what Becky was saying, having assumed she must be receiving a massive telling off for something, considering that not just one but several teachers were with her. They assumed she must be trying to defend herself. But when they heard her telling the teachers about giving up smoking, they became interested, and hung around to listen.

She continued, "You could try fixing a date in the near future, and thinking of it as the special day you'll give up smoking. If you've made up your minds that you'll make a good fresh start from that day on, you might wake up with optimism that day, and not feel stressed and conflicted for days about which cigarette will be your last, because you'll have planned it and anticipated it for a little while, so you'll be used to the idea that you're going to give up right then. So it might be easier. And you'll at least be starting on a high if you've decided that's the day you'll start positive change.

"For the first few weeks after you stop smoking, you'll probably get bad cravings, since part of your brain will be sending out alarm signals, because it'll notice that a familiar substance is lacking from your bloodstream that it's come to expect there, and you'll be remembering how much you liked smoking; but if you know it's mostly just a mistaken alarm signal and hints of misguided nostalgia causing the cravings, they might be easier to tolerate. And when they're dying down later, you can think back to how bad they felt at first, and compare them with what they've come to be like at the time you're looking back, so you can tell you're making progress, because they likely won't be anywhere near as bad as they were at first; and then you can give yourself more of an incentive to stay free of cigarettes with the happy thought that if you never start smoking again, you'll never want to try to give up, and have to go through the stress of the first few days after giving up when the cravings were at their worst again.

"And when you first give up, you can console yourself by reassuring yourself that the stress of having the cravings won't last; they'll get weaker and less frequent fairly soon over time if you don't give in to them, and if you don't consciously start fantasising about how nice it would be to smoke when you have one. The thought that they won't last could make you more optimistic and less stressed.

"Another thing that could cheer you up is often calculating the amount of money you'll have saved since you gave up smoking by not buying cigarettes, and the amount of time you've managed to stay smoke-free for."

The maths teacher was one of the ones Becky was talking to, and he looked uncertain when she said that, as if he wasn't sure he'd manage to remember and calculate that accurately over time. At least, that's what Becky interpreted his look to mean, and said, "There might be apps that help you do that." The maths teacher looked relieved.

Then Becky carried on talking, conscious they were running out of time but really wanting to say more. She wondered if she'd have time to say just a few more things. She decided to try.

Unfortunately, just then, one of the girls in her first year of secondary school came in, dripping snow, and loudly singing an old playground song she seemed to have modified a bit:

> *Glory glory alleluia*
> *Teacher hit me with a ruler.*
> *I threw it at her belly*
> *Which wobbled like a jelly*
> *'Cos it's bigger than the classroom door.*

Becky desperately hoped the teachers would ignore the girl instead of telling her off, partly because she thought it would be a shame if they did tell her off, because the song had made her smile – something she tried to hide from the teachers by putting her arm over her face, pretending she was brushing her hair out of her eyes, even though it was too short to have got there – but also because she thought a telling-off might last till the end of break, and then the teachers might not come back to hear what else she had to say.

The teachers didn't think the girl who'd sung the song deserved to be ignored, but after opening their mouths to all tell her off, they quickly closed them again, since they wanted to hear the rest of what Becky had to say. So Becky carried on:

"It doesn't sound very nice, but you can help to re-train your brains not to crave cigarettes so much if you spend some time each day bringing to mind all the bad things about smoking you can think of, so they'll become easier and easier to remember when the cravings come on, as well as thinking about some good things you'll begin to experience when you give smoking up, so those will come to mind more easily too, so smoking won't seem quite so appealing when you're in the middle of a cigarette craving.

"Feelings have a more powerful impact on the mind than thoughts, because it's easier to remember the strength of a feeling than it is to remember some thought you might have had; so one way of trying to make sure the bad things about smoking and the good things about giving it up will more easily come to mind when you have a craving to smoke is to think of them in a way that makes feelings accompany them each time you practice thinking of them. There's a way you can make it more likely that that will happen, which is if once a day, you take a few minutes to imagine the bad things smoking could do for you in vivid enough detail that you start to get a bit anxious about them, and then imagine how happy you could be if you give up, vividly enough that you actually feel happy just thinking about it.

"Here's one way of doing that: You could first imagine you're walking along a road you could call the Road of Doom, which is ageing you as you go along, till you get to a place where you imagine it's twenty years in the future, when you've got serious health problems because you smoked – heart disease perhaps, or cancer, or severe scary breathlessness where you can't get where you're going easily because you get seriously out of breath quickly and have to keep stopping to gasp for air, and the fact that it's hard to get enough makes you wonder if you'll collapse. Maybe you could imagine having all those things at once. Then you can imagine relatives crying at your bedside after you've got even more ill, and your own adult children being there, who've had breathing problems for years that they got from living with you and your smoke. Spend time imagining how you'll feel if that happens, and how they'll feel, worrying about whether you're going to die."

Some pupils who smoked had stopped to listen a few minutes earlier, and started drifting away when they heard that. But they stopped again when they heard Becky say:

"Then imagine walking back along the road away from it all, towards a place called the Garden of Hope, where you imagine how nice it'll feel when you experience all the advantages of not smoking, such as having a better sense of taste, being able to enjoy social occasions with friends without having to walk away from them and go out in the cold to smoke if there's a smoking ban where you are or they don't want you smoking near them, the knowledge that your health might well improve, your increased chances of seeing your grandchildren grow up, and so on. Daydream about enjoying all the advantages you can think of for a few minutes.

"Then at the times you'd normally smoke, try to remember those nice daydreams, plus the scary ones if it helps."

A few pupils who'd started to smoke a year or two earlier and then regretted it had happened to come along some time earlier, and had started listening when they heard what Becky was saying, and had even given up their plans for a good snowball fight as they stayed to hear what she said. They ended up thinking it was worth it, even though they didn't like the idea of thinking of all the horrible things that could happen if they carried on smoking.

Becky continued, "Sometimes you might have thoughts telling you how nice it would be to smoke. You can talk back to those thoughts if it helps – not out loud of course, at least in public; you wouldn't want to be accused of having the first sign of madness."

She grinned as she said that, and then said:

"But for instance, if you have a thought that tells you you'll go mad if you don't have a cigarette, you can imagine your better nature challenging that thought, perhaps saying something like, 'No I won't. This is only a temporary craving. It'll go soon.'

"Or if you think something like, 'Oh, doesn't that man over there smoking look contented! It brings back happy memories of when I was doing that; and isn't that cigarette smell enticing!' you could say with your better nature:

"'But I know I'm better off not smoking really; it shouldn't really cause me happiness when I'm breathing something in that might give me lung cancer or heart disease or breathing problems! And now I don't smoke, I realise the smell of smoke on a person doesn't seem so nice the next day. I can list several reasons why I'm better off not smoking.' "

Just then the bell went for the end of break. Becky said in frustration and disappointment, "Oh no! I've only got a few more little things I want to say!" She knew asking the teachers to give up another break-time to come and be lectured by her was perhaps a bit much. After all, a few of the children passing had looked at them a bit strangely – a group of teachers being lectured by a nine-year-old. But the teachers were happy to stay there. They all decided they'd let Becky carry on for a few more minutes, and deliberately go late to their classes for the first time in their lives.

So Becky continued, "It's important to plan for what you're going to do when you get tempted to smoke after you've given up. You'll probably be offered cigarettes when you go out to socialise with people you know, if there are smokers in the group, and it'll be tempting to accept them if you have to think about whether to accept one or not on the spot when the cigarettes are right there; but you might be more successful in resisting the temptation if you're prepared for it to happen, and have an answer ready so you can use it before you even start really thinking about it.

"Also, you can plan to do other things when the temptation starts to get stronger – as it probably will for everyone who tries to stop smoking: For instance, you could leave the group and go for a little walk for a few minutes, phone a friend, or anything really that gives you breathing space to calm down and think about what the addiction's really doing to you, and how much better it is to give it up.

"Also, you could try and make sure there are some non-smokers in the group with you, so you won't be the only one refusing a cigarette if they're offered around, so you don't feel as if you stand out awkwardly."

As the teachers got later and later for class, Becky tried to finish off. At first she started talking faster and faster, but they started protesting that they couldn't understand her, especially since she began to stumble over her words a bit. So she slowed down to normal pace, and repeated what she'd tried to say before, saying:

"Another thing you could try when a craving to smoke comes on is telling yourself you'll wait fifteen minutes before maybe giving in; you can tell yourself you won't deny yourself a cigarette altogether, but you'll wait, and if you still want it as strongly in a quarter of an hour, you'll consider whether to give in, or whether you can cope with the craving for a while longer; cravings often die down after a few minutes, so chances are it won't be so strong after fifteen minutes, and you'll realise you can cope with it. But if you're not sure if you can after fifteen minutes, you could decide to wait just another fifteen minutes, telling yourself you can always give in if you really can't cope with the craving after that. And when that quarter of an hour's over, you can do the same thing, and so on for some time, each time asking yourself if you could wait for just an extra fifteen minutes. That way, you won't feel the stress of thinking you have to deny yourself a cigarette for evermore, which might make you long for them more."

It suddenly occurred to Becky that the teachers might be forgetting what she was telling them as fast as they were learning it. It was a dismaying thought, but a couple of them were jotting down brief notes; she just hoped they'd be able to understand them afterwards. She asked them if they thought they would, and they said they felt sure they would. Another teacher looked at the notes of one of them and couldn't understand a word, but the teacher who wrote them seemed to think she'd be able to understand them herself, and said she'd interpret them for the other teacher later if she wanted. So Becky gave them her last piece of advice:

"Sometimes a strong craving to smoke might come on when you haven't had a craving for some time, and you might not understand why. If it takes you by surprise when you're off your guard, you might be more likely to give in to it, because the strategies you've been using to deal with it might have slipped to the back of your mind by then, so it takes longer to remember them, and to even remember to try to remember them. So have a think about what you can do beforehand if that happens, so you're as prepared as possible.

"Cravings will likely come on at times of significance when you've smoked in the past. If you try and work out what those might be, you might not be able to think of them all, but you might be able to think of and plan for some. But whether you can or not, when one comes on, try to remember it's doing it because the part of the brain that monitors your routines is associating what you're doing with smoking because you've often smoked when you've done it before, so it thinks you ought to be doing it this time too. It's just making a mistake, and you can tell it so.

"In case you're not sure what I mean, I'll tell you a story to give you an example: There was one woman I read about who hadn't had a craving for a smoke for nearly a year, but suddenly got one when she was packing her suitcase to go on holiday. It was really tempting for her to give in to it; but then she realised she was only getting it because her brain remembered she'd often smoked while she'd been packing her suitcases before, so it thought it was a good time for her to do it again. When she realised that, she found it easier not to give in to the craving.

"Sometimes cravings might come on at times of celebration if you're used to smoking then, or if you're not on the alert for them when you're at your happiest so they get stronger before you can distract yourself from them. Sometimes they might come on when you're feeling down, if you've been used to smoking to comfort yourself when you've been in a bad mood. But they'll always be coming on because you've been in the habit of smoking at those times, so it's as if the brain's programmed to prompt you to do your usual thing by smoking again. But once you've got into new smokeless habits and routines, the brain will be being re-trained not to do that."

With that, Becky finished lecturing the teachers. They thanked her and went off to class. They walked in shamefacedly, because they were all about ten minutes late, and they hadn't even tried to get in earlier. But they were thankful they'd heard what Becky had to say, and did remember a lot of it, and it helped them.

Chapter 6

Becky Saves Her Mum From a Con Artist Pretending to be Psychic Who Thinks She'll Be an Easy Target

When Becky was about eight years old, a new couple moved in next-door to her family. Becky's mum saw the woman around, and they got chatting.

Becky's mum invited her in for tea one day. The new neighbour said she was a psychic medium, and that if Becky's mum liked, she'd invite her to her house and give her a free psychic reading.

Becky's mum was interested, so she agreed, thinking it might be a bit of fun, and feeling curious to see what went on. She thought it would be interesting if she really could find out things about her future, and thought that even if it was a disappointment, at least it would have been free so it wouldn't matter much.

Becky Starts Analysing a So-Called Psychic Reading Given to her Mum by the Self-Proclaimed Medium Next Door

When she and Becky went round there, the woman who'd said she was psychic created a calming atmosphere with dim lights, incense and gentle music, before doing the reading.

Becky's mum was impressed with what she told her, and discussed the reading with Becky after they went home. She said:

"Wow! I didn't really believe she'd have a real psychic gift, but she said things she couldn't possibly have known before, because I've never told her. She knew I've got a brother with a little boy, and said the boy's got a good future ahead of him! She even knew his name! She actually told me his name's Tom! And she knew my brother's called Steve too! I'm really impressed!"

To her surprise, Becky was disappointingly unimpressed. Not only that, but she seemed to suspect there was some kind of trickery going on. Just the thing to spoil her mum's good mood! She said, "Mum! The other day when the medium came round for tea, while you were out making it, she looked at some of your photos. She saw some with Tom in them. Then she asked me a few questions about the family, and I told her something about some of the people in it, including Tom and uncle Steve. That's how she got to know about them!

"And as for her saying Tom's got a good future, that's a safe prediction – something would have to go dramatically wrong for you to decide that couldn't be right! And it'll be years before you can determine whether it's true, so there's probably no way you can disprove the prediction and discredit what she says for a long time to come; and by the time it's possible, you might have forgotten she even said it, or she might have moved away from here!

"For another thing, there are so many ways it could be interpreted, it would be difficult to prove it wrong. Even if Tom dies in three years' time, you could still think the prediction was right, because between then and now, he might go to a good school, and he could be top of the class and enjoy himself. Even if he grows up to have no job and no hope but he lives a decent life, you could interpret the word "good" to mean that in his future, he'll be a good person! You might believe the prediction's true for years and trust that woman, just because you've interpreted it in your own mind in a way that makes it sound convincing!"

(Naturally, it beggars belief that Becky could have said such things when she was only about eight years old. But as I said at the beginning of this book, this story has some of the qualities of legend ... and you know what legends are like for exaggerating people's achievements all over the place. Still, whatever Becky's real age was, she certainly came out with some wisdom that day.)

Her mum had started to feel a bit hot-and-bothered, and said, "Becky, must you say horrible things? Tom's only a little boy; I don't want to think about him dying!" She didn't like the idea that Becky might be right about her having fallen for a trick either. She wished there were times when a legend-like eight-year-old didn't seem so worldly-wise and clever, and depressing. She said,

"Maybe you're right about the reason the medium knew Tom's name. But she got some things right she can't possibly have known before, because she talked about people I haven't got photos of as well, and you don't even know them yourself, so you can't have told her about them. I mean, before you were born, I had a friend called Frances who married a Turkish man and went to live in Turkey, and the medium told me that, and told me I'd been worrying about whether they were happy together and whether she was being treated well, which I have been. She even told me her name!"

Becky said, "No she didn't. At least, not before you'd helped her along a lot. You've forgotten what you said to give her clues. The medium said, 'You've been worrying about someone recently' . . . well for a start, that's a safe guess! From some of the conversations I hear you and other mums having together, I reckon everyone must worry about someone else sometimes, even if it's just a little bit.

"Then she said, 'I can't quite get the name; I think it starts with a letter in the first half of the alphabet . . . E? . . . H? . . . G? . . . F perhaps.' You nodded your head a bit and sat up straighter when she said 'F', since you'd probably been thinking of someone whose name begins with F; and those were the kinds of clues she was probably looking for to tell her which letter to stop at. Then you helped her guess the name without realising; she said, as if she was trying to decipher the signal she was getting from her spirit guide or wherever these things are supposed to come from, 'Fay? . . . No, Fiona? . . . No, Francesca?' . . . And then you gave her just what she was hoping you would by saying, 'Frances'? She said, 'Yes, Frances!' as if she'd almost known it all along really. Then she called her Frances from then on, and you obviously forgot that you were the one who virtually told her that was the name in the first place."

The Subject Changes, and the Conversation Becomes Amusing for a Little While

The washing had been on, and Becky's mum noticed it had finished, and told Becky she was just going to put it out, relieved to have a break from the process of being disillusioned. Considering there was no sun, and it wouldn't be all that long before it got dark, the washing didn't have much chance of drying that day; but it was warm for that time of year, so Becky's mum thought it was possible.

Becky went outside with her, and saw there was a little bird perched on the washing line. She said, "Oh look at that little bird! It looks happy! It seems a pity to disturb it."

Becky's mum quipped a little impatiently, "What do you think I should do then, just spread out the washing on the grass and hope it dries? Somehow I don't think you'll be very happy if you end up with mud on your clothes!"

Becky grinned and said, "Nor will you! You'll have to wash them all again!"

Becky's mum gave the washing line a little tug and announced, "Come on birdie, it's time for you to fly away now!"

It did so.

She told Becky to wait till she'd finished hanging out the washing before telling her more about what she thought of the medium, so she could give what she said her full attention.

They were both quiet for a few seconds, and they heard a few birds singing. Becky said thoughtfully, "Have you ever seen a bird in a bad mood? I can't remember ever noticing any grumpy birds. Do you think birds ever get depressed? I mean, you hear them chirping the same cheerful-sounding songs whether it's just been raining, or we've just had a storm, or whatever… Well at least, I can't remember ever hearing them sound any different. Hey, what do you think a grumpy or depressed bird song would sound like?"

Becky's mum smiled and said, "I don't know. Maybe it would be slower or something."

Becky replied, "Or maybe it would go a bit croaky like crows; I suppose someone with a bit of imagination might say crows sound grumpy. Or if birds were feeling really really grumpy, maybe their songs would even sound like frogs croaking. If they weren't that grumpy very often so you'd hardly ever heard them before so you didn't know they made frog sounds when they were really grumpy, you might say to me one day, 'That's funny! It sounds as if there are frogs in the sky outside! Flying frogs!' "

Becky's mum smiled again and said, "Actually, I'm not even sure I know what frogs sound like. I can't remember ever hearing any. Have you heard some then?"

Becky said, "Actually I don't think I have; I've just read about them croaking, and tried to imagine it … No actually I think I did hear them on the radio once."

She joked, "Just imagine if frogs only croak because they're always grumpy all the time, and if they cheered up, they'd start singing like birds. Then if we ever went past a pond with cheerful frogs in it, you might say to me, 'Hey, stop; let's go back and have a look at that pond; I'm sure I just heard birds happily chirping in it. They must have all learned to swim!' "

Becky's mum grinned and said good-naturedly, "You do come out with daft things sometimes! Actually, that reminds me: I think I heard somewhere once that there are different kinds of frogs, and some of them do make noises a bit like birds."

Becky said, "Imagine if when birds were in a bad mood, they'd sing in a minor key. Imagine if whenever they had something to be grumpy about, like it beginning to rain, they'd start singing songs that sounded sad. So you might be indoors doing something, and then you might suddenly hear them singing a sad song, and say to me, 'Oh no, I'd better go outside and get the washing in quick; it sounds as if it's about to rain!'

"Hey, imagine if when people had their radios on in the garden, birds would start copying the music; so instead of just chirping, they'd start singing pop songs! And just imagine if they learned some sad songs, and every time it was about to rain, or there was going to be a storm or something, they would start singing the sad songs, so it would be a signal to people like you that you'd better go and get the washing in! Or just imagine if they taught themselves to sing songs in harmony. Wouldn't that be good!"

Becky's mum smiled and said, "I don't think I'd be too impressed if I heard them singing sad songs in harmony when I'd just put the washing out!"

Becky said, "I don't suppose birds can be impressed themselves when it starts raining. Or maybe they don't mind it. I wonder why they're happy to put up with it! I wonder if it takes more for them to get depressed than it does us. And what about other animals? Do you think smaller creatures ever get depressed, like flies? How do you think a fly might behave if it was depressed? Maybe it wouldn't bother flying, but it would just lie around on a cake, comfort eating till it got fat."

Becky's mum grinned and said, "I think if I was surrounded by cake, I'd be tempted not to move but just to lounge around eating it too!"

Becky said, "What if flies never get depressed though, for some reason? I've never seen a fly just moping around as if it was depressed. Or what about slugs? If you found a slug and chucked it into a neighbour's garden, like you do sometimes, do you think its friends might be sad and worried about it, or do you think they'd just carry on as normal? Or what if you trod on one? Hey, do you think the person who invented the word sludge invented it after they accidentally trod on a slug, and squished it so it went all over their foot, and it was all sludgy, but that word wasn't invented then, so the person said to themselves, 'There's got to be a word for this horrid slime stuff that slugs turn into when they're squashed; I know, I'll call it a word that sounds like slug; sludge seems like an appropriate word!' "

Becky's mum made a face and said, "I've got no idea! Becky, why do you want to say yucky things about slugs?"

Becky said, "Why, do you like slugs? If you do, why do you throw them over the fence into a neighbour's garden when you find them? Anyway, I've just been thinking: If slugs never get to be in a bad mood, and scientists one day found out they had special genes that meant they were immune from getting grumpy and depressed and things, and doctors offered to give you some slug genes so you didn't ever get in a bad mood any more, do you think you'd accept the offer?"

Her mum screwed up her face and said, "I don't think so, somehow! Having slug genes as part of my make-up doesn't really appeal to me!"

Becky said, "What about the genes of more cuddly animals then? What if they found out that cats and dogs never got depressed, and it was because they had special genes that made them immune to being in a bad mood? Would you agree to having dog genes or cat genes put in you? Mind you, if you did, things might start happening that you didn't expect. Imagine if you opened your mouth to say something one day, say in front of some of the teachers at my school, and a big meow came out instead! Or a big dog bark if you had dog genes.

"Or imagine if you started growing fur, and your ears started changing shape till they were the shape of dogs' ears or cats' ears.

"Or just imagine if you decided to have another baby, and it turned out to be a dog or a cat. Imagine if you brought a puppy home and said, 'Here's your new baby brother Becky; he's a dog.' "

Becky's mum chuckled and said, "Rebecca! You do come out with funny things sometimes!"

But she didn't find the next subject that came up in the conversation funny at all!

The Conversation Becomes Controversial

Becky was quiet for several seconds, and then said, "Mum, if you didn't disapprove of abortion, would you have had me aborted?"

Her mum at first smiled and joked, "Well, if I found out you were going to be a dog or a cat I might have done . . . although dogs and cats can be quite cute, so I'm not sure. Anyway, what brought this on?"

Becky said, "I'm just curious. I can't imagine myself not existing. But I suppose the only reason I didn't stop existing is because you don't approve of abortion. Would you have wanted to get me aborted if you did approve of it?"

Her mum said, "I doubt I would have wanted to! But I might have got you aborted. I'm glad I didn't though, darling, even when you get on my nerves! It's still nice to have you around ... at least sometimes!

"Actually, I *was* tempted to have you aborted. I was pretty sure I was pregnant for months before I found out for sure, but I waited till I knew it would be too late for me to have an abortion before I went for a pregnancy test at the doctor's, because I knew that if they told me I was pregnant and there was still time for me to have an abortion, I might not have been able to resist the temptation to have one, because it was scary being pregnant with you ... Well, not just because it was you; it would have been scary being pregnant with anyone! And I didn't even know it was you at the time. But it was scary because I didn't know where I was going to live, or what was going to happen or anything.

"I didn't get pregnant with you deliberately; it was a silly mistake I should have known better than to make, especially with that crudbucket of a boyfriend I had ... Well, I suppose I must have liked him at the time, although I can't think why now! Maybe it's just as well I'll probably never see him again. But anyway, as I said, I'm glad to have you.

"But I knew Grandpa and Grandma would be angry when they found out I was pregnant, and wouldn't want me to live with them any more, so I didn't know what I was going to do. But I was always brought up not to believe in abortion, and I like babies anyway, so I didn't want to get rid of you.

138

"Actually, the person who told me I was pregnant at the clinic told me I'd come too late for an abortion, and I said, 'I know', and they were surprised I wanted to keep you, since they said most people who are the age I was then who get pregnant have abortions. But things have turned out better than I was worried they would ... Crikey, I don't know why I'm telling you these things! You're a bit too young to be told about things like this, even if you are advanced for your age!

"But anyway, it was a good thing in a way that your great grandpa and great grandma died not long before I got pregnant with you – I know it sounds heartless to say that, and I don't mean it that way; I actually still miss them sometimes; but it did mean I had somewhere nice to go to live. Grandma and Grandpa inherited their house after they died and were going to sell it at first. They tried, but they couldn't at the time; and when they found out I was pregnant, they decided to let me have it for some years, until I get to be able to afford to get a place of my own."

Becky said, "How come you think it's good that Great Grandma and Great Grandpa died, but you don't approve of people who haven't been born yet dying?"

Becky's mum got a bit annoyed, and said, "Rebecca! I didn't say I'm glad they died! It just meant that a big worry got taken off my mind, because I could come and live here, in a nice area, so you can grow up not having to worry about kids taking drugs on street corners or whatever, and you'd get to go to a decent school."

Becky said, "Well that's good; but it still seems a bit contradictory that you approve of Great Grandpa and Great Grandma dying, but disapprove of people who haven't been born yet dying."

Perhaps Becky's mum should have known better than to try to have a sensitive conversation with her. She was almost longing to start talking about the possibility that she'd been tricked by the woman next-door again, the subject she'd been glad to come outside to escape! She said, "It's not that I approve of anyone dying! But Great Grandma and Great Grandpa were getting into old age and would probably have died fairly soon in any case. And Great Grandma's health was getting so bad before she died that she didn't have any kind of decent quality of life, so she might even have been relieved to die, even though she was only in young old age by today's standards. But unborn babies have their whole lives ahead of them, unless they're aborted or die naturally before they're born. I just think it's nice if people can have a chance at life, and I don't think it's fair if people just take it away from them without asking if they mind."

Becky smiled broadly and said, "Well how could people ask unborn babies if they mind? Most babies won't even know how to talk by then, and they'd have to shout really really really loud to be heard on the outside of the person who was pregnant with them anyway, even if they could."

Becky's mum said, "Oh Becky! You know what I mean! I just don't think it's fair that the unborn babies don't get any say in the matter."

Becky said, "Anyway, why do you think everyone deserves a chance at life? What about people who live in horrible areas, who will grow up having to pass by kids taking drugs on street corners and things if they're not aborted, and who'll be at risk of getting into that lifestyle themselves and then turning into criminals when they grow up, because they need to steal things to pay for their drugs, or because they think crime's exciting because people around them are having fun buying nice things with the money they've got from crime, but then they might end up in prison?"

Becky's mum sighed. She said, "I don't know. I suppose it's difficult to say for sure, but I know that if I'd had to bring you up in an area like that, I wouldn't have had you aborted; I'd have done the very best I could to improve my circumstances over time till we could move out of that area into a better one. Anyway, what made you bring up abortion in the first place?"

Becky said, "I'm wondering if it would've hurt me if you'd had me aborted."

Her mum said, "Maybe. It might depend on how far along I was in the pregnancy – how developed you were. I'm not quite sure how many weeks into a pregnancy babies start to feel pain."

Becky said, "I'm glad you didn't have me aborted; but I wonder whether if you'd had me aborted very early on, I wouldn't have felt any pain at all, and I wouldn't have even known anything bad was happening to me. If I didn't, then I don't suppose I would have cared that I was being aborted."

Becky's mum was starting to get a bit upset by the conversation. She loves babies, and didn't enjoy being made to think about having unborn ones aborted. She said, "Maybe you wouldn't have. But I think I would have done! Can we change the subject please?"

Becky said, "I'm just wondering about one more thing: Imagine if scientists one day develop home pregnancy testing kits that are so advanced that just a week or two after you get pregnant, you can get yourself tested with them, and they'll have a screen on them, and a message will come up saying whether you're pregnant or not, and it'll be able to say things like, 'This baby has got Down's syndrome', or, 'This baby's going to be severely disabled'. If you got a message like that on one, do you think you'd decide you approved of abortion after all and have the baby aborted?"

Becky's mum sighed again. She said, "Well I wouldn't decide I approved of aborting any baby. It's possible I'd be tempted to have him or her aborted, just like I knew I'd be tempted to get you aborted if I'd been to the doctor's for a pregnancy test earlier. It might even be for the best if I got them aborted, although I don't know; when you see a Down's syndrome child, they're often enjoying life; and after all, what counts most in life? I think happiness is more important than being as perfect as possible. I know it would be more difficult as they grew up, especially when I got to old age and they still needed looking after. But maybe we'd find a way. But I know it would be a very, very difficult decision whether I decided to have them aborted or whether I decided not to. But I really wouldn't have felt happy having them aborted whatever was wrong with them."

The Mood is Lightened for a Little While

Becky's mum began to look depressed, and even a bit tearful. But completely oblivious to that, Becky suddenly turned playful, beginning to bounce around and grin. She said, "Hey, imagine if a pregnancy testing kit told you your baby was going to be a cat, or a lion, or a rat. Or what about if it told you that you were going to have a Rottweiler? Do you think you'd rush off to the doctor's in a panic and say, 'What am I going to do? I'm going to give birth to a Rottweiler!' "

Becky's mum laughed and said, "No. Somehow I don't think I'd believe the pregnancy testing kit. I think I'd probably throw it away and go and buy one of a different brand, hoping it would say something more sensible!"

Becky said, "What if it could even tell what the baby was going to be like? What if it said, 'Your baby's going to have genes that make it not like bananas.' If you'd had a pregnancy testing kit like that when you were pregnant with me and it had said that, then maybe you wouldn't keep trying to persuade me to eat them!"

Becky's mum smiled and said, "Well, maybe not . . . But if it said, 'This baby's genes are going to make her especially fond of chocolate', don't think I'd let you have any more of it than I do now!"

Becky giggled. Then she said, "What about if lots of people's pregnancy testing kits said things like, 'Your baby's going to love climbing trees when it grows up a bit. So if you don't live in a house with a garden with trees in it now, move to one that has them.' I wonder if lots of people would believe that without question and move house, just because the pregnancy testing kit told them to."

Becky's mum chuckled and said, "It's possible I suppose; but I think a lot more people would just object to being bossed around by a pregnancy testing kit!"

Becky laughed.

Becky Carries on Debunking her Mum's Supposedly Psychic Reading

When her mum had finished hanging the washing out, they went back indoors, and Becky carried on telling her what she'd thought of the visit to the medium next-door. She said,

"Hey, you talking about us living in the house your grandma and grandpa used to live in before they died reminds me of a joke I read, or it might be a true story even. Maybe you could do something like it! It said someone once asked a medium to get in touch with their grandma for them. The medium said their grandma's spirit was beginning to talk to her, and the other person said, 'That's strange! She isn't even dead yet!' Maybe you could try something like that on the medium next door!"

Becky's mum chuckled, but said, "I don't think I'd feel comfortable trying that, somehow; I don't like deceiving people."

Becky said, "She was perfectly happy to deceive You!"

Her mum said sternly, "Well even if she was, two wrongs don't make a right!"

Becky said, "Well anyway, before we went outside, I was telling you that she didn't really find out the name of your old friend Frances in a psychic way, wasn't I, and that she didn't even know what letter it began with at first. She said it was in 'the first half of the alphabet'. If you couldn't think of someone with a name beginning with F when she suggested that letter, you would probably have tried to help her out in the end by giving her a name that started with a letter nearby, or she would have started guessing names beginning with different letters nearby, till you'd recognised one as being the name of someone you know who you've been thinking about. And it probably wouldn't have taken long till you did; let's face it, who doesn't know someone with a name that starts with a letter in the first half of the alphabet? Again, she made a pretty safe guess when she said you knew someone with a name that does, and that you were worrying about them.

"After all, 'worrying' could mean anything from being really anxious to just having a few concerned thoughts every now and then. So everyone probably does one of the two, or something in between those things sometimes.

"And if you weren't worrying about anyone, you might still know people who are going through hard times in some way, who perhaps you should, in all conscience, be a bit concerned about; so if you'd said you weren't worrying about anyone at all, that so-called medium would probably have asked you if you knew anyone who was having any problems whose name started with a letter in the first half of the alphabet; and if you said yes, and she'd got you to give her a name, she would have told you that that was who she was thinking of, and you would have believed her, because you would have forgotten that she'd originally said you'd been worrying about that person; or you'd have thought the fact that they're having problems was similar enough to you being worried about them to count as that, because you'd have thought that after all, the signals from the spirits or psychic energy or whatever she supposedly uses to know all these things must be quite faint, so she would be bound to have a bit of difficulty deciphering them, so she could easily think they said you'd been worrying about someone when they were really saying you knew someone with a problem.

"So you'd have just assumed she still basically knew what she was talking about and was giving you special knowledge she was picking up with her psychic abilities.

"And when she listed names of people, pretending to be trying to decipher the psychic signals to find out the name of the friend you'd been worrying about, she was looking at you to see if she saw a flicker of recognition when she mentioned any of them. If she had, she'd have stopped and said that was the name she was looking for. She was reading your body language. That's what people like her do. I've read a couple of articles about it on the Internet."

Becky's mum didn't enjoy having what she'd thought was a great experience ruined. She was getting fed up. But Becky didn't stop. She said,

"And then the supposed medium said she was getting the impression that you'd been a bit concerned about how Frances was getting on in her marriage. If you'd said you hadn't been, she'd probably simply have asked if you had any other friends with names that started with letters in the first half of the alphabet whose marriages weren't going too well, or said that maybe it wasn't her marriage you'd been worrying about but her career or something else. She'd probably have hit on something after a while, and if she didn't, you'd have just assumed she was talking about someone else you couldn't think of at the time, and forgotten it when she moved on to talking about something else. You only remember what she seemed to get right, because that sticks in your mind more than all the things she got wrong, because you're so impressed by it. But you shouldn't be.

"It seems you can't remember, but before she said she was getting the impression that you'd been worrying about how

Frances was getting on in her marriage, she asked you if you were good friends with her, which you probably thought she was just asking out of interest or because she cared, whereas actually, she was probably asking in the hope of getting more information she could use to give her clues about things she could tell you later and impress you with if they were right; and you told her Frances had married a Turkish man. Well, considering that there have been reports about some wives in that part of the world being treated like servants and second-class citizens, it was a pretty safe guess when not long afterwards, she told you you'd been worrying that Frances might be being treated like that. You were impressed that she knew, but she almost certainly just guessed from what she's been hearing in the media."

Becky Makes Some Jokes

Becky's mum began to feel embarrassed. But she had to admit she was impressed by what Becky had said, and decided they'd go back for another reading, to see if she herself could detect the tricks Becky was convinced the medium was using on her.

But she said to Becky, "Well, even if you're right about people who call themselves psychics doing that kind of thing, I'm sure there must be some spiritual force out there we don't know about. I mean, the other day I was writing something on the computer, and I'm sure I pressed the wrong key twice in a row, but on the screen, it said exactly what I wanted it to say, as if the computer was thinking, 'I know you well enough by now to know what you really want to type.' "

Becky grinned and joked, "Hang on, are you saying you think computers can read your mind, even though they're not alive? We'd all better watch out! Come on, you probably just didn't press the key down hard enough for anything to come out one of those times! But imagine if computers really could do things like that! Imagine if you were trying to buy a book online, and a message flashed up on screen saying, 'No, you won't want that one; I know about it and it's too depressing for your tastes; have this one instead,' and no matter how many times you tried to buy the one you thought you wanted, it would always scroll itself to the other one instead."

"Oh that would be spooky!" said her mum. "At least it would be if you weren't expecting it!"

Becky said, "And imagine if it wasn't just computers that did things like that. Imagine if you were putting some clothes in the washing machine one day, and you heard a voice coming from it, saying, 'You silly thing! You're putting white clothes in with colours that are going to run!' Wouldn't you jump if you'd never heard that washing machines could do that! And imagine if you put a blouse in your wardrobe and it came hurtling out again, and your wardrobe said, 'I'm not having that in here; it's dirty! Go and put it to the wash!'

"And just imagine if you put your deodorant on one morning, and the can suddenly said, 'You don't need any- where near that much!' "

(Becky had seen her mum putting deodorant on, and her mum had explained what it was for.)

Becky carried on, "And just imagine if you were walking down the road one day and all the hairs under your armpits started talking, and most people's didn't, just yours, so no one knew they could do that. Imagine if one hair said to you in a loud high-pitched squeaky voice, 'Oy! You forgot to put your deodorant on this morning!', And then another one said to it, 'Oh don't worry, there's still enough here from yesterday.' I wonder what all the passers-by would think! And imagine if all your armpit hairs started arguing about whether there was enough to last the day, and then a peacemaker armpit hair decided it was better to start talking about what to do better in the future instead of quarrelling about what went wrong before and whether it went wrong enough to matter, so it said to you, 'OK, never mind about it today; just do your best not to forget to put your deodorant on in future, OK?' "

Becky's mum laughed and said, "I never forget to put my deodorant on! You are funny sometimes!"

She'd begun to cheer up.

Another Visit to the Self-Proclaimed Medium

She decided she'd like to try and work out for herself whether she was being tricked. So when she next met the woman who said she was a medium, she asked if she could come round for another reading. The self-declared medium said she could, for only a small charge.

They went to her house a few days later, and while she did the psychic reading, Becky wandered around the room quietly. After a while, she came towards them. For some reason, she had some coins in her hand that she'd taken out of her pocket. Her mum and the medium weren't taking much notice. Becky dropped them, and crawled under the table they were sitting at, seemingly to pick them up after they'd rolled under there. For some reason, she was under there for a little while. But they were too engrossed in what they were doing to say much.

The woman who called herself a psychic put on some gentle soothing music, and turned the lights down low. She asked Becky's mum, "Would you mind if I take your hand? The power of the spirits comes through the strongest when a medium's in physical contact with the person they're doing a reading for."

Becky's mum said she could, and the so-called medium started stroking her hand slowly in a soothing way.

As she did so, she said, "I feel very strongly that the spirits are giving me a deep insight into your personality. They want to help you understand yourself, and inspire you with knowledge to help you improve your life. Tell me if I'm on the right track here:

"I'm feeling them telling me that at times you are extroverted, friendly and sociable, while at other times you prefer to be alone, and feel like keeping things to yourself and not saying much.

"You have a great deal of unused potential that you haven't turned to your advantage.

"While you have some personality weaknesses, you're normally able to compensate for them.

"You prefer a certain amount of change and variety, and become dissatisfied when you're hindered by restrictions and limitations.

"You pride yourself on being an independent thinker, and don't accept other opinions without satisfactory proof.

"You have a tendency to be critical of yourself."

Becky's mum was amazed at how accurate it sounded! She was impressed, and felt sure the medium must have special deep knowledge and be genuine after all. She regretted having had to give up part of her education to have Becky, since she'd had her not long before she would have otherwise taken her A levels. She'd been given the opportunity to study for them and take them again later, and she'd studied for them in the evenings after Becky had gone to bed. She'd passed them, and then started training to be a nurse. She'd been one for a couple of years. But sometimes she did think she could be achieving more in life by then if she hadn't had a child so young.

Also, although she normally liked to be with other people and talk a lot, there were still times when she liked to be alone to think or relax. She was surprised at how the medium seemed to have picked up on it.

Then the medium said: "If the power of the spirits is here in strength today, it will show you a wonderful sign, especially for you; I'll pick this match stick up, put it in the palm of my hand, and it will move by itself."

She picked it up, and Becky's mum saw it turn round in her hand, and then stand up on end! Again she was amazed! She thought there must be powerful spirits in the room!

Then the medium offered to tell her fortune, and she said she'd like that. The medium told her to position her hand with the palm upwards. She did, and the medium looked at it for a while. Then she said she detected that there were some things in Becky's mum's life that needed to be renewed and cleansed. She asked her to quickly pop over to her house and bring back a tomato if she had one, since tomatoes were used in traditional healing rituals, slowly waved over the body, as incantations were chanted to cleanse the soul. Becky's mum couldn't see the harm in it, so she did. She brought it back and sat down.

Then the medium slowly waved the tomato in front of Becky's mum's face and body, gently talking a language she didn't understand, and then asked her to get up and turn around so she could wave it over her back, saying she could sense there was a bit of a problem there. Impressed, Becky's mum stood up and turned around. Becky had come out from under the table to look.

When Becky's mum turned back around, the medium gave her the tomato and a small knife, and told her to cut it in half, saying that if it didn't look healthy, that would be evidence of a problem in her life.

Becky's mum cut the tomato, and to her horror, a big worm crawled out, and the tomato was full of hair. The medium appeared shocked, and told Becky's mum that was evidence of a curse or something wrong in her life that needed to be cleansed.

Becky's mum looked horrified. But the medium reassured her that she could perform more healing rituals, only she'd have to buy things that would cost a lot of money, such as special candles and special stones and rosary beads that she'd use to perform the healing spells, so Becky's mum would have to pay her.

Becky was worried her mum might be about to hand over lots of money, and shouted, "Don't give her any money Mum! She's trying to con you!"

Her mum was embarrassed, and said in a loud venomous-sounding whisper, "Becky, shut up!"

Becky was indignant and protested, "I'm trying to warn you; she's trying to con you!"

Becky's mum snapped, "Becky, be quiet!"

Then she felt more embarrassed, and felt sure Becky wasn't going to be quiet. So she apologised to the medium and said they'd better go, and that she'd think about having healing spells done.

Outside, Becky, with tears in her eyes, asked her mum why she'd spoken to her like that, since she was only trying to protect her from wasting a lot of money.

Her mum apologised, saying she just hadn't wanted the medium to be offended.

Becky said, "Why not? She obviously wasn't worried about offending *you*! She just wants to swindle you. And isn't it better to offend someone than let you waste your money? When you had your back turned and she was waving that tomato over your back, I saw her put the one you'd given her in her pocket, and take out another one, which was the one she gave you. I've read about tricks like that on the Internet; she'd have made a little slit in it earlier and put that worm and hair in herself. She was going to ask you for money to supposedly buy these expensive things to use in her rituals, and then probably say she'd detected more and more evil every time you saw her after that, and ask for more money to do more spells to get rid of it. That's the kind of thing these people do!"

Becky's mum realised she might have been conned after all, but said, "Well OK, but that match stick moving in her hand all by itself was pretty impressive. Surely there must have been genuine spirits there."

Becky said, "I looked at that match when we first went in. It had a tiny nail sticking to one end. And when I was under the table, you thought I was just picking up the coins I dropped, but actually I was examining it. I found out part of it must have been removed, and there was a magnet there in its place. I wondered if it was a magnet, and I found out it definitely was one, because I held a penny near it and it jumped towards it. The nail in the match must have been attracted to the bit of the magnet on the top side of the table. It must have been a really powerful one. So if the so-called medium put the match in her hand with the nail facing in a different direction from where the table was, the nail would have been pulled towards it by the force of the attraction to the magnet, so that's why the match would have turned round."

Becky's mum was dismayed to have been so easily taken in by the trick. But she said, "OK then, but that personality profile she did of me was pretty impressive. How could she have known all those things about me when she hardly knows me, if she didn't really get the information from spirits?"

Becky said, "It wasn't really a special personality profile of you. It was another trick. I've been reading about them on the Internet; it's called the Barnum effect, otherwise known as the Forer effect. The things she said about you are true of most people. Experiments have been done where lots of people in a group have been given bits of paper with words on them very similar to what she said to you, and told they were individual personality profiles, and over three quarters of them have praised their accuracy, thinking they were specially meant for them, when actually they were all given the same thing. Oh, and she mentioned your backache, but she probably guessed about that from the way you rub your back sometimes and take a while to get comfortable."

Becky's mum felt stupid. She hadn't realised she could be so easily fooled. She decided never to go back to the medium again.

Whenever she met the medium after that, and the medium asked if she was coming back, she felt uncomfortable about saying she'd realised she was a fraud, so she said she might come back, but that she needed to think about it.

Becky Has Fun With her Auntie Diana

After Becky had convinced her mum she'd been tricked, they decided they needed a bit of refreshment. They went around to Becky's grandma and grandpa's house, and had a cup of tea and a chat. Becky's auntie Diana was there for a short visit. She listened to what they said and sympathised.

Then Becky turned the mood more light-hearted by saying, "I don't know how often that psychic cleans under her table, but when I was underneath it, I saw lots of crumbs under there! If she could really see into the future, she'd know she'd better clean them up before loads more end up there, or she might get mice in her house!"

They giggled, and Diana said, "Well there'll be one good thing if that does happen – it might scare away customers."

They sniggered. Then Diana joked, "I spoke to my own personal psychic advisor the other day; I asked him if I'm still going to be alive in 250 years' time. I thought it might be nice to be around to find out what new technologies they've got then; I mean, you never know, one thing is that maybe governments will have cloud zappers that they let weather forecasters use, so instead of just forecasting the weather, the Met Office will Create it! I mean, imagine if summer's supposedly coming, but it's all disappointingly cloudy outside as usual. Instead of saying, 'It's going to be cloudy tomorrow', they might say, 'It's going to be lovely and sunny tomorrow, because early in the morning, we're going to blast all the clouds to bits!'

"Anyway, I was talking to my personal psychic advisor the other day, and I asked him if I'm going to be alive in 250 years' time, and he said no. Then he charged me four times the usual amount he charges me for information, saying the extra charge was because he could be 99.9 % sure the prediction was accurate, as opposed to usually only being 82.4 % sure his predictions will come true. He said his psychic power had been unusually strong at the moment he predicted I'm not going to live that long.

"He said it often wasn't as strong as that, because the forces of nature controlling the particular thing he'd just made the prediction about would often conspire against him after he'd made a prediction, to try to make it fail, because they haven't liked him ever since he was mowing his lawn one day and accidentally cut the heads off a couple of nature spirits, and they had to be treated at great expenditure of spiritual energy by spirit doctors who rushed to the scene with their ethereal medical instruments and welded their heads back on. They've all had a grudge against him ever since.

"He said he was a lot more confident that this prediction wouldn't fail, because the life force he makes predictions about life with and the forces of nature that normally oppose him are so similar it's as if they're brothers or really good friends, so they won't oppose each other in the way forces of nature often oppose the spiritual psychic force that enables him to make predictions.

"I went and told a friend of mine excitedly about the especially accurate prediction he'd made; but she wasn't impressed. I didn't know why! Then she told me she could have predicted I won't be around in 250 years' time herself, for free! I said, 'Wow! What, so you've got psychic powers too? I wish I'd known earlier! I'd have asked you the question instead. Oh well, perhaps I'll come to you for psychic advice in future if it will all be free.'

"My friend said she doesn't have psychic powers, but that she still knew for certain that I won't be around 250 years from now, simply because no one alive now will be, because people just don't live that long.

"I said, 'Oh yeah!' I felt silly for not thinking of that earlier. I got annoyed that my psychic advisor had charged me so much for telling me I wouldn't live that long when it's really common knowledge, and I went and demanded he give me my money back.

"He said he couldn't give me any, because as soon as his psychic powers had led him to tell me I won't be around 250 years from now, they'd grown much weaker for a while, so he hadn't been able to predict that I'd come back and ask for my money back, so he'd spent it all."

Becky laughed. But her mum didn't know if it was a joke, because Diana had said it with a straight face. She thought she might just be crazy. But when Becky laughed, Diana smiled, so Becky's mum thought it must have been a joke after all.

They had a nice cup of tea anyway. Then Becky and her mum went home.

Becky Looks up Information About the History of Hoax Séances, and Some Modern-Day Fake Paranormal Activities

Becky's mum decided she wanted to know more about the tricks people who pretend to be psychic use, so she asked Becky to look on the Internet while she was doing the ironing and tell her what she found. It took her a long long time to do the ironing that day, because Becky kept calling her over to look at things.

First she said, "Hey look at *this* page, Mum! It says there was a big craze for spiritualism in Victorian times, and it started when two sisters called Kate and Margaret played a trick on their parents. They discovered they could make their toe joints and other bones click at will, and they told their parents they'd discovered the clicks were spirits trying to communicate with them. The parents couldn't work out where else the clicks could be coming from, and called in the neighbours to hear them. More and more people came to hear them, and it got more and more difficult for the sisters to own up to just playing a trick, because the more people who'd believed it was spirits tapping, the more people there were who were going to be angry if they said they'd just been making the noise themselves, and they might have worried that their parents would be especially angry, since they would probably have been laughed at or criticised by all the others for believing the girls.

"So they kept on pretending it was spirits knocking, and more and more people came to hear them, till they were famous, and some famous people came to hear them.

"The sisters told them they'd developed a code where different numbers of clicks meant different letters of the alphabet, and yes and no, so they could ask the spirits questions, and the spirits would spell out the answers. For years and years they pretended to talk to the spirits for people. But when they were old, they confessed that it had all been a fraud, and said they wished they'd never done it."

Becky's mum came over and looked. She said she thought it was interesting.

She'd just got back into doing her ironing when Becky called her over again, saying, "Hey Mum! Come and look at this!"

Her mum said, "In a minute, darling. You tell me what it says."

Becky replied enthusiastically, "There's a website here about how there were people calling themselves mediums in Victorian times, who played all kinds of fancy tricks to make people think they were seeing spirits! Mediums usually did séances in a dark or nearly dark room. They said that made the spirits more comfortable, and gave other reasons like that. But people who didn't believe they were really contacting spirits said they thought the real reason was that it would make it much easier to trick people, because they could do tricks without being detected.

"The website says that sometimes the mediums would trick people into believing there were spirits in the room by changing into different costumes in the dark and then showing themselves; or sometimes assistants would come out of trap doors or parts of the room they'd been concealed in, wearing wigs, make-up and costumes, pretending to be spirits wafting around and doing things. Sometimes mediums would get down on their knees and crawl around pretending to be spirit children. One medium was caught hiding a wig and costume in a chair with a false back; that's a back that could be secretly taken off, and there was a space between that and the real back where things could be hidden.

"Sometimes they would blow up little balloons and paint faces on them, and tie them to the line on the end of a fishing rod, and move it around by holding the other end; and in the dark it would look as if little faces were floating around by themselves, and they would say they were spirit faces. Or they'd stuff gloves with things, and tie those to a fishing rod, and brush them against people's faces, and in the dark they'd seem to be spirit hands stroking their faces.

"Or tables would seem to jump around the room by themselves as if spirits were moving them, but a medium was really moving them with her foot, or using some other method.

"Or musical instruments would play, and it seemed as if no one was playing them so it must be spirits doing it, but really the mediums would be using tricks, such as one where a violin had a thread draped over it, with a weight on one end to stop it flying off, and the other end was being held by someone secretly in a room next-door with the door shut, and the thread was running through the keyhole to the violin. They'd pull their end from side to side, and it would make the thread move over the violin strings, and it would make a quiet noise that sounded like ghostly music.

"Sometimes the mediums would pretend that something they called ectoplasm was coming out of their mouths or noses or other parts of them, and they said it was a substance spirits were producing. But when people who didn't believe them examined it, it was often found to be made of really chewed-up bits of paper or cloth covered in grease. Some mediums would even swallow things so no fraud investigators would find them before the séance started, and then make themselves gag and bring them up again when the room had been darkened, so they could say spirits were making the things appear; and then they'd get rid of them before the end.

"And they did lots of other tricks like that.

"Some scientists and magicians who could do similar things but would be honest about it being trickery went round trying to prove the mediums who did things like that were frauds, and quite a lot of mediums got found out. But mediums started doing tricks to try to fool the scientists into believing they were really contacting spirits.

"One thing that happened was that they'd sit in a cabinet and get someone to tie them up, supposedly so they couldn't move anything themselves, so that would prove that spirits must be causing whatever happened. They'd tell everyone in the room to come and examine them to make sure they didn't have anything on them, saying that would prove they were telling the truth about not having anything. But someone in the room would often be in the conspiracy with them, and they'd be the last person to examine them to supposedly make sure they weren't concealing anything they could fool people into thinking they were hearing or seeing spirits with; but even while that person was saying they couldn't find anything on them, they'd secretly be giving them things they could use, and untying them."

Becky's mum came over and had a look at what Becky was reading. She thought the information was interesting.

She went back and got on with some ironing again. But no sooner was she halfway through ironing something, when Becky said again, "Hey come and look at this, Mum!"

"Soon," said her mum. "Just tell me about it for now, Noodles."

Noodles was Becky's mum's pet name for her, for some reason.

Becky said, "This website says some celebrities who say they're psychic and have got television programmes today are still just fraudsters. It says one used to claim he could turn pages of books and move pencils on a table with the power of his mind, but he was caught blowing gently on them, and exposed as a fraud on television!

"And there was a man who attracted big meetings of Christians, and told them he knew things about several of them that he'd been told by God. He would tell them things about them that they were impressed he knew. But it turned out that he was told them by his wife, who was asking people in the audience questions about themselves before he came on stage, not saying who she was, but just pretending to be an ordinary member of the audience making small talk; and also she read what they'd written on 'prayer cards' they were given to write on if they had concerns they wanted prayer for; and then she would secretly give her husband the information through a little earpiece he was wearing."

Becky's mum joked, "Wow, that's not nice! . . . Still, it's nice to hear about a man who thinks his wife is God!"

Becky giggled.

Then she became serious and said, "There are people claiming to be psychic mediums who have television shows in America who tell people they're contacting dead relatives of theirs, who might use techniques a bit like that, as well as the ones the supposed psychic next door used on you the first time we went there, like listening to people and looking at their body language to pick up clues about what to say, and using information that was really found out before to make people think they've got special psychic knowledge about their families.

"I think it's pretty common for people who call themselves mediums who aren't celebrities and don't use the kinds of tricks the one next-door used on you earlier today to use techniques like reading body language and listening out for clues about what to say, and things like that."

Not long after that, Becky said, "I've found one website that says sometimes no fraud's going on, but people still get fooled into thinking paranormal things are happening when they're not really. It says that sometimes people can cause things to move, thinking they're moving all by themselves, but really they're moving them a bit without realising they're doing it, with tiny involuntary muscle movements directed by their subconscious minds. I know that sounds a bit unlikely; but I'll explain the kind of thing I mean: One thing it says is that there's a thing called a Ouija board, where the letters of the alphabet are put in order on a table in two semi-circles, and the words yes and no and numbers are put there too, and everyone sitting around it puts a finger on an upside-down glass or something similar, and they try to ask spirits questions, and they often find the glass moving to letters of the alphabet and spelling out words or moving to yes or no, and they think it's spirits answering them.

"It's possible to buy ready-made Ouija boards, where there's a pointer for people to put their fingers on instead of a glass. Actually, it seems they've been pretty popular at times.

"A lot of people who've looked into Ouija say it's not really spirits moving the glass or pointer, but it's the people themselves just giving the glass or pointer a slight push in the direction they're expecting it to go in without really realising they're doing it; and when most of the people in the group do it, it starts to move there. One psychologist did an experiment where he turned all the letters face-down, telling the people who were about to do a session of Ouija that surely the spirits would still be able to read them; but when the people around the table couldn't see what letter was what, the glass didn't move much.

"And when everyone around a table's been blindfolded in experiments where scientists are watching, the words that are spelled out have made a lot less sense than they would normally.

"The website says there are horror stories about people using Ouija boards and ending up thinking they've been possessed by demons, or that they've received spookily accurate answers to things they didn't know the answers to themselves before, but that the claims might well be exaggerated or made up, or sometimes the result of people just getting paranoid so their own minds are making them feel bad, or caused by them remembering things or letting their hunches influence them while they're playing the game that lead them to direct the pointer to the right answers, when they didn't realise they knew them before. They might get more accurate answers because they're more open to the first ideas that come into their minds in their enthusiasm to play the game and to be directed to the right answers, while normally they would doubt them, so their uncertainty blocks them from deciding they're right. And it might make it more likely that the answers will be right if more than one person thinks the same thing."

Becky's mum got back on with the ironing, till Becky said, "I've found a website that says a lot of so-called psychics are part of organised crime families, and they con people into thinking they have to give them money to buy things to perform rituals that they say are necessary to remove a curse on them, or because it's an essential part of a spell they say they have to do to bring them good fortune, or to safeguard them against something bad happening, or something like that. They sometimes tell them they'll get their money back when it's been used in the spell; but then they don't give the money back, or they don't spend it on buying things to perform the rituals they say they have to perform, or whatever they've claimed they'll do, but they spend it on luxury living for themselves. I wonder if the supposed psychic who tricked you's part of an organised crime family."

Becky's mum felt a bit scared at the thought. But she still wanted to hear more.

When she'd finished the ironing, she sat down to carry on listening to what Becky had to say.

Not long afterwards, Becky said, "I've found some web-sites about companies that run phone lines where people can ring up and supposedly get psychic advice, but they're cons really, because the supposed psychics aren't really psychic at all, but they're just trained to gain the confidence of people and encourage them to keep talking for as long as possible, so the companies will make more money, since the calls cost a lot per minute – or at least, the first few minutes sometimes might not, as an incentive for people to phone up in the first place; but the calls will normally take a fair bit longer than that, so the higher price will kick in long before they end. And most of the first few minutes will often be taken up with a recorded message and menu options anyway.

"It seems a lot of people phone those lines for reasons such as that they've recently had a relationship break-up and they're wondering if it's possible they'll get back with the person they're in love with, or they're wondering whether to leave a relationship they're in, or marry someone, and they want an answer from someone they think will have special insight.

"One of these websites says the supposed psychics on the lines are trained to say vague things and flatter the people they're talking to, to give them hope and make them feel better about themselves, so they'll be encouraged to carry on talking in the hope of getting more of that. The supposed psychics ask callers questions about themselves, partly to encourage them to talk, so the calls will last longer, and partly to find out more about them, to help them work out what the best things to say about them will be. If a caller asks them why they need the information, since they should just know it if they're psychic, they're trained to say things like that since they're not in the same room as them, the only way they can pick up on their vibrations is by having a conversation with them.

"And some of them will pick up on clues about what kind of lifestyle a caller's living by listening out for background noises, such as children or pets, busy traffic and so on, to give them more ideas about how to say accurate things.

"A lot of them use a script with certain questions on it that they can ask, to give them ideas about what to say. I'm reading stories from people who've worked on these psychic lines, who say they were told when they signed up to work there that it didn't matter if they were psychic or not, since the skill of talking to callers was all in the techniques they'd be told about, such as ways of encouraging callers to say more about themselves.

"There's a story here about someone who says that on the psychic line he worked on, after the supposed psychics had been speaking to callers for a long time, they'd ask for their names and addresses, and then later someone would send them a letter saying a psychic had discerned that they were in trouble and needed psychic help; and when they visited them, they'd ask for money to supposedly use psychic powers to make the problems go away. It seems that there are psychic lines that entice people to give them their names and addresses by offering to send them a free deck of tarot cards or something like that.

"One of these websites says people can genuinely be helped by phoning psychic lines, because a lot of callers are lonely and unhappy and really want a listening ear, someone they can pour out their troubles to in order to get their feelings about them out of their systems. And some of the people who work on the lines are caring people. But it seems a lot of callers would be better off finding a befriending service they can phone, or going for therapy, because it's possible that they could be given false hope or misleading advice by some of the people who are claiming to be psychic, and a good trained therapist might give them better help.

"But a lot of people phone people they think are psychics because there's a lot of uncertainty in their lives that's worrying them, and they want some supernatural insight into how things will go if they take one decision or another. It seems that the supposed psychics are trained to pretty much tell them what they want to hear, sometimes encouraging them to take the decision they'd prefer to take, whether it really would be the best idea or not.

"It seems a lot of people find phoning those lines addictive, so they can end up spending all their money on them and even going into debt.

"Sometimes psychic hotlines are exposed as cons in the media; but a lot of people probably assume there's just a problem with those individual lines and the rest are OK, so they keep phoning them. But according to what I'm reading, they're pretty much all really just money-making schemes."

Becky's mum joked sarcastically, "I've been learning all kinds of tricks tonight, Becky. Perhaps I'll set *myself* up in business and make people think I'm psychic! Just think about how much money I could make!"

Becky was a bit shocked, and asked, "You wouldn't really do that, would you Mum?"

Becky's mum laughed and reassured her that she wouldn't really.

Becky Has Some Ideas for Halloween Party Games

Then Becky had an idea. She said, "Hey let's have a party at Halloween, and invite all the friends you're still in touch with that you made when we used to go to those mother-and-toddler groups with their kids, and we could invite some of the kids in my class with their parents. We could pretend to do some of the things those mediums did in Victorian times. We wouldn't tell them we were really contacting spirits or anything; we could just say it was a magic show, just a bit of fun. Then we could make the room dark, and you could say you were doing a séance and you were going to see what spirits turned up.

"Maybe we could ask auntie Joan to pretend to be the spirit of Queen Victoria. She could find a wig and other things that made her look like whatever Queen Victoria looked like, and she could put on a different voice, and hide till the room went dark, and then come out and say something like, 'I'm the spirit of Queen Victoria. Now something I don't think the history books say is that I used to love tickling people. I still do! I'm going to tickle you now!' And then she could go round tickling people.

"And maybe we could invite uncle Steven over and he could pretend to be a spirit dog. He could dress up as a dog and hide till the room went dark, and then come out and crawl around on all fours doing barking noises. And Joan could have got a dog lead from somewhere, and she could put it on Steven and lead him round the room, saying to people, 'Say hello to my dog.'

"And she could tell stories, like saying, 'Let me tell you about some of the funny things that happened in my palace! One day, I was holding a huge banquet for all my cousins from overseas and lots of European diplomats and politicians. My cook had made a huge fancy cake. She'd made lots of others, but that one was the biggest. It was brought into the room just before the banquet started. All the guests were there. But when no one was looking except me, one of my naughtiest children grabbed a pepper pot, ran over, and sprinkled pepper all over the cake! I didn't want to tell her off because I thought it would be embarrassing if my guests found out what naughty children I had! So I didn't say anything. I didn't have the cake taken away, because I knew my guests would be disappointed, and they might protest, and I'd end up having to tell them why.

"'So instead I told the servants to fill the guests' dinner plates as full as possible, hoping they'd be so full after eating dinner they wouldn't have any room for the cake, so they'd never find out it had pepper on it. But they still wanted to eat it after their dinner.

"'They can't have liked the cake, but no one said a word of disapproval when they ate it. I did see some trying to resist the urge to make faces. It seems they all thought it was very important to be polite on international occasions, and didn't want to risk offending anyone. So they all pretended to like it. In fact, some praised it so enthusiastically I was almost convinced they really did like it, and thought of telling my children to put pepper on the cakes at all the banquets I held from then on. I decided I'd better not though.'"

Becky's mum laughed. But she said, "That fake séance sounds like a nice idea, but I don't think it would work. Some of the little brothers and sisters of the kids who used to be in the mother-and-toddler groups when you were are very young; they might be scared. Tom was scared of Joan when he was a little baby, and she wasn't even dressed up!"

(They were talking about Becky's mum's older sister Joan.)

Becky laughed. But then she protested, "Oh Mum! It could be such fun! You could tell all the kids not to be scared, saying it's just a game. Then you could do that trick with the fishing rod, and dangle balloons with faces painted on them in front of people's faces! And you could put cloth in your mouth and then spit some of it out and pretend it's ectoplasm."

Becky's mum laughed again, but said, "I'm not shoving a load of cloth in my mouth, thank you! And I don't want to dangle balloons in front of people's faces either. You can't trust kids to just stay still and watch like you can with adults; they'd probably give the whole game away by grabbing the balloons and shouting, 'Hey, this balloon's not really floating in mid-air by itself; I think it's attached to a fishing rod, and I bet Becky's naughty mummy's holding the other end and moving it around!' Maybe sometimes adults are easier to trick than children."

So they didn't have a party where they did a magic show. But on the evening of Halloween, they went round to Becky's Grandma and Grandpa's house nearby, where other members of the family also went for the evening, and there they had fun playing some more traditional Halloween party games, like apple bobbing, where Grandpa put water in a washing-up bowl and put some apples in it, and everyone took turns trying to catch them with their teeth – no hands allowed; and they also played the game Murder in the Dark, where each of them took turns pretending they were being killed and falling down dead, and they all took turns playing a detective asking all the other people in the room in turn what they'd been doing at the time the play-victim died, trying to work out who the 'murderer' was.

(The identity of the 'murderer' was decided beforehand by giving everyone in the room except the one who was going to play the victim a card before each round of the game, while the 'detective' was outside the room so they wouldn't know what was going on; the cards were chosen from a little selection of them that had been taken from a pack before the game, that had one ace in it; and whoever got that would be the 'murderer'. They and the others had to tell stories, making up alibis about where they were when the crime was committed, with the 'murderer' trying to make theirs as clever as possible so as not to be detected; and if the detective guessed which one was the murderer with a false alibi, they won that round of the game, which meant they could have another go at being the detective.)

———

About a year later, it turned out that some real crimes had been going on right next-door to Becky's mum's house, although nothing as serious as murder. A police car pulled up almost outside the door one day. Becky and her mum rushed to the window to see what was happening. They saw the police arrest the woman next-door who'd told them she was a medium, and take her away.

A few days later, they read in a local newspaper that she'd been taken to court for trying to defraud several people out of lots of money.

Chapter 7

Becky Helps a Girl With a Dog Phobia At the Beach

One day when Becky was about seven, she went on a day-trip to the beach with her mum. They had a nice time. Becky was already quite a good swimmer, and they had a race in the sea, which Becky won. Maybe her mum was a slow swimmer.

Later Becky and her mum played a ball game on the beach. Becky's mum told her that years before, her and her family had played with a ball on a beach, and it had gone in the sea and been carried out with the current and lost; but amazingly, several months later, they'd gone to a beach nearby and they'd found it again, washed up on the sand! They felt sure it was the same ball, because it had the same markings on it. But it had a puncture, so it was all squashed, and they couldn't use it again.

Becky and her mum spent a while sunbathing. They were sitting drying off after going in the sea when Becky said, "I've seen something in the shops that says one of the ingredients is sun-dried tomatoes. How could you possibly dry a tomato in the sun? There's so much juice in it. And it grows in the sun for months without drying out. Surely at least the sun would have to be much hotter than ordinary sun to dry them. Do they chop them up small and put them somewhere where the sun gets especially hot, like on a beach where the sand gets really hot in the sun or something? This sand's so hot it's like a radiator that's on . . . Our feet wouldn't start drying out, would they, if we spent ages and ages with them on this sand in the sun?"

Her mum said, "No! They probably drain the juice out or something before they start trying to dry them. Anyway, the outside of you might start looking like a ripe tomato if you don't put any more sun cream on; I bet some of the cream you put on before washed off in the sea. Go on, put some more on."

Becky did. Then they spent some time happily sun-bathing.

When they were walking back to the car afterwards, they saw a girl of about thirteen walking along in front of them. Someone came along with a little dog, and the girl dropped what she was carrying, turned and ran onto the beach. When the dog had passed, she came back, looking a bit upset and embarrassed. Becky helped her pick up her things. The girl thanked her, and explained apologetically that she had a phobia of dogs that gave her an urge to run away whenever she saw one coming. She said it was so embarrassing, the embarrassment just made things worse than they already were.

Becky had been reading about phobias on the Internet not long before. She asked the girl if she'd ever tried anything to cure hers, and the girl said no, and that she wouldn't know what to try.

174

Becky said she'd read about a few things that could help. She gave the girl some advice, although the bit she gave at first should probably have at least waited till later.

She said one thing that could help, if the girl could do it without feeling panicky or upset, and maybe when she'd started trying other things that had started working so the phobia was beginning to get less intense, was if she found out as much as she could about dog behaviour, and different dogs' temperaments, and dog body language – like how to predict what they might be going to do by the way they looked, such as that when they put their tails up straight and wag them stiffly, it means they're annoyed rather than happy, so it's different from when they wag their tails in an ordinary way. She suggested the girl could also learn something about how dogs think – as far as anyone knows – what upsets them, what dogs are the most placid and soppy, what they enjoy, things that can sometimes pacify dogs when they're becoming agitated, how they like to play, all the reasons why the ones that get vicious do that, and how some can be ill-treated by humans.

She said part of what often keeps phobias going is assumptions people make without even thinking about them, or the way they can unwittingly fuel their anxiety by imagining the worst, such as by worrying that any dog they meet might want to bite them, and that they'll be helpless to cope if the dog does something unexpected, like shows particular interest in them. She said that when the girl had learned some new things about dogs, she could challenge any assumptions she realised she was making like that in her mind, asking herself what evidence there was that they were really true, so she could reassure herself with everything she could remember that she'd learned about most dogs not being harmful most of the time. She said the more the girl found out about dogs, the easier that would be to do; and also she might feel she had more ability to control her fear levels when she actually saw a dog, and to be able to control dogs around her, if she knew what dogs like and don't like, and how different breeds are likely to react in different situations, so she could predict their behaviour better.

The girl told Becky that that was all very well, but that she knew not all dogs were going to bite her; it was just that her phobia made her frightened before she even had time to think about that, so she was running away before she had a chance to reassure herself that there wasn't really anything to worry about.

Becky said she knew that's what phobias are like, but that if the girl studied different things about dogs and felt she could predict their behaviour better, she might feel more confident that there wasn't likely to be an incident that she couldn't cope with when she came across most of them, and that might stop her being so frightened. Or she might feel more in control, thinking she knew a lot about them, so the thought of dogs wouldn't seem so overwhelming, because fear of the unknown might be part of what was keeping the phobia going. She said that as well as that, if the girl started feeling sorry for some dogs that had been badly treated, rather than always worrying about what they'd do themselves, and if she came to think it was cute that some dogs are so obedient and loyal to humans, she might feel less threatened by them, so that might help her feel calmer.

The girl said, "I know you're trying to be helpful, but I don't think this would work. I don't even like thinking about dogs. I don't even like hearing or saying the word dog! I think it might make me just want to be sick if I thought I had to look up information about them!"

Becky said, "Well, I'm not suggesting you do it right away. Just after you've started doing other things to make your phobia fade away. And if looking at information about dogs would seem too much at first, you could work up to it by doing things that are less stressful first, till you got used to them, like just drawing little pictures of outlines of dogs, or writing the word dog a few times every now and then for a while."

Then Becky wondered if suggesting the girl look at information about dogs being mistreated might have been a bad idea, since it might be depressing. So she suggested that the girl didn't look at much of that, and didn't look at any till she'd spent quite a bit of time looking at information on other subjects that would help her learn about dogs and how to get over a phobia of them, after she'd perhaps worked up to doing that over time by just doing things that would mean she had to think about dogs for mere seconds at a time at first, and then gradually think about them for a bit longer and longer as time went on.

Then she said, "And you probably don't need telling at all, but try to avoid websites with nasty stories about dogs biting as well at first; I'm pretty sure it's much more usual to have nice dogs than nasty ones, at least in this country, but if you get into browsing websites with horrible stories on them, because you start thinking you ought to find out as much as you can about them so you'll know what to look out for to protect yourself or something, you might end up convinced all dogs are nasty, because you're filling your mind with those stories most, so they might seem to be by far the most significant things, and your phobia might get worse than it was before.

"Maybe you can read a few stories about the bad ones when you've taught yourself about all the other stuff, so you've come to feel sure that some dogs are normally just soppy, and you understand the reasons why some dogs get nasty, and you're well on the way to getting over your phobia. You could maybe read some after that just to prove to yourself that you can manage to read things like that without getting all anxious again, which might lift your spirits when you later think about how you could do that without anything bad happening, and reassure you that if you come across things like that unexpectedly in future, your phobia probably won't come crashing back again, and you won't feel as upset to read horrible stories as you would now – although that kind of detail will still be upsetting, as it would be for most people."

Becky's mum was a bit concerned that what Becky was saying might make things worse, so she said sarcastically, "Gosh, this is helpful! What are you trying to do, give the girl nightmares?"

Becky said in protest, "No! Hang on, I'm getting to some of the more helpful things!"

Her mum remarked, "You could have started with those!"

Becky said with a little irritation, "I didn't have time to get my thoughts in order before I started!"

The girl was cringing and making faces, since just listening to someone talking about dogs made her feel squeamish, and as if she would rather not hear about them.

Becky guessed what she must be thinking. So then she told the girl that if the thought of looking at any information at all about dogs still gave her a yucky feeling after she'd started to get over her phobia, then before she sat down to do that each time, she could maybe try doing something to help herself stop taking dogs so seriously, such as first using a technique to relax deeply to make sure she was calm – and she said she could tell her about one or two ideas for how to do that if she wanted – and then having a go at doing something like daydreaming about miniature dogs doing odd amusing things, like having sausages attached to their tails and then chasing them to try to get them, or wearing funny hats and shaking their heads a lot to try to get them off, or jumping on swings to try to have a go on them and falling off the other side and doing accidental somersaults, and things like that. Becky told the girl that if she made herself laugh with her daydreams, she might feel more in the mood to find out about dogs afterwards.

Becky's mum was skeptical about whether what Becky was saying could work. She said for fun, "I suppose that just might work. Or maybe you could make up funny limericks. Maybe something like, um, this, for example:

> *There was once a dirty old dog*
> *That wandered into a bog.*
> *It sank in the mud*
> *Till at the price of its blood*
> *It was pulled out by a vampire frog.*

"Or how about this:

> *There was a young dog from Reading*
> *That ripped up all of its bedding.*

Its owner said 'Right,
You'll sleep outside tonight.
Your vandalism's doing my head in!'

Becky's mum had meant to make a bit of gentle fun of Becky's suggestions, by implying that they themselves were a bit daft, so they were deserving of being made fun of, to try and lighten the mood, in case the teenager was feeling awkward at having to listen to her; but Becky said to the girl, "Actually, that might help. You could try it, before you ever try looking at websites about dogs after your phobia's begun to fade away, and you could see if having a bit of fun making fun of them makes you feel a bit less anxious about them.

"Also it might help lighten things up and make you less scared of dogs if besides making your own funny ideas up, you manage to find some amusing 'daft dog' stories on the Internet one day. You might not feel like doing that till you've got over the phobia a bit. But after that, if you can start thinking of some dogs as sometimes funny and daft, most dogs probably won't seem so frightening any more. You might not be in the mood to do that for some time after your phobia begins to get better, but one day, maybe you'll feel more like giving it a try; or you could read just one story to start off with. Anyway, since you'll be in control of what you do, you'll know you can stop at any time if you begin to get upset, and that'll probably reassure you."

The teenager was surprised to be given so much information by someone as young as Becky. She didn't know if she could trust information from someone that little. As if reading her mind, Becky said, "I've got some information I could give you from some really good psychology websites.

I might do a psychology degree in a few years' time when I've left school."

The teenager was amazed. But then she thought, "Oh yeah? A degree long before most people have even finished school? And you're going to finish school that soon? And how would you know which psychology websites are the really good ones?" She sniggered a bit. But Becky carried on talking, and soon the girl was interested. Becky said:

"Alright, I'll give you some information you can use right now, instead of you having to wait till your phobia isn't so bad. First, just let me explain something: I've read that when people find themselves near something they've got a phobia of, they feel a sudden sense of fright that makes them want to run away. If they do, they feel upset and feel convinced they can't control the phobia, since it makes them run away even though they know it's not sensible to be so frightened – they can't help it. I know you know this already, because you told me about it. But the thing is that every time they run away, it's as if they're accidentally programming their brain to sense danger sooner than it did the last time they ran away, because the brain controls what they do, but also learns from it, and the more they run away, the scarier it'll think what they're running away from must be.

"Different parts of the brain control different things. For instance, one bit in particular regulates emotions, and another bit has to do with the sensible things we think. The fact that someone with a phobia has run away convinces the part of their brain that controls emotions even more than it was convinced before that there's danger, so it'll quickly give them the fear signal again next time they encounter what they've got the phobia of, because it'll be convinced that's what they need as a warning, even though it was itself the thing that made them run away in the first place. And the fear signal will be way too strong for the part of the brain that helps us think sensible thoughts to override. So the person will just run away, before they can even think about what to do.

"But actually, the part of the brain that thinks things through can have a good go at controlling or calming the part of the brain that sends out the fear signals, whenever it's possible for it to anticipate that they might come on, or just when thoughts of them come on, and there's time to think before the person's in the presence of what they've got the phobia of, when they'll be at risk of the emotional part of their brain taking over so the fear gets too strong for any thinking to be able to happen. When a person's got time to think, because they know there's unlikely to be a danger of the thing they've got the phobia of unexpectedly appearing just then, the part of their brain that thinks things through can reassure the emotional part that there's probably no need to be frightened of what it's afraid of; you can think as if one part of your brain's talking to another.

"You could try doing that every so often, just when you're alone and there's no dog nearby, or if you take on the challenge of going to look at someone's dog at a safe distance, when you know full well it's under control and can't come near you, and won't have any idea you're scared of it, so it won't be thinking you're weird or anything for looking at it – if dogs ever actually think like that about anyone; but when you're there, or alone, you could try imagining that the sensible side of your brain's calming the emotional side down, thinking up reasons it could tell it about why it doesn't have to get as scared as it does.

182

"It won't be easy to calm the emotional part of your brain down at times when the fear suddenly comes on at first; but even if you do see a dog unexpectedly, if it's in your mind to do and you remember, you just might be able to manage to start calming yourself before the panic really sets in, if you've been practising a lot.

"One thing you could try is to say to yourself something like, 'Oh, this is just the emotional side of my brain giving me a strong fear signal by mistake, because it's been programmed over time to instantly decide this is a scary situation when it isn't really.'

"Or when you've learned about dog body language and which breeds are the gentlest, and that kind of thing, when you see a dog coming, the very second you start to feel the fear signal, or before if you can, you could try and have a quick conversation where your brain's talking to itself, where it says something like, 'No, emotional bit of my brain, I don't need to be frightened. Don't worry. I know about this kind of dog; it's a soppy one that only usually attacks if someone hurts it first, and it doesn't look about to attack; it's all absorbed in running after that ball. So there really is no need for this fear signal.' Or whatever."

Just then, someone who must have been the teenage girl's big brother came up to them, and, obviously not scared of him, though maybe embarrassed that he might hear her being taught by a little girl half her age about ways of getting over the phobia she'd always been embarrassed to admit to having in front of him, she said, "Oy you, get your big ugly mug to the car; I'm coming in a minute."

Her brother walked off obediently.

She then told Becky that what she'd told her was beginning to sound helpful, and it gave her hope that she could get over her phobia, but she had some doubts, because the reason she'd got the phobia in the first place was because she'd been bitten by a dog when she was little, and she was sure it would have done worse things to her if its owner hadn't pulled it away. She said she thought about that sometimes, and the memory was so scary and upsetting that she always felt more scared of dogs afterwards, so even if she stopped herself being scared a few times, she felt sure she'd just start feeling scared again after the next time thoughts about being attacked when she was little came into her mind, so it would keep getting harder to control her feelings.

Becky sympathised. Then she told the girl that she'd read that there were ways people could stop memories of scary things upsetting them so much, so when they thought about them afterwards, they'd just feel a bit bad, not really upset. She said she could think of one way, which she'd heard was really supposed to be done with a therapist, but that people had managed to go through it on their own, and then felt much calmer than they had before when they had the memories that used to be so upsetting. She'd at least heard of one person doing that.

Becky was about to continue when she spotted a little family with a little dog coming along. She was worried the girl would run away and get scared again, so before she even really thought about what she was doing, she ran towards them, waving her arms with her fists clenched, and shouted, "Shoo! Shoo!" in an aggressive voice at the dog.

The dog stopped and huddled up close to the legs of the man who had it on a lead. The mother was startled, and shouted at Becky, "Hey!"

Then Becky realised that what she'd done was in danger of making things worse than they would have been if she'd done nothing, because it could possibly cause an argument, which would make the dog stay around for longer. So she quickly walked back to where the girl and her mum were standing, looking sheepish, hoping the family would decide to ignore what she'd done and just quickly walk on by.

They did just walk past, looking puzzled. The girl with the phobia managed to stand still without getting too frightened.

As they went past, Becky and the others heard the boy in the family say, "Why did that little girl run up to us and shout like that?"

The father said, "I don't know! Weird things have been happening all day today, starting when I went down to make breakfast and found a bar of soap in the food cupboard next to the cans of sardines!"

Perhaps another one of the family explained how it got there; but Becky and the others didn't find out, because the family walked out of earshot.

Becky felt embarrassed at having run and shouted at the dog, but the others were laughing. Becky's mum said, "Perhaps they'll still be puzzling over the mysteries of the little girl who told their dog to shoo and the bar of soap in the food cupboard this time next week."

When they stopped giggling, Becky asked the girl with the dog phobia if she'd like to hear what she'd been going to say before the family had come along. The girl said she would. So Becky continued,

"Well, about that technique that some psychologists believe can help people stop being upset about scary memories: They say that before you start trying it, it's best to make sure you're in a relaxed frame of mind; and you can try putting yourself in one by sitting for several minutes imagining you're doing something you love, if you can think of something. It doesn't have to be relaxing; it could just put you in a good mood; sports fans could imagine they're playing their favourite sport and competing against other people, starting to feel exhilarated and happy, for example. But try to imagine something that makes you feel good, anyway, whatever it is. It's best if people try to imagine things as realistically as they can, so it's as if they're feeling the same good feelings all over again that they've felt when they've done the thing for real.

"For instance, if you like sunbathing on a beach, you could imagine sitting there, actually feeling the sun on you, and enjoying the sights and sounds on the beach. See if you can imagine it so vividly you actually feel the enjoyment.

"Or if a person can't think of anything relaxing or enjoyable they've done that they can get absorbed in a daydream about doing again, they could try thinking of something they think they'd enjoy doing, if they can still imagine it vividly enough that it makes them feel good."

Becky's mum was a bit skeptical, and said in a tongue-in-cheek way, "So if you're a video game fan, you could fantasize about fighting monsters in a game and things, and that would put you in a relaxed frame of mind? And if you're a chocolate fan, presumably you could dream about enjoying a lovely big bar of your favourite chocolate! . . . Or if you love popping bubble wrap, perhaps you can fantasize about doing that for minutes on end . . . Or if you really enjoy challenging yourself to trying to get your big toe in your mouth, for some reason, you could daydream about doing that . . . But hang on, why can't people do those things for real?"

Becky said, "Mum, don't interrupt! I bet no one would really want to dream about trying to stick their toe in their mouth and popping bubble wrap! I don't know why people are supposed to just daydream and not do things for real; the article I read that described what you do didn't say. But I think you're supposed to be in a bit of a dream-like state when you finish, so it's better to dream about doing things; and anyway, if you did something nice for real, you might enjoy it so much you wouldn't want to stop, so you might never get around to doing the rest of what you're supposed to do for the technique. And anyway, some of the things people will want to daydream about are things they'd have to travel a long way or make a lot of preparations to do for real, like sunbathing on a beach, if they don't live right near the coast."

"Yeah, they'd especially have to do that in winter! . . . Or actually most of the year round in this country!" said her mum.

Becky said, "Yeah. Anyway, after several minutes of being engrossed in a nice daydream, it'll probably take a bit more to upset you than it might normally; so that'll be a better time to tackle upsetting memories. But you don't need to think about them enough to get really upset by them all over again.

"This might sound a bit weird, but you'll understand the reason for it in a minute: When you're in a bit of a dream-like state and feeling good, you imagine you're gently floating out of your body."

"Like a ghost!" joked her mum in a loud whisper.

"Mum! Take this seriously!" Becky said in a raised voice.

Her mum apologised. Then Becky continued,

"Anyway, you imagine you're floating out of yourself, and then imagine sitting to the side of yourself, watching yourself;

so it's as if there are two yous, one that's still in your body. But it's not as strange as it sounds.

"Then you imagine there's a television screen in front of your body, and you imagine one of your horrid memories is being replayed on the screen, as if it's a film of it. You haven't got a very good view of it, and it's all blurry; but you're watching yourself watching it, knowing it's being replayed. It can be replayed on fast speed. And it goes forward to a time after the horrible thing happened, when you felt safe again.

"The reason that technique's recommended is because it'll probably be less upsetting to go over the memory again in your mind if you're just imagining yourself watching yourself watching blurry images of it on a television screen, than it would be to imagine it's replaying in front of you, or to relive it in your mind just as it was.

"After you've imagined watching yourself watching it, you imagine you're floating back into yourself . . . but there's only one you in you. You're not you and the other you that materialised; you're just you."

Becky's mum and the girl were beginning to laugh. But Becky carried on:

"Then you imagine you're watching your bad experience on the television screen, but you imagine it's going backwards at fast speed, back to a time before the nasty thing happened when you felt safe. When it's finished, you imagine it's fast forwarding over just part of the memory, then rewinding over just that bit, then fast forwarding over that bit again, then rewinding, then fast forwarding; and you imagine it going back and forward over just that little bit again and again till you can look at it without feeling any emotion.

"You see, the way this is supposed to work is that it gives you new memories of it, and disrupts the way the brain thinks about it, since usually what will have happened before is that the memory will have come to mind, and then a painful emotion will have come on straightaway, so the memory was always upsetting. But if when the memory comes to mind after the technique's been tried, the brain just thinks of a bit of it, and thinks of it whizzing backwards at high speed and then forwards fast and backwards again and things like that, it won't be nearly as upsetting as it used to be.

"Anyway, when you've managed to rewind and fast forward one part of the horrid memory till it's stopped bothering you, you pick another part, and do the same with that. And you do that with all the parts of the bad memory. Then lastly you imagine it rewinding the whole way through, back and back till you're at a place in time when you felt safe. The technique's actually called the rewind technique.

"If you've got lots of horrid memories, like one memory of being bitten by a vicious dog, but lots of other memories of feeling really humiliated because you ran away from dogs when people were looking, you can take one memory at a time and do the technique with it. Maybe you could do one a week or something, or maybe more often if you feel like it, till you've done them all.

"But if you're doing one and you begin to feel a bit upset, it might be best if you stop, and try getting absorbed in something you'd prefer to do to take your mind off it, and don't try the technique yourself any more. After all, there are other things that could work, and you could always try seeing a good therapist. So you don't need to feel discouraged if you don't get on with that technique.

"After all, as I said, it's really supposed to be done with a therapist anyway. Maybe if other things don't work for you, you could look for a therapist who does the technique; most don't. But some do, and they guide people through it, and make sure they're relaxed enough first, and that they aren't getting upset. At least, they're supposed to.

"But actually, if the technique does work for you, either on your own or with a therapist, you could use it to try to get over the phobia itself, besides using it to help you stop getting so upset by bad memories, because if you imagine watching scenes of you running away from dogs going backwards and forwards and backwards and forwards on fast speed in your mind, it'll be a bit like deprogramming your brain from giving you the strong fear signal that makes you run away every time you see a dog, because when you encounter a dog after that, the emotional part of your brain that will have been giving you the strong fear signals before will have been calmed down by the memories being messed around with like that in your mind, because the memories of what's happened before when you've seen a dog will just be mingled with the scrambled memories, so the emotional part of your brain probably won't recognise them as its cue to trigger off a strong fear signal any more. It might be worth giving it a go anyway."

The teenager with the phobia said she thought that was interesting, and that she would think about trying it.

Then Becky said, "And what I said earlier about you looking up information about dogs online eventually's relevant here, because if you do that, it'll help you change your memories of what happened a bit too, in a way, or at least it might change the way you think about them, since you might understand what happened better, since, say if now you think, 'I've got a dog phobia because when I was three, a vicious dog bit me', one reason it might seem scary is because it might seem as if it was just a random unpredictable sudden event that happened out of the blue, and was beyond anyone's control; but if you get to understand more than whatever you do now about what can make dogs lose their tempers, or what kinds of upbringings make dogs more vicious, or what kinds of breeds are the most aggressive, and the reasons why, then you might understand the possible reasons for what happened to you more.

"For example, say if the story that flashes through your mind when you think about what happened is now, 'I was bitten by a vicious dog when I was little and that's why I've got the phobia', which is a scary story, it might turn into something more like, 'I got the phobia after I was bitten by an aggressive dog that might have got to be that way because it had an irresponsible abusive owner that made it aggressive by taunting it every day, so it ended up fired up with temper all the time and hostile to people, because it might have thought they might all taunt it like that', or, 'I realise now that pulling a dog's fur and standing on its feet will hurt it, and it probably bit me just to try to make me stop', or that kind of thing.

"Thinking of what happened as the consequence of a chain of events, and not just something uncontrollable and dangerous that suddenly happened out of the blue, might help you think of it more calmly, because it won't seem like just a shock, but you'll think through why things might have happened more when you're reminded of what happened, and think about what might have been able to have been done to have prevented them from happening, so that kind of behaviour will seem more controllable, so it'll seem less scary."

Becky didn't have any personal experience of what she was talking about; she'd never had any full-blown phobias herself, though the sight of spiders and worms had made her cringe at first; and she couldn't remember any upsetting memories. But she was fascinated by the way the mind works, in the same way she was interested in the mechanics of an engine. So she'd been curious to learn a lot about it. That's not to say she didn't genuinely care about people; she did.

Just then, the teenager's dad came along, and said to her, "There you are! We've been waiting ages, wondering what you were doing. Mark said you ordered him to get back to the car, saying you'd be with us in a minute. That was some time ago. What are you doing? And how long do you think you'll be?"

The girl said she'd met someone who knew a lot about how people could get over dog phobias, who was giving her advice, and that she probably wouldn't be too much longer. She apologised for keeping them waiting.

Her dad knew about her dog phobia, and was pleased. He agreed to go back to the car and wait a bit longer. He assumed Becky's mum was the one giving his daughter advice about how to get over a dog phobia; he certainly wouldn't have expected a girl as little as Becky to be the one doing it.

He thanked Becky's mum, and then went off and left them for a while.

The teenager started to feel a bit awkward about keeping her family waiting, and fidgeted a bit as she asked Becky if she had any more advice.

Becky felt a bit resentful that the girl's dad had thanked her mum and not her, but she realised the girl probably didn't want to hang around too much longer, so she ignored the feeling, and said she did have more advice. She said,

"One more technique you could try to help yourself get over being scared of dogs is first doing something you find relaxing so you're feeling calm, just like you would do with the technique to help with bad memories, and then just imagine there's a dog standing at the end of your road."

Becky's mum interrupted to say, "You know, I feel funny standing here in nothing but a swimming costume. I don't really like showing off all my flab to the world. I'll take our stuff to the car, and get dressed and come back, if you're going to stand here chatting for ages."

Becky said, "Well I don't think it will take ages! But OK." Then she turned back to the girl and continued,

"Anyway, when you've relaxed, and you're imagining there's a dog at the end of your road, just imagine you're not feeling scared of it at that moment, and that you're going to go and stroke it. Imagine setting off, getting the door key and going out. As you're doing that, if you start to feel even just a little bit scared, imagine you're coming back and sitting down, and then do something to unwind, maybe what you were doing to relax before you started imagining getting up to go, till you feel calm again. It might not take ages; it might just take a minute, or even less time.

"If you don't think dreaming of something nice will work to relax you – and after all, you'll only be doing it for a short time, so it might not – you could try something else, like clenching your fists tightly for a few seconds and then very slowly unclenching them, so you actually feel the nice feeling of the tension easing in them. You could do that a few times, thinking about how nice it feels to release the tension in them each time, and then your whole body might feel more relaxed, as well as your mind.

"Then when you feel relaxed again, imagine you're getting up and starting off towards the door again. Imagine going to the same place you went to before, like the front door or wherever it was; and then even if you're not feeling anxious this time, imagine coming back, and do something for a few minutes to relax, and then imagine going to that point again in your mind. Go there and back in your imagination till you get bored of going there. Don't move on when you've just stopped feeling twinges of anxiety about going there; wait till you're downright bored before moving on, so the anxiety's less likely to come back.

"Then go further in your imagination, till the next point where you start to feel a twinge of nerves. Then come back in your imagination and relax, and then imagine going there and back again, and again and again, till you're bored of going there too.

"Then go a bit further in your mind, till the next place you begin to feel a bit anxious. Then imagine coming back, and do something to relax yourself, and then imagine going there again.

"Carry on going like that, further and further towards where you imagine the dog to be. Every time you're feeling even just a little bit scared, imagine coming back and sitting down again, and then starting off several seconds later when you feel better again, going to the same place you stopped again, and again and again till you're bored of imagining going there. You might find you can imagine going further and further without feeling scared.

"Then eventually, you might imagine getting right up to the dog, and even stroking it, and not feeling scared. When you can imagine stroking it and not minding one little bit, maybe even feeling bored, like you did after you imagined going to the places on the way several times, you may as well stop. That'll help train your brain not to mind when you see a dog for real.

"And then for an extra confidence boost if you like, if you know someone with a friendly dog who's sympathetic to your problem, you could ask them to stand at one end of a room with the dog on a lead so it's under their control, while you stand at the other end of the room, and then gradually walk towards it, and back when you feel a twinge of nerves, towards it and back, again and again till you're a bit bored of doing that, using a technique to relax whenever you need to, and then going a bit further towards it and back, and so on, slowly closer and closer, in the way you did in your imagination, till you can stroke it for real without feeling scared.

"If you're wondering what else you could do to relax each time you need to when you go back, one technique you could try is to breathe in very very slowly, and then breathe out just as slowly, and when you do, imagine your anxious feelings are blowing out of you with your breath, and wafting up to the ceiling, and dispersing into bits around the room. You could try breathing in and out very calmly and slowly several times, imagining that kind of thing, and see if it relaxes you. If it doesn't, try something else, like daydreaming of chocolate or something."

Becky told the girl she hoped the advice would help her, and then said to her mum, who was still there despite saying she'd go, having changed her mind halfway through picking up the things they'd taken down to the beach like their towels, that she'd put on the ground at the start of the conversation, "OK, I think that's all I can think of to say."

Becky had an email address, and she and the teenager, who turned out to be called Stephanie, said goodbye and exchanged email addresses; and Becky asked her to contact her after a while and tell her whether what she'd said had helped. They left each other smiling.

A few weeks later, Stephanie did email Becky. She said she'd tried some of what she'd recommended, and it had worked; for the last few days, she'd been going past dogs, and not minding at all.

Chapter 8

Becky Advises a Worried Mother of a Girl Who's Got an Abusive Boyfriend and Doesn't Want to Break Up With Him

Becky got a reputation at her school for being able to help people. One day, the mother of one of the girls there, Caroline, took her aside after school while Caroline was doing an after-school activity, and confided in her that she was worried about Caroline because her boyfriend was unkind to her. Caroline was in Becky's class, and she wouldn't have liked it if she'd known her mum was discussing her with Becky. But she never found out, as far as Becky knew.

Her mum said to Becky, "I really don't like Caroline's boyfriend, and I'm upset that she won't stop going out with him. He tries to control her, and gets angry and insulting any time she doesn't want to do what he says. I think she's losing her confidence in herself because of the way he criticises her all the time. It even makes her cry. I hear her crying at night sometimes. She used to want to go to university, but now she isn't sure she's brainy enough, and wants to try and get a job instead for a while. I'm sure it's him that's made her change her attitude. It would suit him if she stayed around here because he can keep her with him, so she's a lot less likely to meet nicer boys and start going out with one of those instead.

"I've often told her I don't think he's right for her because I hate the way he upsets her, but whenever I criticise him she defends him and gets annoyed with Me, saying she's old enough to do what she likes! But it really upsets me to know she's often being upset by him. I don't know what she sees in him! I suppose he must be loving towards her sometimes."

Becky replied, "I've got a few ideas that might help, that I've picked up from some of the things I've heard. There's another tactic you can try, that might work better than pointing out her boyfriend's faults, especially because there's a problem when a person criticises someone's horrible boyfriend or anyone else they like, which is that even when what they say would persuade anyone else of what he's really like, someone who's in love with him won't want to hear it, so they probably won't really be listening, but instead they'll likely leap to his defence, thinking about what to say to argue with what's being said, instead of really thinking about what the criticisms are. And the more they think up things to say to defend him, the more they'll be convincing themselves that they're right to stay with him because he's decent really. It's as if they'll be persuading themselves.

"And when they walk away from the person doing the criticising at the end of the conversation, instead of thinking about whether what they said might be true, their head will be full of angry thoughts about them, and how annoyed they are that they criticised their boyfriend, especially if the conversation turned into a heated argument where the one doing the criticising said some things they took to be insults.

"But there is a way you could hopefully encourage Caroline to think more seriously about what she's doing, and that's by asking her questions that'll hopefully make her think more deeply, in a way that makes it sound as if you're just curious, not trying to get her to admit he's no good for her.

"You could try saying to her something like, 'I've decided not to criticise your boyfriend any more. You know what I think of him; but you're right: You're old enough to make your own decisions. Just know that I'm here for you if you ever need me. I'm not saying you ever will; I'm just saying I still care about you; but then, you already knew that.'

"If you say something that sounds touching like that, she might be less likely to ask you what's made you change your mind about criticising him, so it might be less likely to turn into an argument again.

"Then at some point when it seems that she's feeling thoughtful, or not too preoccupied to be willing to have a decent conversation, you could try asking her something like, 'What do you think you might be doing with your life five years from now?'

"When she tells you, you could ask other questions, like, 'Imagine it's five years in the future: What do you think might have been the ups and downs of life with your boyfriend during the time between now and then?' 'What do you think the advantages and disadvantages of life with him might be?' 'It might be difficult to know, but what do you think you might have achieved in life if you're still with him, and what do you think you might have achieved in life if you haven't been with him for a while by then?' 'Imagine it's further on into the future: What are the good things and the bad things about the kind of father you think he'll make for any children you have with him?'

"Try to make it sound like relaxed conversation, so it doesn't begin to sound to Caroline like an interrogation, which it might if she feels a bit pressured to say things about her boyfriend she'd rather not. And if she says good things about him you don't agree with or really don't enjoy hearing, try to resist the temptation to argue for the time being, even if you think it's really important she doesn't go on believing those things, and it's really stressing you out to hear them. The trouble with contradicting her will be that it'll be more likely to turn into an argument where she just starts defending him again, and she stops taking in what you're saying, because she's so preoccupied with thinking about what to say to contradict you. You might well get the chance to question her about what she's saying later, in a way that doesn't feel like criticism to her.

"You can try to remember all the good things she says about him, and think about each one in turn later, maybe writing them down so you don't forget what they are, and then thinking of any reasons you can as to why they might not be quite the advantages Caroline thinks they are. Then you could try to think up questions that'll make her think for herself about whether they're really the advantages she thinks they are.

"Even if she seems to be refusing to even think about whether there could be anything about her boyfriend that isn't as good as she'd like it to be, don't lose hope, because if your questions have made her go away thinking about the things you brought up and what she said about them, and she thinks about them some more over the coming days, she might decide for herself that he isn't everything she'd like him to be, and that she wouldn't be happy to be with him long-term after all.

"And listening to what she's got to say about him might help you understand what she sees in him. You might cringe when she says good things about him, but the more you know about the reasons she feels the way about him she does, the more you might be able to come up with questions that might cause her to go away thinking about whether she's right to want to be with him so much, and it might help you come up with ideas that could persuade her she doesn't need him as much as she thinks she does.

"One example of the kind of thing I mean is that if she says she wants to be with him because it's nice knowing he loves her so much, you can go away and think up a question that doesn't sound like a criticism, but will still get the point you want to make across to her if she thinks about it, like, 'You say he loves you; but when he's saying insulting things to you, does it still feel as if he loves you? Do you think it can really be love if he says things like that?'

"And then you can go away and think of more questions to ask in response to anything she says in reply that defends him.

"One question you could try asking her is, 'What do you think you'd miss out on in life if you weren't with him?'

"The thing is that it's possible that if you find out what she thinks she'd be deprived of in life if she wasn't with him, you could try to think of alternative ways she could get those things, within reason; and then if she does get them, she might not be so reliant on him for them, and also it might draw her attention away from him. This is the kind of thing I mean:

"Say if one thing that attracts her to him is that being with him makes life more exciting, because the drama he creates gives her an adrenaline buzz that puts her on a high sometimes, and also she gets to go out to nice places she thinks she just wouldn't get to go to without him, or that she'd feel too self-conscious to go to on her own. You could maybe start trying to work out other ways she could get an adrenaline buzz in life, and trying to think of other places she could go that she might enjoy just as much, and then see if she's interested. If she is, she might become less attached to her boyfriend, because she won't need him to provide them so much because she's getting them from another place. Or you could gently suggest that she could go to the same places just as easily with another boyfriend, or with someone else, who might be nicer. You could actually ask her what she thinks she could do to substitute for the things she values about her relationship with her boyfriend if she ever stopped going out with him.

"For instance, if she'd really miss his humour, you could encourage her to try to think of other ways she could get humour in her life if she ever stopped going out with him. Or if she says she thinks she'd be lonely, you could discuss with her ways she could stop being lonely, such as going to places where she might make friends, such as doing evening classes in a subject she's interested in, where she'd be filling her mind with things she enjoyed thinking about, and she might be making new friends, and might even find a new boyfriend.

"Or sometimes, she might say something that sounds awkward, like that she values doing a certain thing, like being given expensive things, or being taken out to places it's expensive to go to; but you wouldn't have to worry that they'd have to be substituted with other expensive things. If you ask her the reasons why she values being given expensive things or being taken out to expensive places, you might find out that the reasons go deeper than her just liking expensive things, and that she could get a lot of what she gets out of being given expensive things in other ways.

"For instance, if she says something that roughly means she values being given expensive things because it gives her a sense of worth and boosts her ego, and that makes her happier, because she thinks it means someone cares about her enough to buy those things for her and must think she's classy if he does that, and that the places they go to are exciting, and being a part of the group of friends he's in gives her a cosy feeling of belonging, you could talk through with her other ways she could get a sense of worth and an ego boost and a sense of excitement and belonging. You could ask her if she can think of any other ways she could get those things.

"Then you could maybe ask if she likes the idea of doing things such as joining an amateur dramatics class – she might make some good new friends and feel a sense of belonging there, and rehearsing and playing in front of an audience might give her an adrenaline boost and a sense of excitement, as well as a sense of status and self-worth, and pleasure at being admired. And if she gets them from something like that, she might not feel such a need to be with her boyfriend to get them.

"You wouldn't have to suggest she does them instead; you could maybe just ask if she'd like to start doing them. If she decides she'd like to and enjoys them, it might mean she spends more time away from her boyfriend, and that in itself might be a good thing, because it'll mean there's less time for him to be upsetting her. And the more time she spends away from him, the more she might realise she wants to do other things with her life.

"Also, if she gets to be more self-confident because of her achievements, she might be less tolerant of whatever her boyfriend says that makes her think she isn't good enough. So she might be more likely to split up with him.

"That might happen even if he decides to go to the new things she's going to with her. So don't be too discouraged if you persuade her to go to some new thing, only to find he's tagging along too.

"Or if she values the expensive things for themselves, maybe you could help her think up creative ways of earning enough money to pay for them herself one day, and talk to her about the importance of getting a good career, hopefully one she'll enjoy too. If she knows that might well mean doing something her boyfriend would disapprove of, that might eventually encourage her to split up from him.

"Or if she says she feels flattered by all the compliments her boyfriend gives her, and she enjoys feeling good about herself because of them, you could maybe think about whether you and other family members could start complimenting her on more things, such as when she's helpful or looks especially nice or has done something skilful, which might give her some of the same kinds of feelings, so she wouldn't feel the loss of them so much if she stopped going out with her boyfriend.

"If she thinks she'd miss the physical affection a lot if she stopped going out with him, maybe you could try hugging her more over the coming weeks, and then try to find out if she'd miss it just as much, or any less, because she's got other affection in her life.

"Another thing is that you could ask her if she thinks it's possible that there are things about his behaviour she interprets one way now, that she might interpret in another way in the future. Here's the kind of thing I mean:

"One thing is that it's believed by a lot of people that abusive men as a rule are far more charming than men in general. That can attract women to them, but it's not really a sign of a good thing, because the way they get to be so charming is by using a lot of flattery most men wouldn't give because it would be dishonest. People without much of a conscience don't have any problems using a lot of insincere exaggeration, like telling women they look like film stars and they're the most beautiful women they've ever seen, and that if they were with them, they'd like to lavish them with gifts, even though they're saying it knowing full well they wouldn't do it really; and they can say a lot of things like that. And they have no conscience about putting on a considerate courteous act to get what they want, whereas a lot of men would just be themselves a lot more; they might be on their best behaviour at first, but their normal selves would probably show through sooner.

"A woman can feel flattered by the charm, and the feeling of being admired might make her feel loved and good about herself, so that might be one thing that can attract a woman to an abusive man, especially because he probably won't be abusive at first, because he'll know that showing his abusive side too soon will put her off him. He'll often wait till he's sure she's fond of him before getting abusive to her, because by that time, he'll think she'll be more reluctant to break free of him, because she'll lose out on the good things.

"That doesn't mean every charming man will be abusive, and there might be a lot of abusive men without an ounce of charm in them. But a lot of them can seem charming, so a woman can think a man like that is really nice at first, and it might be a long time later that she starts thinking his charm must have been fake, only put on because it was his way of getting what he wanted. Even during the days when he's at his most abusive, there might still be times when he's charming, because he'll know it'll help to keep her with him.

"It's also been said that abusive men as a group are far more fun to be around than average men. But again, that isn't the good thing it might seem to be at first, because one reason they can be more fun is that, having less of a conscience, they might have no qualms about making fun of other people, so there's more opportunity for them to have fun than there would be for a lot of men, and they might sometimes do it in a witty way that makes people they're with laugh . . . apart from the people on the receiving end of it, of course. So a woman might be attracted to an abusive man who makes her laugh, loving the way he gives her more enjoyment in life by the way he puts other people down in an amusing way, and it might only be later when he's turned his liking for making fun of people on her that she starts to realise it's not a nice character trait after all. But by then, she might be too attached to him to find it easy to leave him, both emotionally, and physically – say if they've moved in together and she's pregnant with his baby.

"Another thing that might be interpreted differently at the beginning of a relationship than it is later is behaviour that can seem fun and bold and courageous at first, but reckless and irresponsible later, such as if a man's not very good at holding down a job, because if his boss isn't very nice, he's got no hesitation in telling him so. It might be hilarious to sit and listen to him tell the story of how his boss tried to bully him so he stood up in front of everyone and bawled at his boss that he could take his job and stuff it where the sun doesn't shine; and a woman who's attracted to the man might think, 'Wow! He must be brave to have done that! So many other people must dream about doing that but haven't got the guts. He must have a strong personality and be full of confidence! I bet he'd stand up for me if someone tried to get abusive to me!'

"But he might still be doing that kind of thing years later, when she's trying to bring up their kids; and then that behaviour might look totally different to her, when she's got all the worries of trying to pay for the things they need. Behaviour like that might seem irresponsible and reckless then, and instead of taking it as a sign of a strong person, she might take it as a sign that he hasn't got the will to stick at anything, and that he can't love her, because otherwise he'd care more about bringing in money to support the family. She might be upset by the behaviour, even more so if she tells him she wishes he'd stick at a job and he just gets abusive.

"Or if when she first starts going out with him, he does things on impulse, such as responds to a taunt by someone who says they bet he can't drink as much as they can without falling under the table by immediately bellowing an order for a dozen whiskeys and gulping them straight down, it might make onlookers laugh, and seem as if he's a fun person to be around, and that life with him will be exciting.

"But some time later, if he's still spending a lot of money or drinking a lot on impulse, a woman who used to think that kind of behaviour brightened up her life by making it more amusing and exciting might come to see it as over-extravagance and irresponsibility, and worry a lot about it, especially if he buys big things on impulse when they can't really afford it; or if he drinks a lot, she might realise he can often be a danger to be around because he's more abusive when he's drunk. Or she might realise the behaviour that seemed fun was just a dangerous lack of impulse control, when the same character trait might lead him to do things like hitting out at their kids at the slightest provocation.

"Another thing is that he might phone her up several times a day and ask her what she's doing and who she's with, and tell her he loves her; and at first, she might think it must be a sign of caring and devotion, and love him more because of it. But some time later, if he's still doing it, and he isn't so nice to her, and she knows more about what he's like, she might realise it's really a sign of obsessive jealousy and distrust, and one way he uses to try to control her movements, because he's doing his best to make sure she isn't with anyone he disapproves of. So the same behaviour she thought was touching at the beginning of their relationship might seem upsetting and annoying then.

"Or whenever a friend or member of her family criticises her or the boyfriend, and she gets a bit upset or angered by it, he might tell her it's best if she doesn't see them so much any more; and at first that might seem to her like caring, as if he's concerned about her welfare, and doesn't want her to be upset. But when she knows him better and he's started being abusive, she might realise it's really just another way he's trying to control her, because he's trying to isolate her from people who might manage to persuade her to leave him, or help her think of his behaviour from other points of view so she's more likely to see it for what it really is.

"Sometimes a woman beginning a relationship with a man who's going to turn out to be abusive will realise there are things about him that aren't very nice, but she's getting so much out of the relationship, like fun and excitement and the feeling of being loved, that she doesn't want to let him go; and only after some time, when there's more abuse than fun in the relationship, will she start to wish she hadn't stayed with him.

"The thing is that you could say all that to Caroline, not saying her boyfriend might be like that, but just saying you heard it somewhere. You won't have to ask her if she thinks her boyfriend's like that at all, or even mention him at all unless she brings the subject of him up; if you just leave her to go away and think about what you said, she might see signs of it in her boyfriend, and decide for herself that he isn't all she thought he was.

"One last thing is that it might help her think about whether she and her boyfriend really are a good match if you give her some of the same advice people who run marriage preparation courses would give couples, which is that before they decide for definite that they want to be with each other for good, they should have a very serious think about how compatible they are, both asking themselves a series of questions, and then comparing their answers, to see if any of their attitudes to things might be so different from each other it would cause conflict in the future.

"There are websites with lots and lots of questions on them that each member of a couple can answer, so as then to compare their answers with their boyfriend or girlfriend's and debate them – questions like, 'What would you do if there was an accidental pregnancy before we're ready to settle down together?' 'What are the ways you think children should be disciplined?' 'Do you believe in saving a lot of the money you earn, or spending freely?' 'Do you like to gamble?' 'In a marriage, who do you believe ought to be responsible for deciding how much money gets spent and what it gets spent on?' 'Who do you think ought to do the majority of the housework?' 'How important is it to you that you go out with your old friends on your own sometimes?' 'How would you feel about your husband or wife going out with friends and leaving you on your own in the house in the evenings?' Questions like that.

"It's possible that if Caroline went through a questionnaire like that with her boyfriend, even if he didn't answer all the questions honestly, but said what he guessed she wanted to hear sometimes, there still might be enough differences between them to make her think more deeply about whether she really wants to be with him for any decent length of time. She might realise things about him she didn't know before, or suspected but didn't want to think about before.

"So you could recommend that Caroline and her boyfriend do one of those questionnaires together. You could find what you think is a good one. You don't have to make it sound ominous, as if you think she'd better do the questionnaire if she doesn't want to risk being unhappy; you could sound bright and cheerful about it, as if you just think it's a really good idea for any couple to do, which it is really.

"Or Caroline could answer the questions on her own, just guessing how her boyfriend would answer from what she knows about him.

"I hope things work out the way you want."

Caroline's mum hadn't been expecting a lecture. But she was grateful for the advice and thanked Becky.

When she was in the fourth form at school, Becky heard more and more worrying news stories about global warming, about how if all the ice in Antarctica melted, it would turn into masses and masses of water that would pour into the sea, so much that it could even make the sea rise by a metre, or even a fair bit more over time, and that would mean there would be floods in lots of parts of the world, because the sea would come in further in a lot of places than it had before, and cover a lot of land where people were living. Then she read an article on the Internet about Antarctica, which said the ice there contained about seventy per cent of all the world's fresh water. She'd heard things about water shortages in some parts of the world, and people going hungry because it was difficult to grow crops there because of that. So she thought:

"That frozen water shouldn't be wasted by just being left to fall in the sea! Wouldn't it be good if they could take all the ice away from Antarctica before it melted, and dump it on deserts and other places where it doesn't rain much but people live, so crops would grow, and the people wouldn't have a problem feeding themselves any more; and they could use some of the water to drink too. If engineers or people like that took the ice away bit by bit over decades, there could be a constant supply for a while, till those countries were better off. And then maybe they could start importing lots of water or something.

"Then wouldn't it be good if Antarctica was artificially warmed up somehow so crops grew there too, so not enough ice to raise sea levels if it melted would ever build up there again, and a lot of people could go and live there. That would help to solve the problems of earth's population getting too big to be fed, and earth getting overcrowded, if those two things get to be problems. Having the deserts turned into fertile places that can feed more people by having tons of melting ice dumped on them will help with those problems too, since a lot more people might go to live there, and a lot more food will be able to be grown in the world because of all the food that will be grown in the newly fertile land that used to be deserts.

"And Antarctica could be turned into a great place for masses of refugees from wars and famines and things to go to, so they can make new lives there, instead of having to try to escape to already-crowded countries that sadly don't really want them."

Becky came up with some fairly elaborate ideas for how such a thing could be achieved.

She thought it would make a lot of sense for governments to group together and fund a project to transform Antarctica and do something useful with the ice there, since after all, if nothing was done about the ice and it melted and flowed into the sea, raising sea levels by a fair bit, it might cost billions or even trillions of pounds to build sea defences in coastal areas all around the world to protect communities living near coasts, especially in low-lying countries, so the money may as well be spent on removing the ice and doing something worthwhile with it.

Not everyone shared her enthusiasm though. She found the email address of a scientist who'd worked in Antarctica for a while, and emailed him to ask if her ideas could be put into practice. He emailed her back saying removing the ice caps and heating up Antarctica could actually cause a problem, since the ice caps help to cool the earth, and without them some countries could have more extreme heatwaves than they have now, endangering life. Becky was a bit concerned, but hoped he was over-estimating the problem. She didn't have the scientific knowledge to be sure one way or the other; but she thought it would be such a pity to waste all the water in the ice caps that instead of trying to find out, she thought she'd make more enquiries about whether her ideas could be achieved if a group of senior scientists and government advisors thought they might work.

She wrote to the British prime minister explaining her ideas. After a while, she got a brief and maybe tactful letter back, saying they sounded interesting, but that Britain couldn't fund such a thing alone – perhaps the European Union could help. Becky wrote to its president, but didn't hear anything for some time, and then just got a little letter back saying the European Union had no plans to fund projects like that.

So Becky decided to write to the American president and ask if America could do it.

She seemed to be having more luck, as she got a letter back saying the American president would like to speak to her about her ideas if she could come to America and see him.

She excitedly showed her mum the letter. Her mum wondered why the president felt he couldn't just speak to Becky over the phone. But Becky said she'd love to go to America again anyway; she'd had such fun last time, when her and her mum had been there on holiday.

She asked her uncle Simon, who'd found her mum and her a good bargain trip there a couple of years before, if he could find them another one. He had a look, and found them a return flight with a price they could quite easily afford.

So they decided to go. Becky made an appointment to see the president, and they decided to spend several days enjoying themselves while they were there.

During the Easter holidays, they were off.

Chapter 9

Becky Finds Herself Advising the American President, About Things She Didn't Expect to

Becky went to America with her mum not long before Easter, so Becky could tell the president about her plans to save the world.

On the day they'd been invited to the White House, her mum sat in the reception area with a book, while Becky was invited into the president's office.

She told the American president about all her ideas about how global warming could be prevented from damaging the planet, and about how some of the world's other big problems could be solved. The president said the ideas were interesting and he'd think about them. Then he asked her to tell him something about herself, saying he'd heard she was a child genius.

Becky told him a bit about her life. When she told him she'd done a counselling course and was going to do a psychology degree, he seemed to want to know more. He told everyone else in the room to leave. Then he asked her about it. When she told him, an unexpected thing happened:

The president lowered his voice to not much more than a whisper, and said, "I need help from someone. But it has to be someone I can trust not to run off to the press with the information I tell them. Can I trust you? I'm thinking you seem too young and unfamiliar with the bad ways of the world to betray my trust. If I tell you something private, will it stay private?"

Becky assured him she wouldn't tell the press anything.

Then he shifted awkwardly in his seat, and began, stammering a bit:

"I get upset by the things people say about me in the media. I'm getting really fed up of reading horrible things day after day. I've read magazine articles that accuse me of being a psychopath, and interviews with old teachers of mine who talk about all the mistakes I made at school, calling me a dunce. It's bad enough having all the responsibility of leading the country and knowing there will be bad consequences if I make mistakes. But when the media not only delight in analysing those, but bring up things from my past, it gets to me. Running this country's becoming too much of a burden for me, but I can't resign, because I'm scared of what my family and all my supporters would think.

"I don't think I could keep going without medical help; my body's loaded down with antidepressants. I take a few kinds at once. And sometimes I take tranquillisers too. But some people in the media have found out, and I've read articles saying my decision-making must surely be affected badly by being sedated with drugs. But I'm only on them because I made such bad decisions before that the doctors said I needed something to help me have a cooler head."

216

Becky was surprised to hear him say that.

All the while the president had been speaking, they'd heard a cat meowing outside. Then they heard a loud angry voice, that sounded distinctly like Becky's mum's, coming from outside, saying,

"Oh stop that gloomy yowling you mournful beast! You ought to go and live in a graveyard, and then you can spook passers-by at night with that noise."

Becky was embarrassed, realising her mum must have just insulted the White House cat. She apologised, saying her mum didn't like cats, and that she'd been in a bad mood ever since she'd dropped her phone in a snow drift that morning. She'd managed to fish it out, but she hadn't dared try to use it since, in case she found out it was broken. Becky said,

"I've never seen such big piles of snow as the ones here! It's spring sunshine at home, but it seems to be still winter here! If this is global warming, I hate to think what it was like before it started!"

The president laughed and said winter often liked to inflict one last fierce snow storm on them before it disappeared, and that it was alright about the cat. He said Becky's mum was probably sitting in the chair his wife sat in when she greeted visitors, and that the cat often did great screeching meows in protest whenever anyone else sat there, as if he thought they'd invaded the chair and might not let his wife have it back.

Then he got serious again and said, "Winter reminds me of the people who don't like me in a way; it seems out to get us, like my enemies. I wish I could stop people saying nasty things about me. I've read articles that bring up things from my childhood I'd much rather weren't publicised, like all the times I used to tie frogs to fire crackers and then explode them to watch the frogs get blown to bits.

"And they bring up the fact I used to be an alcoholic and I'm now officially in recovery, saying alcohol probably damaged the part of my brain responsible for complex thought, and that's why I've made some of the awful decisions they say I've made. They accuse me of 'stinking thinking', as they call it, saying it's what alcoholics have even when they've sobered up, thinking in extreme ways, and as if issues and solutions to problems are more simple than they are, because they can't see the complexities in them, such as if they categorise leaders of countries in their minds as either good leaders we can be friends with or evil leaders who need to be destroyed, and that's that – nothing in between. They say that means I haven't realised some important things I could have realised if only I'd made an effort to get the old brain into gear despite its failings and thought about things more carefully."

Coincidentally, suddenly a noise like a thousand beer bottle tops was heard rattling in the distance. The president quickly reassured Becky it was only the percussion section of the White House band beginning the weekly band practice. Then he carried on:

"Those people talk about the countries I got America to invade, saying I was psychopathically keen to invade, and that I just thought in terms of evil and good – that we had to get the bad guys and that was it, with no thought for whether what came afterwards might be worse, or whether despite the headline-grabbing terrible things the leaders did, they had also done a lot of good, so most people in their countries would be better off if they stayed in power than they would be if war was brought to their countries that might cause violence for years; and they say I didn't give a thought to whether there was anything that could in any way justify any of the bad things they'd done, which would mean they weren't quite as bad as they looked. People say I was just focused on the one thought of invading and getting rid of them."

Becky asked him whether he thought there was any truth in what his opponents said. He looked uncomfortable. Then he admitted, while his face went a bit red with embarrassment:

"Well, I realise I've made some terrible mistakes, but I wouldn't dare admit it in public, because then my party might lose the next election, and lots of people might blame me! So many lives have been lost because of my decisions, they'd never forgive me. I was so eager to get our troops to invade those places, I wouldn't listen to anyone who told me it wasn't a good idea.

"But after we'd taken over the latest country, we realised we hadn't planned for what to do next. And then, because no one was ruling the country properly any more, some nasty groups of people rose up and started fighting each other for control of it. We held elections there, but it didn't stop the fighting, and then we realised that one reason the dictator who'd ruled before had seemed so evil was that he was ruling a country with several nasty groups of people in it, who would have loved to rise up and fight if he hadn't had such a reputation for crushing opposition.

"They rejoiced when he wasn't there any more. We thought at the time that so many people rejoiced because they were glad to see us liberate the country. But we found out later that a lot of the people rejoicing were those groups, who were pleased because they knew it meant they could rise up and fight each other for power in an attempt to take over the country themselves without worrying about what he'd do."

A big fly flew in the window and landed on the president's head. But he didn't seem to notice at all as he continued:

"We hadn't even realised those groups existed before. It hadn't occurred to us that it would be a good idea to do some research into what kinds of groups might be there that would want to struggle for power if the dictator wasn't there any more. We just thought he was evil and needed to be defeated. That was that. We hardly gave any thought to what we'd do next, or whether anything bad could happen as a result of the dictator being removed. And we didn't think about the soldiers on both sides who'd be injured and killed, or how their families would manage without them, or how others would cope looking after permanently injured men for the rest of their lives, and whether a lot of civilians could end up being killed and suffering."

At that point, the president shed a few tears. Becky was touched to think he cared about the soldiers and their families now, even though it was a bit late. But then he said,

"And even some respectable newspapers and magazines have started criticising me for being so enthusiastic to invade without thinking of anything like that. And my ratings in the opinion polls are going down and down. A few journalists have somehow got hold of the information that I'm very depressed, and they say depression's as bad as alcoholism for making people think in extremes, not seeing the more complex and subtle things about a situation, but just thinking it's either all one thing or all the other, like all evil or all good. So they say depression on top of alcoholism makes me dangerous when I'm in charge. I can't stand it any more!"

Big tears began to fall from his eyes, and he sobbed uncontrollably for a few seconds, before making an effort to calm himself, and apologising.

Becky tried to comfort him by saying, "Well, if you recognise that you really do have problems with the way you think, it won't necessarily mean you've got them forever. And realising you've got them means you'll actually be a lot better off than if you didn't, if you want to improve things. The teachers on my counselling course said that recognising you've got problems that need solving in the first place is an encouraging step on the way to solving them – provided there is a solution you're happy to try out, of course; so it's as if you've already made progress towards solving the problems, even before you start. If you know you've got that 'stinking thinking', you'll hopefully recognise when it's happening again after a while, so you can stop it."

The president said it wasn't that simple, since when he got carried away and really wanted something, he felt sure he was thinking about things the way they really were, rather than thinking in extreme and simplified ways and so on. It was only afterwards when the media criticised him and he thought back on things that he realised that maybe he had been thinking in over-simplified and extreme ways after all.

Becky suggested he write out reminder cards, and stick them on the walls in his bedroom and in other private places in his home where no one or only family members would ever see them, that said such things as:

"Might things be more complicated than I think? Can my past experience of making mistakes teach me lessons that give me wisdom about ways I could handle situations I'm in now, and warnings about things not to do because they could lead to difficult problems if they were done? What lessons have I learned from the past?"

Then she suggested he could make cards to put around his desk where he'd often spot them, that said things like:

"Could I achieve what I want to achieve by doing something different that will harm fewer people? In what alternative ways might it be possible to achieve it?"

"Do I really need to take such extreme action as I think I do? What are several good things that might happen, and bad things that won't happen, if I don't take the action I want to take?"

"Is there anything that might justify the way the person/people I want to punish/depose/or whatever is/are behaving? Is what they've done just a case of them being nasty, or could there be more to it? What other possibilities are there?"

"What bad things might happen as a result of doing what I want to do? What might possibly go wrong?"

Becky told the president it didn't matter if other people saw those cards, since they wouldn't necessarily know he'd written them to remind himself not to make the same mistakes he had in the past. She suggested he could always call in advisers too to help him think of alternative less harmful courses of action in future if he was tempted to send his military to invade somewhere.

She said that as for all the bad press he was getting about the past, naturally he couldn't change what he'd done, but if he tried to organise good things that would benefit the people in the places he'd invaded, he'd get praised by a lot of the media, and end up looking better. She did caution him that it had better not be anything too ambitious, since trying to achieve too much at once, or in areas where doing things like building hospitals and setting up good electricity supplies was difficult because there was fighting there, would likely doom the projects to fail, so he would end up looking worse than he did already.

The president thanked Becky for her advice. They talked some more, and then he said he had an appointment so he'd better go.

Unfortunately, Becky concluded with disappointment after a while that he must have forgotten all about her suggestions for warming Antarctica and solving the world's water shortage and population problems. She never heard any world leader mention them again. But the president was impressed with the way she'd counselled him about his depression, and recommended her services to several of the White House staff and politicians he knew who had depression, not telling them she'd helped him, but just praising her achievements like having done a counselling course at such a young age. They thought the president had gone a bit barmy, telling them a child who was just a month short of her seventh birthday was so clever, and would be able to help them get over depression. But he arranged a meeting for the very next day where they could meet her, and she could give them a lecture and give them group therapy, teaching them about things that might help them. Out of curiosity, and because he was, after all, their boss, they decided to go along.

Chapter 10

Amid a Bit of Controversy, Becky Gives a Talk to Some American Politicians About Ways of Overcoming Depression

Becky went to the White House the next morning to give the staff and politicians with depression some advice and group therapy. Again, her mum waited in the reception area while she spoke to them.

They turned up because the president had told them to, but they were very doubtful about whether a six-year-old could teach them anything, and wondered if the president was losing his mind for telling them she could help them. Still, because he'd told them to listen respectfully, they'd decided to try their best, and at least not voice out loud any uncomplimentary thoughts they had.

Becky Talks a Bit About the Causes of Depression

The first thing Becky said, though, impressed them so much they started listening respectfully for real . . . at least for a while. She said:

"Wow there are a lot of you! Working for the government must be depressing! The president's asked me to tell you some of the things I've learned on the counselling course I did at school and in a couple of books I read in my spare time.

"One thing I learned is that depression can be caused by a variety of things. Sometimes it can be brought on by vitamin or mineral deficiencies, such as vitamin B12 deficiency or magnesium deficiency, or by not having enough thyroid hormone, and other physical things like that, I think because the brain chemistry gets altered so the brain gets depleted of the chemicals that can help people feel good. There's even scientific research that's finding that some people grow up more vulnerable to depression and other mood disorders than the average person is because an infection their mothers had when they were pregnant with them caused changes in certain kinds of brain cells that were growing in their brains. That doesn't mean nothing can be done about their depression though. And sometimes it might have a cause that's part-biological and part psychological.

"But a lot of the time, depression's caused when bad things happen to people and then they think about them more and more, and feel hopeless about them, as if there's nothing they can do to change things. Sometimes they can start thinking things are even worse than they are, and that they'll never change, so they get more miserable. Often things aren't really hopeless, but some of the people who think they are got into the habit of thinking there was no hope of getting out of bad circumstances when they were children, when they had less or no power to change bad things that were happening to them; and they never got out of the habit of thinking that way, so they still do, even though they have more power to change things now. But feeling hopeless about them can be what puts them at risk of sinking into depression.

"So if you find yourselves feeling a bit hopeless about something, it might often be worth you reminding yourselves that there might be more you can do to change the situation than you think. Then you could start trying to work out what you could try to do about it."

Becky Starts to Talk About Emotional Needs That can Damage Mental Health if They're Unmet

Becky felt as if she was getting into her stride, and relaxed a bit, carrying on, "Also though, some psychologists believe that everyone has several needs besides physical needs that they have to get met for them to be happy, and that anyone who doesn't have some of them met over time will be likely to have some kind of mental health problems sooner or later. I'll tell you what the needs are, and then I think you'll have to work out how you can get them met later on your own, because our counselling course and those books I've read didn't tell us much about how to do that, I don't think, and besides, it'll probably be a bit different for each individual, depending on what you want out of life, and what's causing your problems.

"One need people have is for control over their lives and what happens to them, and the freedom to make their own decisions, free from being pushed into doing things they don't want to do, or left out of things like decisions that are going to affect their lives in big ways. But people also need a balance between having freedom to make decisions, and feeling over-burdened because they're expected to make more or bigger decisions than they feel they have the skill and information to."

Trouble Erupts in the Room

One of the White House staff interrupted Becky to ask a question and tell her about something that was bothering him. He said:

"That strikes a chord with me! I'd like to hear more about these needs and what to do! I'm depressed because I feel as if I can't control things I'd like to. It really bugs me that I can't do anything about things I'm unhappy about – at least I don't think I can.

"I think the president makes terrible decisions sometimes that mean our soldiers have to go and put themselves in harm's way, and a lot of innocent civilians get killed; but I feel as if I can't protest to the president, because he could just tell me that if I don't like it, I can feel free to get another job; or for all I know, he could make things awkward for me; he wouldn't just fire me, because it would be illegal to fire me just for a disagreement – even he has to obey the law I guess, much as he might not like the idea.

"But I'm worried that instead, he could persuade people to start making life difficult for me, by doing things like not telling me things I need to know, so I can't do my job so well; and then he could start accusing me of being incompetent, so then he would have an excuse to fire me. Or he could take away my responsibilities so I have to do tedious work instead that I don't get any enjoyment out of or opportunity to use my skills in – I've seen it happen to others – not here, but with friends I know in other jobs; and I'm worried it'll happen to me if I say much."

A growl was heard from somewhere in the room. There were no dogs there, so Becky concluded that it had to be one of the politicians, perhaps a supporter of the president.

The man who was talking continued: "I did speak up once – I did my best to be polite, and wrote a message to the president telling him he shouldn't be ordering the invasion of the places he'd decided America should invade because it would be the worse for America in the end, and he didn't speak to me for days! He just gave me frosty looks whenever we met! And since then he's been short-tempered with me, snapping at me impatiently at the slightest excuse, and barking orders at me and expecting things to be done right away, instead of asking nicely and being willing to wait if I'm doing other things, like he used to. So I feel pushed around, and I'm worried about what would happen if I said another thing!"

One of the other men in the room, a staunch supporter of the president, had been looking more and more annoyed, and eventually said angrily, "You cheating sneak! The president's kindly told you about this meeting because he wanted to help you, and now you go and try to ruin his reputation! I always knew the likes of you were no good!"

The man who'd said he was unhappy replied, "We're here to get help! It's only right that I should say what's bothering me! People like you make me sick anyway! You've got such blood-lust, you'll support the president no matter how irresponsible his decisions are!"

The other man said, "People were talking like you talk all the time while Hitler was building up his army, insisting it was best not to do anything about it so as not to risk people being hurt and killed! If you'd been in government then, we'd probably never have gone to war with him, and his descendants would be ruling the world now! That's what happens when people refuse to do anything about the problems these tyrants cause!"

The first man who'd spoken said, "Don't be stupid! You can't possibly compare the dictators of little countries you thoughtlessly voted for America to invade with Hitler! You're incapable of telling the difference! You think it's all a sport anyway, don't you, like fox hunting! You've got a psychopathic streak; you wouldn't have any understanding of the feelings of people who have to watch their friends get killed, or of mothers grieving for their sons!"

The other man leapt to his feet, fists clenched, and shouted, "You've got no right to insult me like that, you limp-wristed pathetic weed! I take the decisions I think need to be taken for world security! If it was up to you, you'd probably let any dictator get away with anything he wanted, trampling over other countries, burning their houses and terrorising their people!"

The other man also got up, and angrily shouted, "I'd take the decisions I thought were best for our people and civilians in other countries! And don't you call me limp-wristed! I'd be happy to fight you any day!"

230

The other man shouted, "Oh yeah? Come on then!"

Becky was scared they'd have a fight right there and then! Others joined in the shouting, some speaking up for the president and his policies and condemning anyone who'd oppose them, and others shouting about how terrible they thought they were!

Then more of them stood up, and Becky was scared they'd all have a brawl right there and then in the White House, smashing up the room! She briefly wondered how that would look, with her right in the middle of it! She certainly wouldn't be invited back to talk about depression again, she thought. And she worried it might get into the newspapers and be international news! She didn't want that kind of fame! She was planning to do a psychology degree when she left school. She didn't know what she wanted to do afterwards, but she imagined what might happen if she ever decided to try marriage counselling: She imagined a couple coming in, realising the counsellor was her, and one saying to the other, "We'd better get out of here. Up to now we've been arguing a lot, but I know this person's reputation; if we stay much longer, we'll probably end up physically fighting on the floor of the therapy room!"

Becky wondered if she'd better run for safety quickly and just leave the politicians and White House staff to it. But then she thought it would be best if she tried to stop the argument quickly. She stood on a chair, and yelled, "Please, can you be quiet and listen to what I've got to say?"

No one took any notice; they were all too busy shouting at each other. She wondered what to do. Then she had an idea. Nearby there was a bookcase. She took a big hardback book out. She wondered if it might belong to the president. But she thought something needed to be done regardless; she banged it hard on the desk several times for attention, and yelled, "Silence!" She hoped she hadn't damaged the book! But it seemed alright.

To her relief, the tactic worked. It got everyone's attention, and they remembered they were supposed to be listening to her.

She was a bit worried about what would happen next. But she told the man who'd spoken up at first that she'd try to answer his question. She said:

"I'm not sure I can give you any good advice really; after all, I haven't even finished school. But I can think of a few things you could try:

"I know it'll be hard, but try not to take the president's attitude too personally. Try making excuses for him whenever he says something bad-tempered to you; it could be that at least part of his attitude to you comes from the fact that he's depressed too. When people are depressed, they can just brood on what someone's done that's annoyed them, and get more annoyed about it till it's the only thing they think about when they think of the person.

"Anyone can do that. But depressed people will likely do it more. And some depressed people can easily be offended, especially because they can get so focused on themselves and what's going wrong for them it doesn't occur to them to try to think of things from others' points of view, so when someone does something they don't like, they don't think of reasons why they might have done it, but just condemn them for it and feel annoyed. They seem to lose the ability to think of different ways of looking at things, but just think in extremes, as if things are just one thing or the other, such as that either people are doing the right thing, or they've behaved badly and need to be condemned."

Becky saw several of her audience looking at her disapprovingly, but couldn't work out why. So she carried on:

"I knew a girl at school like that. She was depressed. Whenever someone did something she didn't like, like when she asked a teacher for help with her homework, and the teacher said it would have to be later because she was busy, she always insulted the teacher behind her back, swearing about her and calling her names, and saying it just wasn't good enough that she hadn't helped her, not thinking about what else the teacher might have to do, or whether she might have had a hard day and needed a break to get over it . . ."

Suddenly Becky remembered that she was talking to a room full of depressed people, who might be offended at what she was saying, besides the fact that the person she was actually advising was depressed! And she was saying it so soon after they'd nearly all started fighting too, when she'd worried about what kind of reputation she'd get if it was reported in the papers that she'd been trying to give advice and therapy in the White House and it had resulted in a fight! She stammered a bit, and then said,

". . . Sorry, I don't mean to be offensive; I know all of you are depressed; I don't mean to say that all depressed people are inconsiderate scumbags or anything like that."

She realised that was even worse! She went red with embarrassment. She thought she noticed several of them making little movements towards the door, not standing up, but turning towards it in their seats and looking at it as if they'd like to walk out; and she realised they might be even more offended than they probably were at first. She reflected that public speaking seemed to be more complicated than she had ever imagined! She said,

"Hey, don't get up and go away! I'm not trying to say all depressed people will be annoying to be around. I'm just trying to help you, like the president told me to. Sorry if you feel offended by one or two things I've said. You know I'm not an expert . . . You know, I don't think the president would like it if you walked out; he seems to be a fan of mine."

At that last sentence, they all stopped making little movements towards the door, and turned back and started listening again.

Then one of the White House staff said, "We can tell you're not an expert on depression. Not all depressed people complain like the person at your school you told us about! But it reminds me of something I half-remember, about someone telling me about a Charles Dickens novel they read once, where there was a woman who would often sit around feeling sorry for herself, complaining about being lonely, as if she was hoping people would feel sorry for her; but one day, some kind of crisis happened, and she fetched and carried for people all day, and managed to do it without a thought for herself and her emotional problems, as if suddenly having something meaningful to do perked her up a lot."

Becky felt a bit embarrassed that one of the people she was lecturing had said they could tell she wasn't an expert. But then she saw some humour in what he told her, and said, "That's interesting. Yes, maybe if schools taught things that were more meaningful, or we had more meaningful things to do there, this girl I told you about who got so critical of people so quickly would have got so involved in them she wouldn't have worried about her problems so much! Maybe that's one solution to people being depressed – schools teaching things that are more worth learning! . . . No, actually, I don't know if that would work really, and I know that's not quite what you were saying. Actually, I'm planning to say something about how having more meaning in life can help people get less depressed later. I'll just say some other things first."

Becky Gives a Man Advice About Better Government and Personal Communication Skills

Becky then changed the subject, and said to the man who'd told her he was unhappy that the president had become bad-tempered with him after he told him he was unhappy about the wars he'd started,

"Here's one thing you could try: I read an interesting article on the Internet about something decent President Kennedy did. It said that dangerous things can happen because leading politicians get ideas into their heads . . . I'm sorry, I know a lot of you are politicians; I don't mean to say all politicians are like this." Becky was beginning to feel self-conscious about the words she was using, thinking it seemed to be very easy to say words that might offend people. She kept on trying to say what she wanted though. She continued:

"Anyway, the article I read said that President Kennedy realised after making bad mistakes at first that he had to be very careful about the decisions he made, since America had hostile relations with the Russians, and he didn't want it to turn into World War III. He started worrying that he might make bad decisions, and he worried that if he did, maybe no one in his government would dare to raise objections to them, because they might think they'd be punished for challenging him, or else they might want to flatter him by seeming to support everything he said, because they thought it would be to their advantage if he stayed friendly towards them and thought they were good supporters . . . presumably even if World War III did break out! So he wanted to find a way of making sure people felt free to speak their minds properly.

"So when he was deciding on a particular policy after that, he would split his advisers and politicians into groups, and send the groups off into separate rooms, not telling them what he thought should be done, but telling them to come up with their own ideas, and then come back and tell him what they were. And he gave certain people the task of finding things wrong with whatever was suggested, even if it was him suggesting it. So he made sure he'd get a lot of different ideas about what to do, and they'd be thought through carefully, rather than just suggesting some idea himself and not being told what was wrong with it.

"Maybe you could tell the President about that; don't criticise what he's already done, since when people are criticised, they tend to stop paying attention to what the person criticising them's got to say, because all they want to do is defend themselves."

Becky suddenly wished she'd remembered that little gem of wisdom a minute before, feeling sure some people must be thinking she should take her own advice and not criticise depressed people in front of a room full of them! But she bravely carried on:

"So the president might not listen to you if you criticise him; but maybe you could just rave to him about how wonderful this Kennedy plan sounds, saying you reckon it would be a good idea for the government to do that nowadays."

Then another thought came to her, and she said, "As for him being short-tempered with you and ordering you around, you could confront him about his behaviour, but instead of complaining to him, tell him how you feel quickly, and then suggest a way his behaviour could be different in future, so the conversation doesn't get bogged down in accusations about the past, but it's all about how things could be changed for the better. I'm thinking you could say something like, 'You know, I think it would be really nice if we could speak to each other in a more civil way; it bothers me that we're not getting on. I'd like to feel warmer towards you. I think I can do that better if in future, we try to speak to each other in a more friendly tone of voice, so the things you ask me to do sound like polite requests; it's just that at the moment, although it might not be your intention, they sound like orders, so it'll be nice if we try to speak respectfully to each other from now on.'

"Naturally it's possible that he'll say he doesn't know what you're talking about, and deny having done anything wrong; but requesting he be more friendly in future might still work, and in any case I'd say it's worth a try."

The man thanked her, and Becky said she'd move on to talking about the next need people have to have met if they're not going to risk getting mentally ill.

Becky Tries to Talk About Another Emotional Need, but Ends up Giving the Man She's Been Advising More Help With his Personal Concerns

She said, "Another need people can't do without if they want to stay mentally healthy is the need for security and privacy; people need to feel safe and free from fear; and they need to have time to themselves when they want it, as far as possible. A person's mental health will suffer if anything in any part of their lives makes them feel fearful or vulnerable or lacking in confidence or worried, especially if they know they've got good cause to feel that way. I know that seems obvious, but it's worth people thinking about what they can do about anything like that in their lives."

The man who'd spoken up at first did so again, saying, "Security's what's bothering me! Not my own, but the country's! With all the bad decisions the president takes, I'm scared terrorists are going to get angry and want to attack America worse than they ever have before!"

Becky cringed when she heard him speaking up again, and said, "I know you feel that way. But first when I tried to give you advice, there was nearly a fight, and then people nearly walked out! I don't think I can spend much more time trying to suggest things that might help, sorry! Still, there are a few things you could try if you try what I've already suggested and it doesn't work, or as well as what I've suggested. If the president isn't interested in that thing about having different groups of advisers who come up with as many new ideas as they can that I told you about – and actually I think he might be, because he told me he regrets some of the decisions he's made; but if he isn't . . ."

Becky suddenly felt a pang of conscience that made her more ashamed and embarrassed than ever, because she'd just remembered that the president had asked her not to tell anyone what he'd told her . . . Then she felt a bit better, as a memory came up from the back of her mind that it was only the press that he'd said he didn't want her to tell . . . at least, she thought she'd remembered that's what he'd said. She still felt uneasy about having just said what she had though, when he'd spoken to her in confidence. But she knew she had to carry on giving the people in the room advice. So she said to the man who'd just complained,

"Well, if you try things and they don't work, if you still feel bad about not being able to control things you think are going wrong, and pushed around because the president's short-tempered with you and won't listen but just tries to make you do what he wants, and anything else he does that makes you unhappy, there are other things you could try:

"One thing that might help you feel as if at least a bit of the pressure on your emotions is being relieved is if you resign yourself to not being able to stop the president doing things that worry you, and do things in your spare time that might compensate at least a little bit for your feelings of frustration and other feelings about not being able to control things at work – I know your concerns are very serious; but still, as well as trying to change the president's ways, it might at least be a bit of consolation and boost your morale a bit if you search around for hobbies or other things you can do in your spare time that do make you feel as if you're in control of at least certain areas of your life, and where you can enjoy yourself. Those things might at least give you a bit more hope and optimism that life isn't as bad as you think it is now – at least for you personally – because there are at least some parts of it that are good and within your control.

"Also, you could let off steam by writing a diary, where you express all your thoughts and feelings. You could even give yourself satisfaction by daydreaming about giving it to the press one day before you die, so even if it's years into the future, people will find out about your views on the bad decisions the president made. You'll know it should be kept secret for now because you need your job; but you can still dream about some time years in the future when you can tell everyone. Maybe you never will; but the dream might make you happier. And people can feel better once they've vented all their feelings by writing them down, so maybe you will. And don't forget that the president can't stay in office for all that much longer, so there's hope that someone whose policies are more to your liking will be elected next.

"Or if you don't like the idea of just waiting and hoping, maybe you could try blogging anonymously, broadcasting any of your views to the Internet that you can get away with without anyone becoming suspicious that it's someone with inside information doing it. You might be able to say a whole lot about what you think the president's done wrong without giving any clues as to who you are, and your blog might get so much publicity it could even influence the government to change its ways, because it doesn't want to lose votes at the next election, you never know."

A few people cleared their throats in a disapproving way, and Becky remembered that a number of people in the room were members of the government. She got a bit embarrassed again. But she thought the best thing to do was to carry on talking as if nothing had happened, and continued:

"Also, if you're really unhappy here, and nothing changes, you could try daydreaming about telling the president what you think, and being sacked, and about what it would be like afterwards, perhaps imagining trying to get new jobs and experiencing the problems that would cause, and then dreaming about finding another job eventually that you're happy with. You could try to imagine all that as realistically as you can. And at the end of all that daydreaming, if you think trying for a new job would be worthwhile, perhaps you could try getting one, or telling the president your honest opinions, in the knowledge that you're willing to go through the hassle of trying to find a new job if it should come to that. Or you might have realised while you're daydreaming that things would likely be worse for you if you left here, so you might decide that you're at least better off here than you would be somewhere where you had even less chance than you do now of being able to find a way to influence government decisions.

"Also, a few little things that might make you feel a bit better, before I really need to start talking to everyone here again – because that's what I'm supposed to be doing, rather than just talking to one person here like I am now … actually, thinking about it, these suggestions might make everyone happier though. There are a few physical things that people who are depressed can do that can lift the mood, according to the things I've learned: regular exercise can help, and so can enough sleep; chronic sleep deprivation can mess with the brain and cause depression and other things. And good light and sunshine can help too.

"Also, life might seem all bad, and you might have good reason to think that, but you might just be forgetting good things along the way; it's easy to do. So perhaps before you go to bed each night, and at any spare moment you find you have during the day, you could try thinking of three things that have happened during the day that you can be grateful for, or three things about your circumstances you can be glad about, for example at least having enough to eat, and being able to keep warm, and not being in pain all the time or seriously ill, or having enjoyed a nice conversation with someone that day, and other things like that. If you often manage to think of things, you might realise life isn't quite so bad after all, at least for you, and get a bit more optimistic. So you'll feel better."

The politicians and White House staff seemed interested, and stayed fairly quiet during the rest of what Becky said, so she managed to finish her lecture to them without any more trouble . . . Well, at least not much more.

Becky Says More About the Emotional Needs People Have

She said, "Anyway, I want to say more about the emotional needs I mentioned at first. I meant to say more about them before, and I just want to make sure there isn't any misunderstanding. I wasn't just talking about big things like whether or not it's a good idea to invade other countries when I said it can be depressing for people to feel as if they haven't got as much control over their lives as they'd like to have, and that they haven't got as much freedom to make decisions as they'd like. Even in small ways, not having those things can make people less mentally healthy over time. I mean, obviously the worse the things are that are causing problems, the more stressful they're going to make people's lives, and the worse their quality of life will be over time, and the more depressed they'll be at risk of getting. But smaller things can still count.

"Here's one kind of situation some of the people at my school have got themselves into, and told me about later:

"Say, for instance, that a couple goes out to a party, and the boyfriend goes off and starts flirting with other women, leaving his girlfriend trying to make good conversation with someone she wouldn't normally mind talking to, but who she doesn't really feel like talking to just then, because she'd prefer to be finding out what her boyfriend's up to, but she doesn't think she ought to just walk away from them to go and challenge him about what he's doing, because just getting up and walking off would seem rude to her, and explaining the reason why she'd like to do it would be embarrassing for her, because she worries that they might wonder why she would even go out with someone like that if she brought it to their attention. So she might feel as if she hasn't got much real choice but to just watch him flirt, not being able to think of any other way to stop him at the time. Mind you, I suppose what she did would depend on her personality.

"But that's one little way she might feel as if circumstances aren't really under as much of her control as she'd like, and that she isn't as free as she wants to be to make decisions about the things that affect her life. Imagine if when she does confront her boyfriend about his flirting later, he just accuses her of being too sensitive; and then the same thing happens at other parties they go to, or other places they go out to.

"There are ways the girlfriend could take more control, such as by telling him she refuses to go to any more parties with him if he's just going to do that. There might not be any ways she can think of that don't seem to have disadvantages that make them less worth trying though, such as if he's likely to just say that's perfectly fine, and go on his own from then on, where he might be doing who knows what, for all she knows. So the situation might make her feel a bit demoralised over time, especially since a boyfriend who's as inconsiderate about her feelings as that will probably be doing other things she doesn't like too, and not caring when she protests.

"It could work the other way around too though, say if really, the girlfriend was just a really jealous person, and the boyfriend was just talking normally to his friends at parties, and just looking at other women without thinking of flirting with them, but she got suspicious every time he did that, and got angry with him about it. He might end up feeling as if he was the one who didn't have enough freedom to make the decisions he wanted, like the decision to talk to who he wanted and look around in a relaxed way without worrying who he might spot, and he might feel as if control over parts of his life was being taken away from him, by feeling as if he needed to be on guard all the time in case he accidentally offended her and she got annoyed with him. So his own mental health might be affected badly over time.

"To give another example of how even small things can harm a person's mental health over time if they don't know what they can do about them, imagine a person's at work, and it's half an hour before the time when they expect to be able to go home. Imagine they're looking forward to it, planning what they're going to do with the evening, and enjoying the thought of seeing a little child they have before it'll be the child's bedtime. Imagine if they've got all the work they think they need to do in the office for the rest of the day planned out, knowing what they want to do when, and expecting that it'll just take about half an hour.

"Then imagine if the boss comes along, dumps a load of work on their desk, and says it's really important that they do it right then, even though it means they're going to have to go home late.

"The person might not be happy, especially since taking a later train home will mean they might not be home till after their little kid's gone to bed, and they won't have as much time to do the things they wanted to do that evening; and the work they had all planned out that they expected to be able to get done before going home will have to wait, and they know they might not feel like doing it so much the next morning.

"If that kind of thing happens quite a bit, it's going to make them feel as if they haven't got such a good quality of life, so they're not going to be as happy, partly because control over part of their lives is being taken out of their hands, and their ability to stick to their own decisions is being obstructed, whether the boss means to do that or not.

"I heard that people who just have to do what they're told at work, who don't have the power to make decisions for themselves or to control what they do when, can be more stressed and depressed than people who have more control over what they do, who can make more decisions about what to do when, and so on. That might not be the only reason why they're more likely not to have such a good sense of mental well-being, but being ordered around will probably get demoralising for a lot of people, especially if they don't think it'll be easy to change their jobs, because, say, they're worried about whether their family's living standards will go down if they take time off to train for something better.

"To give another example of people's need for control over their surroundings and their decisions being impeded, imagine if a couple would like to go out for the evening to a friend's birthday celebration, but they wonder if they can, because there's only one person they can think of who they trust enough to baby-sit their child while they're out. Imagine if one of them phones her and asks if she'll be free to baby-sit for them, and she says she isn't sure but she'll get back to them about it. Imagine hours and hours go by with her still not getting back to them, and they email her and ask her if she's made up her mind, but she doesn't reply. Imagine they don't want to risk making her feel as if they're nagging her by phoning her up again, so they just wait, getting more frustrated, wondering if they can go out.

"Imagine if the reason she isn't replying is that all along, she knew she didn't want to baby-sit for them, but she didn't want to say so, because she thought it might hurt their feelings and then they'd disapprove of her. But imagine if they would much rather have been told one way or the other right at the start, because they're sitting there thinking, 'If we knew for definite that she wasn't going to baby-sit for us, we could go ahead and make alternative plans for doing something nice indoors this evening. But not knowing whether we can go out tonight means we have to put all arrangements on hold; and we can't even let the person organising the celebration know if we're going to be there or not!'

"If that kind of thing happens quite a bit, it's going to make their lives more stressful, so they won't have such a good quality of life, partly because they can't use their decision-making skills like they want to, and control of some of the things they do is being taken out of their hands more than it needs to be.

"Another example is that it can be depressing if someone has to spend time with people who are so easily upset or offended that they're reluctant to speak their minds in front of them and criticise them in any way, because they know it might well start an argument or lead to some other kind of scene; so their freedom to express their needs and wants or just to be themselves gets stifled.

"Mind you, it's not just the things that other people do that can lead to people feeling as if life's depressing or stressful because freedom to make decisions and control's being taken away from them.

"I mean, take the cases of people with sleep disorders, for example. Imagine if you're all set to do some work you want to do at home, when suddenly you feel really sleepy, and the next thing you know, it's three hours later, and you realise you've just been asleep, and you're disappointed, because you realise you haven't got nearly as much time to do what you planned to do as you thought you'd have; so either you have to carry on the next day, or you work into the night doing it, because you really want to get it finished, or because you're annoyed that the time when you wanted to do it was unexpectedly taken away from you, so you want to stay up making up for it; but then you end up going to bed later than you should, waking up later the next day, and struggling to get up in time for work, knowing you might flop off to sleep while you're there, because you haven't had a good sleep the night before. Imagine that happening often. That's going to get stressful and depressing after a while!

"Or imagine if you keep coming home after a hard day's work, hoping to get a few hours' worth of enjoyment before you go to bed, but partway through the evening, you drop off to sleep, and only wake up when it's around the time when you need to go to bed. That's going to get a bit soul-destroying after a while, because of all the me-time you're missing out on; it might make life feel like more of a drag, because it'll come to mostly consist of slogging away at work . . . Well, maybe your work doesn't feel like a slog; but I'm sure a lot of people's does. But even if yours isn't too bad, you might come to feel as if control of your life's being taken away from you by your tendency to fall asleep a lot during the spare time you were hoping to use to do something you like.

"I know a bit about what that's like, because my auntie Diana's got a sleep disorder, where if she doesn't get enough bright light, she falls asleep, no matter what time of day it is. One day she read a scaremongering news report about how someone had said Russia's preparing for a massive war with the West, and then she promptly dozed off into a peaceful dream; and another time, she was listening to a documentary where the presenter was talking about the symptoms of the plague people used to get a few hundred years ago, and how the bacteria that caused it were spread, and the next thing she knew, she was waking up from a peaceful sleep. She'd missed the rest of the documentary!

"But as well as the way sleep disorders could disrupt your life, so you haven't got as much control over it as you'd like to have, there are other physical problems that could do that, such as if you've got a medical condition that means you're often in too much pain to do what you'd really like to do, or your memory starts deteriorating, so you're not in so much control of your surroundings, because you've started doing things like putting something on to cook, and then forgetting you've done it, and only remembering when you smell burning, so you can't eat what you'd planned to eat.

"All those things can be thought of as examples of control being taken out of people's hands. If the problems that are causing them can be solved, or other things can be done to limit the effect of them, then people are less likely to end up feeling stressed and depressed.

"Anyway, I've told all of you about two needs that psychologists tell us that people have to have met to stay mentally healthy now . . . Or is it three? Actually, I think it might be three. Oh yes, the need to feel secure – safe and free from fear, the need to have some privacy, and the need to have control over the way life goes, and be involved in decision-making in a way that counts, and that kind of thing . . . Actually, maybe that's four needs, but never mind. Anyway, I'll tell you about the rest."

Becky had just started saying what she wanted to say next when they heard a couple of dogs barking excitedly outside the window. She felt a sudden burst of irritation that what she was saying might be drowned out by them, and asked her audience on impulse, "Do any of you like eating roast dog?"

Some of the audience looked a bit shocked, while others sniggered. One said with a smirk, "Those are the president's dogs! I don't think he'd appreciate it if we ate them!"

Becky was embarrassed yet again, and blushed. She realised it hadn't been a wise idea to ask that question, and said, "Sorry, I don't really approve of anyone eating dogs . . .

Well, not if they're people's pets anyway . . . Well, not ever really. Mind you, I don't know why anyone thinks eating dogs is really any worse than eating cows and sheep and things, just because some of them are more cuddly or something. What if you had cows and sheep and pigs as pets, and you let them climb on your furniture and sleep in your bedrooms, and eat in your house, and you cuddled them every day, and got really fond of them? Then you might start disapproving of people eating those animals."

She suddenly realised she'd better get back to talking about what she was supposed to be talking to them about, in case what she said led to a conversation, and they ran out of time while they were still discussing the merits or otherwise of having pigs and cows and sheep as house pets. So she said,

"Anyway, never mind about that. I'd better get back to talking about depression."

She hoped she hadn't ruined her reputation by suggesting they might want to eat the president's pet dogs or have pigs as house pets, because she didn't want any of them to decide it couldn't be worth listening to someone who was insensitive enough to suggest such ideas, and tune their minds out.

Some of them started listening to her more intently instead though, wondering what other controversial things she might say!

She said, "Another emotional need some psychologists say we have is the need to give and receive attention. They say people need to feel as if at least some others are interested in what they'd like to say, and that they have people they can relax with and chat to. If people spend too much time alone, or they're often with someone who steals the limelight and can be overbearing so they don't often manage to express themselves or let their hair down and chat, or get to feel as if they matter because others are paying them attention, they can end up feeling dissatisfied with life.

"So anyone who feels as if they could do with more attention could think about how they could try to get it. For example, doing your best to become genuinely interested in other people and showing them attention can mean you get attention in return. I know that's not as easy as it sounds, especially for people who are isolated so they don't come into contact with other people often; but it's one thing that might sometimes work. And maybe attention on Internet forums is just as good as face-to-face attention sometimes.

"Another need psychologists say people have is the need for emotional connection to others. That means they think everyone needs to know at least one person who understands them, who they can share their hopes, dreams and ideas with, and who they can relax and just be themselves with; someone they can trust to talk about their worries with, and who they feel as if they can identify with in some way."

Just then they heard a great screeching meow from outside the door! Becky thought, "Oh no, I bet my mum's upsetting the White House cat again like she did last time we were here! She's not sitting in the president's wife's visitor-greeting chair again like she did last time, is she? I warned her the cat doesn't like it when people do that! Oh well, as long as the cat doesn't meow so loud it's louder than me, it doesn't matter much."

For a second or two, she wondered if she should go and see what was upsetting the cat. But she thought she'd better just carry on giving the depressed politicians and White House staff advice. So she continued:

"Another need psychologists say we all have if we're going to be mentally healthy is the need to feel connected to the wider community. That means we need to feel as if we're part of something bigger than ourselves, which could either mean working for a cause or charity, or being part of a team – anything that takes our focus of attention off ourselves, and gives us a sense of belonging and purpose in life.

"People who spend a lot of time thinking about themselves and their worries can end up feeling worse and worse about them, till they blow them out of proportion, and get much more miserable than they would if they were working to achieve things for others and not thinking about themselves all that much; people can realise their worries aren't as important as they thought they were if they're not on their minds so much, because the more people worry, the worse they'll feel, and then they'll often assume their bad feelings must mean that what they're worrying about is bad. But if they're working with people who are worse off than they are, they can get their own problems in perspective so they don't feel so bad about them.

"I suppose you could say that helping others with their problems might mean people just end up with a whole lot more to worry about; but if they're part of a team that's helping people solve problems, or making some other kind of progress, they can get to feel more optimistic than they would if they were just worrying and feeling hopeless about things.

"... Well, I suppose there are some exceptions to that rule, such as if what they've chosen to do for others is so stressful they'd have been better off not doing it, or if what they're worrying about is a problem they've got that's genuinely terrible. But Still.

"Another need people have is the need to stay physically healthy, as much as possible. Everyone knows people ought to eat fruit and vegetables to try to stay healthy, but eating them can also help to lift the mood. When people are depressed, they often don't feel like making the effort to prepare anything much, so they can live on junk food, which can be easier to prepare, so it can make it easier to bother to cook at least something; but then their health can suffer. But making the effort to cook something which is actually nutritious can be worth it, even if it takes a bit longer, since sometimes vitamin and mineral deficiencies can badly affect a person's mood.

"Also, people need a decent amount of sleep every night, because sleep deprivation can mess with the brain and cause mood problems after a while. Also people need good-quality light really, plus exercise and fresh air regularly. Those things aren't just good for physical health, but they can stop people feeling so depressed, and make them feel happier too.

"It's best not to exercise too near bedtime though, at least not vigorously, since then people can feel as if they've got so much energy it's harder to get to sleep, because of the amount of adrenaline that's been stirred up in them. But exercise at other times of day can help people feel less depressed."

Immediately Becky mentioned junk food, as if it had set off a craving for it in one of the politicians, he said, "Excuse me!" and went to a vending machine just outside the door, and got himself a chocolate bar. He ate it in front of everyone; but to Becky's relief, everyone else managed to resist the temptation to copy him and get one, which would have spent some of the time she'd been given to talk.

Also, by what was perhaps a strange coincidence, when Becky mentioned sleep, a snore came from one of the White

House staff, and everyone noticed he'd fallen asleep. The person next to him nudged him, and he woke up and apologised, saying politics often sent him to sleep. That was regardless of the fact that Becky hadn't actually been talking about politics, and the fact that he was actually an advisor to a politician, so he was in the wrong job if politics really did do that!

Becky carried on, "Another thing is that drinking a lot of alcohol can cause depression, and anxiety as well. If people's circumstances aren't all that good, they might assume it's their circumstances causing the depression. People are probably bound to try to work out what the cause is. But their circumstances might not get them nearly so depressed if their body chemistry's more healthy because the things they've been putting into their bodies are good for them. I know it might not be easy, because it's another one of these vicious cycles, where people want to drink alcohol to feel better if they don't feel very good, but then drinking alcohol a lot can make them feel worse, so they want to drink again to try to feel better, and it goes on like that. But if you drink a lot, it might be worth having a go at cutting down a fair bit, to see if it helps."

Becky suddenly wondered if suggesting they might drink a lot might sound a bit rude; so she said, "I mean, I'm not suggesting I think some of you might be on the booze right at the time when you're advising the government, or voting on important decisions or something."

She realised that saying that actually sounded worse, even if some of them really did do things like that; and she blushed.

But then she noticed that some of them were grinning. Maybe they thought what she'd said was amusing; or maybe they were thinking of people they knew who could genuinely be accused of doing that; Becky didn't know. But she felt reassured that at least they didn't seem offended.

She continued, with a change of subject: "Anyway, another need psychologists say we all have is the need to have a sense of meaning and purpose in life, and goals to work towards. We need to be challenged a bit mentally as well as physically, so that we have to put our imaginations to work finding solutions to problems, and so we feel as if we're making progress with things, so we can be more optimistic, or so we at least feel as if our brains are getting a good work-out sometimes, and that they're being made to function at the best level they can by being challenged, not necessarily all the time, but for a bit of time every day, or a few times a week, even if it's just by working out answers to puzzles, for people who like doing that kind of thing.

"Some psychologists say that if we don't often put our imaginations to work thinking up creative solutions to things, or by working out how to do things that'll help us feel as if we're moving forward with things in life, in a way that gives us a sense that our brains are being stimulated, our imaginations can be under-used, and then they can brood on things that are unhealthy for us to keep thinking about, like little concerns we have; the more we think about those, the more they can come to seem like big problems, because they're occupying our minds so much, till we get more and more miserable about them. Thinking up solutions to them instead of just worrying and worrying about them, and also thinking about a variety of other things too, can make us happier. And if we come up with solutions to problems, or start getting absorbed in interesting things that take our minds off ourselves, we can feel a pleasing sense of satisfaction."

Becky Explains How she Got Interested in Psychology

While Becky spoke, at least one of her listeners seemed to be getting more and more agitated. Eventually, as if he couldn't stand it any more, one of them stood up and said indignantly, as if something was upsetting him:

"What are you doing talking about all this stuff? This worries me. You're only about six years old, surely! You should be playing with toys, not knowing anything about this kind of thing! You shouldn't have had to cope with depression at your age!"

Becky thanked him for caring, but said it was alright, since she'd never got all that depressed herself, just a bit sometimes when the piles of homework she'd had to do had seemed endless; it was tough getting through school at her age; she was still only a few weeks off her seventh birthday! She said she'd been at school ever since her mum had started her there when she was one year old.

She told them the reason she'd become interested in psychology was because when she was a baby, she'd noticed that grown-ups did strange things sometimes, and she hadn't been able to work out why, so she'd become curious.

One example was when she'd started swimming lessons; she said she was only about six months old. Her mum was holding her, along with other mums who were holding their babies. There was a man on the side of the pool that her mum called the teacher, and he was telling the mums to do things with their babies like dabble their hands in the water, and the mums were just doing everything the man said, without asking why. He told them to splash their babies' faces. Becky hadn't enjoyed that at all! But then he told the mums to put their babies' heads under the water for a second or two. Becky had thought that was horrible, and she loudly whined in protest to her mum, asking her why she'd done it. Her mum said it was what the teacher had told them to do, and Becky had wondered why her mum would do something just because some man called a teacher told her to! She shouted in protest to the teacher, telling him it was horrible of him to have told the mums to do that, and asking him why he'd done it. He just said, "Don't be cheeky; that's just the way it's done."

Becky didn't think that was a good answer, but her mum said something similar when she asked her why she'd obeyed the teacher and just done what he said. She'd said something about helping babies to get used to the water; but Becky had wondered why on earth they couldn't be allowed to get used to having their bodies in it before they had to put their heads in there. She wondered for a long time why on earth her mum would just do what some man said, and why on earth he'd say it in the first place. And she noticed other strange things going on like that in other parts of life.

When she'd heard about psychology and found out it was the study of the reasons people behave the way they do, and things like that, she'd wanted to know more! So she'd started reading psychology books before her fourth birthday. Still, she said that although she'd learned lots of interesting things that were bound to be useful to know, she'd never quite discovered why mums will just obey swimming teachers when they tell them to put their babies' heads under the water for a second or two.

She said she'd got over it quickly though. She told them, "My mum got me swimming lessons when I was a bit older, and I'm glad about that, because now I can swim, it means I'm safer around water . . . or other liquid, like if I accidentally fall in one of the huge big mugs my auntie Diana uses to drink tea out of or something . . . Well alright, maybe they're not quite that big . . . They might be in the future though, if she ever decides she wants to drink even more at once than she does now . . . Well, she probably won't. But anyway, I think there are real ponds and things it's nice to feel safer around."

The depressed White House staff and politicians were impressed with What Becky was saying, and thought she must be a very clever little girl!

Becky Tells the Group About the Last Two Emotional Needs People Have

She told them she just had two more emotional needs to mention, and that when she'd done that, she'd stop talking for about a quarter of an hour, and they could all write down what needs they thought they had that weren't being met, and start planning what they might be able to do about it. If they wrote things down, she said, they wouldn't have forgotten them by the time she finished her lecture, which they might do otherwise. She told them it could be a kind of short group therapy session, since they could discuss their needs with each other if they liked, and anyone who thought someone else had an unmet need could perhaps mention it to them, and they could try to come up with ways of solving the problem together.

She told them that when they were planning what to do about the needs, they would have to make sure they didn't plan to achieve too much at once, in case they failed and got discouraged and gave up altogether. She told them to plan little things they could do that would mean they gradually got closer and closer to making big changes for the better in their lives.

Then she told them that the second-to-last emotional need that some psychologists say people have is the need to feel valued, or to have a sense of importance and status, not necessarily importance and status in a whole community, but in the mind of at least someone. It could be status as a good mother or father, or as a valued member of a team at work or sports team, or some other thing. Then she thought about the people in front of her, and said, "But I don't suppose that's a need any of you are lacking, you being politicians and White House workers and things!"

They smiled. Then she told them that the last emotional need was the need to have a sense of achievement or competence at doing something, since that would raise people's self-esteem, and make life seem more worthwhile. She said people could get more of a sense of competence and achievement partly by finding out about and learning new things, and by improving skills they already had. She said psychologists said doing things like that could increase a person's sense of purpose and enjoyment in life, and make them feel fairly talented, so they'd feel good about themselves.

She thought about joking that the politicians must already have a sense of achievement, though possibly not competence. But she realised that would be a tactless thing to say, so she didn't. She didn't want to upset them again!

Then she let them all have a break, and they all started working on what she'd told them to do – working out which of the needs that she'd mentioned wasn't being fulfilled in their lives, thinking about how they might be able to go about getting each one met, and talking with others there about what needs they thought might not be being met in the others' lives, and how the others might go about getting them fulfilled. They all seemed glad to be there, learning what she was telling them.

Becky Advises the Group on how Calming Worries and Sleeping Well can Help Cure Depression

After they'd done their bit of group therapy, Becky called for quiet, and said: "I'm going to talk about another reason people can get depressed now, and a reason why depression sometimes won't go away in a hurry. When people are depressed, their sleep can get messed up, and then they feel even worse. One reason it can get messed up is that they can worry so much. Part of the problem is that worrying can stop people getting to sleep. But something else can go on too: A psychology book I read said that when depressed people worry and worry about things, they'll get to be in more and more of an emotional state, till something in the brain thinks things are reaching crisis level; and then it floods the brain with so many emotional signals that it blocks the intelligent part of it from functioning. That'll mean, among other things, that making good decisions, and thinking up good ideas to solve problems, will get much, much harder."

A temptation came over Becky to say, "That might well be why some governments make such terrible decisions." But in time, it occurred to her that the group of politicians and others who worked for the government that she was speaking to might not appreciate the joke, so she stopped herself, and just carried on:

"You might think that worry's good for people, because you might assume that the more that problems are thought about, the more likely it'll be that solutions will be found. But actually, it's possible to worry and worry all day without coming up with any solutions at all, not because the problems are so difficult, but because worrying too much causes people to become more panicky, and it's much more difficult to think of good ideas in that state. Solutions to problems are most likely to be found when people think about them with a clear head. In a state of high emotion, thoughtful decisions are harder to make – even little ones like what to have for tea.

"The reason the brain works like that is that the emotional part of the brain's programmed to assume there's an emergency when a person's in a high state of emotion, because after all, it does get to feel like one with all the stressy emotions flowing around; and its emergency procedure's a bit like a program that causes the brain to act as if taking time to think could waste valuable time, and as if all its resources need to be concentrated on doing one thing to change things quickly, to escape the stressful circumstances; and it'll want it to be something that hardly needs any thought to do, so it can be done without hesitation, like running away quickly.

"That means that if there's a choice to be made between even only two little things that are equally as appealing, like whether to have chicken or fish for tea, it'll still be difficult to make it, because the brain will find it hard to put even the little bit of concentration that's needed into thinking a problem like that through, because the emotional signals it's being flooded with are blocking its thinking powers, and giving it the impression that the person should only concentrate on making a quick getaway from the problem.

"Only being able to think about one thing might be useful if you were being chased by a criminal, and stopping to think about where it was best to run would mean he caught up with you, so the best thing to do would be just to run without thinking about it. That's the kind of situation the emergency procedure in the brain's designed for. The emotions are meant to motivate a person to quick action, after which they're designed to die down.

"But if there isn't a real emergency, but people have just got into a state of emotion because they've been worrying so much, their brains will still act like it's an emergency, but the people won't get up and do something in a hurry to solve the problem, because they haven't got the kind of problem that can be solved like that; so instead, they'll likely often just sit there while the emotions flood their brains, making them feel worse and worse and worse.

"So they won't feel like getting on with their daily routines. And because intelligent thoughts are being crowded out by emotional danger signals – even though people won't realise they're misguided danger signals unless they've found out about what goes on, and they won't realise their intelligent thoughts have been crowded out, so they'll mistake the thoughts they do have for ones that are as intelligent as the ones they normally have – it'll be much more difficult for them to think of ways of solving a problem, and much harder to look at it from different points of view, and to realise it's maybe not as bad as all that.

"So depressed people can think things are hopeless and life's ruined, when neither of those things are true. There just isn't any room in their brains at the time for thoughts about how things could be improved, and how they might not be as catastrophic as they're thinking they are anyway. And the more they think the things about life being terrible, the worse they'll feel, and the worse they feel, the more they'll think those things, and the more they carry on thinking those things, the worse they'll feel, and so on, with them just getting to feel worse and worse and worse as their emotions build up more and more.

"People will probably normally assume it's their circumstances that are making them feel so bad; but really, it'll often be the way they're unwittingly misusing their imaginations and brains, having depressing little tracks like 'This is terrible' going around and around and around in their minds, till that in itself depresses them as much as what upset them in the first place. They won't realise that, because what they're telling themselves they feel so bad about is their circumstances, so they'll blame the circumstances for their depression, not what they keep mentally torturing themselves with by telling themselves.

"And the next time they start worrying about their problems, the emotional part of their brains will remember how bad they felt before, and trigger all the emotions off again quickly, because it thinks they're in the old emergency situation again, where that's what's needed.

"In fact, the reason some people commit suicide is because their brains are so flooded with emotional emergency signals because of all the worrying they've been doing that they just feel really bad, and can't think of anything they can do to solve their problems, and just think they have to get away from them quickly, like the emergency signals are giving them the impression they have to. And because they can't think of different options for dealing with their problems at that point, but just want to get away from them really quickly, suicide seems to them to be the only possible way of doing that.

"So it's best if people don't wait till they've got themselves worked up into a state like that with worry before they try to calm themselves down. One thing that can help you not to get more and more stressed with worry is if the very moment you realise you're beginning to worry, or that your bad feelings are getting stronger, you make a conscious effort to try to calm down. You could tell the part of your brain that's causing the emotions that it's alright; it doesn't have to do that because you're not in an emergency.

"And you could try talking back to any bad thoughts you have. For instance, if you have a thought telling you things are hopeless, if you remember, you could ask yourself, 'Is this really true, or could this be my brain having to cope with so many emotional signals that it's shutting down the intelligent side of itself for a little while, so I can't think of all the other possible perspectives on the situation?' "

Becky said they could try making a habit of talking back to their thoughts. For instance if they started feeling bad and thinking that an entire evening out had gone badly, they could ask themselves whether that was true, or whether there were really some good things about it, and whether the things that really had gone badly had gone as badly as they were thinking they had, and also whether it mattered as much as they were thinking it did that they had gone badly.

Becky had been standing all the time while she was talking to the people in the room. But she started to feel tired, and suddenly wondered why it hadn't occurred to her to sit down before, though lecturers she'd seen on television had always been standing up. She decided to plonk herself down on a seat right then, hoping her listeners wouldn't mind, but thinking there was only so much standing that legs that weren't even quite seven years old could be expected to do!

So she sat down as she continued the lecture, saying, "Try and distract yourselves from your bad thoughts too, and try it before you get more and more upset about them; the worse you feel when you try, the harder it'll be. So if you try and catch them early, it'll be easier. There are several ways of calming down by distracting yourselves from upsetting thoughts. One is getting absorbed in something you like to concentrate on. Chatting to someone you enjoy talking to can help as well. Exercise helps some people too. And another thing that helps some people is to do relaxation exercises, which I'll tell you a bit about in a minute."

Someone had opened a window a bit earlier, and suddenly they heard a sinister-sounding laugh from outside. Some of Becky's listeners thought it might be someone who'd found out that a group of politicians and White House staff was being lectured by a child not quite seven years old yet, and began to look uncomfortable, and shift awkwardly in their seats. But then they heard a couple of people walking by, one saying to the other,

"And after a couple more glasses of wine, he leapt up and started dancing around the room, jumping over furniture and shouting, 'Cheers to all those who defect to the West!'

Then he had another drink. We had to almost carry him back to his embassy! The next morning he woke up and remembered what he'd done, and phoned us up in a panic. We had to promise not to tell his . . ."

Just who they promised not to tell, the group never found out, because the voices faded away.

The people in the room smiled and sniggered a bit, and then Becky continued, saying: "If a depressed person goes to bed in a state of emotion, it'll be very difficult for them to sleep. So they'll wake up feeling bad the next morning, and likely start the day feeling as depressed as ever, with no motivation or energy to do much at all. But that's not the only reason they can wake up feeling depressed and as if they don't feel like making the effort to do anything. A psychology book I've read says that when people have spent a lot of time worrying or being upset in a day, their sleep that night gets disrupted, so even a lot of the sleep they do get isn't good-quality sleep.

"There's more than one kind of sleep: There's a deep sleep that's especially good for us, because during it the body repairs minor damage and tops up our energy levels and we get refreshed. Then there's dreaming sleep, which is a lighter sleep. The book says it's been found that depressed people get more of that and less of the energy-boosting sleep, so they can wake up feeling as if they haven't got any energy, so they can't be bothered to do anything, so they feel lousy and depressed. Even if you never remember any of your dreams, you'll still be having that dreaming sleep.

"The book says every one of us needs the dreaming sleep, because that's the time when all the tension from the day's worries and upset gets relieved and discharged out of the system. But it says depressed people have so much upset and emotion to relieve, they need loads of dreaming sleep to do it, so they get that instead of the energy-refreshing sleep for some time each night. And also having a lot of dreaming sleep can make people wake up feeling worn out, because that itself uses up energy. So having a lot of dreaming sleep means there are two reasons depressed people can wake up with no energy and don't feel like getting up and doing things.

"But there are ways of getting better-quality sleep."

A gentle breeze was blowing in the window, and suddenly a gust of wind came in, and a piece of paper was blown off a desk that one of them was sitting at. A man who'd come in late picked it up for the person sitting there, and looked at it before putting it back. It said:

"Half pound rice; Four cloves garlic; generous pinch chilli powder; knob ginger root; chopped onion; chopped celery; sweet peppers; top with grated cheese."

The man turned pail. He assumed it must be the ingredients of some medicine Becky had told them they ought to take to cure their depression. He wasn't a fan of most of those things. He asked shakily, "Is this what we need to take to get over depression?"

He showed it to the man sitting at the desk, and was reassured to find out it was just a recipe one of the other staff working there had given him, and he'd jotted it down just before coming to the meeting.

Becky Gives the Group a Few Relaxation Tips, and Advice About Mindfulness Techniques

When they'd settled down again, Becky continued:

"If depressed people manage not to work themselves up so much with worry, they'll likely get better sleep, because they won't get so much energy-sapping dreaming sleep, and they'll get more of the deeper energy-boosting sleep, so they'll wake up feeling more energetic, and less unmotivated and depressed. One way of going to sleep feeling less troubled is doing relaxation exercises to unwind at night, and whenever emotions seem to be getting stronger during the day if possible. I'm not talking about just chilling out; I know that's difficult if you're worried about things. I'm talking about set techniques that you really make an effort to concentrate your mind on, and part of the reason they relax you is because you can't have two thoughts in your mind at once, so if you're concentrating on the techniques, the worries just have to fade away for a while, because they're being crowded out. I know relaxation and concentration sound like opposites, but you'll be concentrating on nice things, so it'll make you feel more relaxed in the end.

"One thing you can try is imagining you're sunbathing; and while you're imagining that, breathe in very very very slowly, and when you breathe out, very slowly too, imagine your upsetting thoughts are coming out with your breath, and rising up with the air into the sky, where they're blowing or floating away on little white clouds. Breathe in and out several times like that, imagining that more and more of your worrying thoughts are rising into the sky and just gently blowing away each time you breathe out. Concentrate on that hard. See if you enjoy it.

"Or alternatively, you could have a different daydream, imagining you're lying in a cool wood, with scented trees and plants all around, and a little brook babbling near you; and whenever you breathe out, you could imagine your upsetting thoughts are flowing out of you on your breath, and being carried to the brook by a gentle breeze, landing on leaves floating in the stream, and being carried away by the current.

"You could also try a kind of meditation that's been found to help some depressed people, called mindfulness meditation. It can help people notice what thoughts they're having without getting all absorbed in them and upset by them; and if they practise it often, they can actually get into the habit of not being so upset by their thoughts, because they'll have got used to observing what they are, but not thinking of most of them as being important enough to get worked up by.

"You focus your mind on one thing – it could be anything that stays still, so it won't move around and distract you, with the chance that you'll forget what you're supposed to be doing. It could be a table or chair, or a nice picture, or anything you find relaxing. Try to look at it for a long time, thinking of nothing but that. It'll be impossible, so you're not really expected to do it that well. But the idea is that if any upsetting thoughts come into your mind while you're looking at it, you gently push them away, and start focusing on the thing you're trying to concentrate on again, so the thoughts don't stay in your mind.

"Don't start thinking about the thoughts that come into your mind, but just notice them and mention them to yourself, such as saying, 'Now I'm having a thought about how nice it would be if half the world just vanished in a puff of smoke!' Or whatever you're thinking. Once you've observed what thought you've just had, let it go. Imagine it floating away on a log in a stream, or imagine it suddenly turns into a car and zooms past, or something like that, so it goes away quickly.

"If it's an important thought you don't want to forget, you could make a quick note of it, and then put the note somewhere out of sight to save for later, when you'll try your best to think of how to deal with it, rather than just worrying over it; but then imagine the thought disappearing for now. Then you pull your mind back to the thing you've decided to concentrate on – a chair, the end of your nose, or whatever. And you think about that till the next thought comes into your mind. When it does, just observe what it is again, and then imagine it fading or zooming or drifting away, or whatever you've decided it does, and bring your mind back to what you've decided to concentrate on. And carry on like that for minutes and minutes, or even half an hour or so if you like. At the end of it, your mind will probably be much calmer and clearer.

"Also, if you get into the habit of just observing what your thoughts are and then letting them drift or zoom away for a couple of minutes or so when you've got a spare moment, several times throughout the day, you might well end up not getting so upset by so many of your thoughts from then on, because when depressing thoughts come on, it'll be as if you've been training yourself to just observe what they are and then let them go, instead of getting absorbed with brooding on them till you just get more and more upset by them."

Becky Gives a Few Last Tips on Recovery and a Few Little Ideas About Preventing Relapse into Depression Before Finishing her Lecture

Becky realised it was about time she finished the lecture. She'd been allowed quite a bit of time, but now it was getting near the time when the politicians and White House staff needed to get back to their duties. She just told them about a couple more little things, saying:

"Another thing you can try to improve your mood is trying to take a bit of time out each day to do something that makes you laugh or makes you happy. You might not be able to think of anything you find funny or enjoyable at first, but if you really have a think, you might; maybe think back to the last time you had fun, and what caused it, and whether it's something you could do again. Then think about what you could do each day to make yourself smile.

"And you could do more things you can get pleasurably absorbed in, like reading good books, that take your mind far away from yourself and your surroundings for a while, and give you more of a variety of things to think about afterwards. It's possible that'll be easier once you've begun to recover from depression.

"If you're finding that some things are helping you with your recovery, such as making things, or painting pictures, or browsing interesting websites, or meditation, or whatever, then those things might help stop you relapsing back into depression too, so it might well be worth keeping them up, even when you're well again.

"And if you're just starting to notice you're getting depressed again after feeling well for a while, you could try to think of all the things that helped you recover last time you were depressed, and take them up again where it's practical, before you slip so far into the depths of depression you really don't feel like it, to see if they help you recover again.

"It might be worth you writing a list of all the things you notice are helping, and keeping it handy, so you can easily remind yourself of the things that helped last time, if you start feeling depressed again.

"I mean, obviously they might not always be the solution – you know, say if the reason someone's getting depressed again is because a hated aunt has just re-entered their lives after years in another part of the country where they never heard from her or something; I mean, the solution there would probably be for them to cut her out of their lives, if that was possible. But I mean, the other things still might help, and they might be especially good for people who keep on having bouts of depression, where there aren't any obvious circumstances that are causing it.

"I mean, medication might be the best way of keeping a lot of people's depression under control a lot of the time, or, if it's come on because of some physical thing like a vitamin or mineral deficiency, changing their diet or taking supplements might be the most important thing to do. But other things might still help too, even when the cause is something like that.

"Also, if you suddenly start feeling depressed, it can be useful to think back to what happened just before the feeling came on; and if it was something that caused a problem, you could try thinking up a solution as soon as possible, before depression takes over and makes you just worry about it.

278

"Or if you realise you're missing out on one of those emotional needs psychologists say we all have that I was talking about earlier, you could have a go at working out how you could get it met."

Becky decided to end her lecture there. She told them she'd finished. They were all pleased to have heard her, and thanked her.

One or two said they'd forgotten what she'd said earlier and asked if she could repeat it all. She thought they surely must be joking! She hoped so. It was alright, because others said they'd made notes and would go through them with them if they liked, telling them what they remembered.

After the lecture, Becky met her mum outside in reception, and they went out into the bright sunshine and relaxed.

A senior member of the White House staff met them and invited them in for refreshments with him and a few other senior members of staff, and they had a nice time.

Then they left. They spent the next few days exploring Washington and the surrounding area. Then they went home happy.

Chapter 11

Becky Spots Errors Almost Everywhere, and Investigates Whether Some Pain Can Be Altered By the Way People Feel and Think, as Some People Claim

Mistakes in Films

One day, supposedly just after her ninth birthday, Becky read some funny articles on the Internet about mistakes that have appeared in popular films. She laughed.

One said there was a film about some things that took place in 1973, with a song in the background that didn't really exist then because it was made in 1974. It said that another film had a Boeing 747 aeroplane appearing in it, only they weren't invented till six years after what happened in the film was supposed to have taken place.

Another article told of how in a film called *The Ten Commandments*, about things said to have happened a few thousand years ago in Bible times, at least one person could be seen wearing a modern wrist watch, as if people had somehow managed to make them in those days. And it said that in a film about the Romans, a padlock on a door could be seen, when they weren't actually invented till the nineteenth century. It also said that in a film about ancient Egypt, a plane could be seen flying by.

Another article said there was a film called *Braveheart* about battles long ago in the Middle Ages, and a van appeared on the scene, as if it must have been brought there by someone time travelling. And in a film about the Titanic disaster in 1912, one of the main characters talked about having fished on a certain man-made lake, which in reality didn't exist till it was made five years later.

Becky said, "I bet I wouldn't make mistakes if I made films."

Her mum said with a smile, "Don't be so sure! Putting films together is a lot of hard work that takes some time; it's easy to miss the odd thing."

Becky thought making films sounded like fun, and that it would be a good challenge to try making them without any mistakes; so she thought she'd love to try it one day.

Becky's Loud Irritation with a Radio Programme

Not long after that, she heard a programme on the radio about young people trying to find work. She thought it sounded boring, and said so. Her mum said, "Perhaps it's too grown-up for you." But Becky felt sure that wasn't the reason, and had a good think about what she thought was wrong with it.

When she worked it out, she said, "I know why I don't like this! It started by saying there was going to be some advice for young people about finding jobs, but since then, they've hardly given any decent advice at all! The way they've done things is that three people have been interviewed about what the experiences they've had in their jobs have taught them that can help them give people advice; but they've all got jobs that are very unusual, and it's all about how they got them, not about advice people can use; and they were asked for tips on how people who want to get jobs like them can go about trying to get them, but since the jobs they have are so unusual, the way they got them will be irrelevant for most people, because most people won't want jobs like them! Silly programme! It's over halfway through now, and these people are going to be interviewed for the entire programme, so it's very unlikely to suddenly get better; and if it does, there won't be much time for anything of any worth to be said!

"Its makers might have thought it would be more entertaining doing the programme the way they have, but it doesn't do what it said it would do!"

Her mum joked, "Why are you even listening to a programme about finding work? Are you trying to find a job already at the age of nine then? Somehow I don't think you'll find many employers willing to give you work. When it says 'young' people, it probably means people in their late teens and early twenties!"

Becky said with a little irritation, "I know that!"

She carried on listening regardless of what her mum said, and a few minutes later, her mum almost jumped, when Becky suddenly fumed loudly with irritation:

"Stupid! The presenter of this programme seems to be an expert in taking an interesting subject and making it deadly boring! And one of the people he's interviewing isn't doing much better! He's talking in these vague figures of speech that won't mean anything to anyone he hasn't told about what he's talking about in more detail already so they'll understand it!

"He just said, 'My mum was unhappy at first about me having the freedom to do this, and we had big arguments about it, and even careers officers held me at arm's length a bit.' How does he expect us to know what in the world he means? What's the point of him even mentioning it if he's not going to explain what he means in enough clear detail for us to understand what he's really saying! I mean, he doesn't explain just what kind of freedom his mum didn't want him to have, or why careers officers and his mum weren't happy about what he wanted to do, or just what he means the careers officers were actually doing! It's not as if it's obvious because the career he's doing's dangerous or something! It doesn't sound dangerous to me!"

Her mum said, "Becky, calm down! It doesn't matter; there'll be other programmes about how young people can get into work more easily if you want to learn about it."

Becky said, "You'd do a better job on that programme than him! At least I understood what you just said!"

But she didn't take her mum's advice in enough to do what she said and actually calm down. At least not before she'd fumed just a little bit more. Several seconds after her last fume, she said:

"This is annoying! Even if those people being interviewed did jobs that loads of people do, this programme still wouldn't do what the presenter said it was going to do, because he said the people were going to let us know about whether it's getting easier for young people to get jobs, and whether it's easy to get promoted, and that kind of thing. But they're only telling us about themselves; and even if they told us they personally found it easy, that wouldn't tell us a thing about whether most people will find it easy! No one can say that their personal experiences are what everyone would experience. So the programme presenter told us the programme would do something it just doesn't do. It's stupid! And this is national radio! Standards should be higher than this! It's pointless! This programme's supposed to be helping people! I think they've all forgotten."

Becky's mum sighed and said, "Well, maybe you can go into radio when you grow up and show them all how it's done, eh?"

She was just joking, but Becky said seriously, "Maybe I will!"

Becky was interested in working out what else was wrong with the programme. And from then on, she spotted mistakes and bad things about quite a few radio and television programmes! To be fair, she also spotted a lot of good things – way more good things than bad ones, in fact; but the bad things often stuck in her mind more, because she often gave them more thought, and quite a bit of noisy criticism too, whether her mum liked it or not.

Becky is Skeptical About a Television Programme About the Mind and Pain

For instance, one evening, there was a television programme where the presenters claimed they were going to prove that the mind has more to do with the amount of pain people feel and how much pain relief they experience when they take painkillers than people think. Becky thought that idea might or might not be correct, but that they didn't do as good a job of proving it as they thought they'd done. In fact, she didn't think much of the way they tried to prove it at all!

They tried to convince viewers that people get more pain relief with trusted brands of painkillers than with much less well-known cheaper versions with exactly the same ingredients, that also have the same amounts of the ingredients in them. The theory went that if they could prove that that could happen, it would mean that something other than the painkillers must be causing the well-known ones to have a more powerful effect than the others, so some pain and pain relief must be to do with something psychological.

Becky speculated that if that can really happen, then maybe the pain relief might be partly caused by people's extra confidence in the ability of the brand-named tablets to work, which might make them stop worrying about the pain so much because they might be confident that it will soon be gone; and one effect of them worrying less could be that they might find it easier to get distracted from it, which could help because distraction will often result in pain that's mild or sometimes even moderate not feeling so bad – at least if it's enjoyable distraction – because the mind of the person in pain is absorbed in other things, so the pain's bothering them less, so much so that they're even feeling it less, maybe because the brain's attention is so taken up with thinking about the things they're doing or thinking that it's not paying so much attention to processing the pain signals being sent its way.

But Becky felt sure that that could only go so far, because she was certain that painkillers would often work better than distraction, since after all, people would be unlikely to be distracted continually for as long as they were in pain for, so there would still be times when all their attention was drawn to the pain; and she thought distraction must only help up until the point when pain makes it difficult to concentrate on anything for long enough to get absorbed in it, and if people aren't worried about what's causing their pain or whether it's likely to get any worse, so they can be relaxed enough about it to allow themselves to get distracted instead of worrying about whether they should be doing more about it, such as by seeing a doctor.

She also thought that if what a person's doing isn't interesting and absorbing, then surely pain will be a distraction from what they're trying to concentrate on instead, making concentration more difficult.

She also wondered why in the world anyone would ever buy painkillers that didn't have a recognised brand name if they were less confident they would work. She doubted anyone would. So she wondered if the programme would be making an issue out of nothing, if it said an important reason why people trust brand-named painkillers more is because they have more confidence in them. But she thought she'd watch it out of curiosity anyway.

Becky's Auntie Diana Tells her About Some Pain she Experienced That was at First Put Down to Stress

Becky told her auntie Diana that there was going to be a television programme on that evening about whether the mind has more to do with pain and pain relief than people think. Diana screwed up her face with displeasure at the idea, but then chuckled. She said to Becky, "A lot of people won't like that idea! Well, not unless someone on the programme gives a really really convincing explanation of how it could happen. People don't like to be told by doctors that their pain is all in their heads! I know that from experience as much as from anything else. Not that I minded what happened to me much:

"A couple of years ago, I was diagnosed with skin cancer. I don't know if you remember that. I think that with me being really fair-skinned, with reddish hair, I might be genetically predisposed to it. That's what I heard on a science programme on the radio not long ago anyway . . . Well, I mean, I didn't hear that I'm personally predisposed to it, obviously – that would have been spooky, especially since I don't suppose the presenters have ever heard of me! But I heard that people with especially fair skin and red hair seem to have a gene that makes them more likely to get it. I think it's partly because people like me never tan, but only get sunburned. Mind you, I think loads of people get skin cancer nowadays, but the most common forms are much less likely to spread to other parts of the body than most cancers are. It's still best if the ones that don't often spread much are cut out though, because they can cause problems in the areas where they're growing.

"Anyway, when I had skin cancer, they cut it out, and they cut some of the skin around it out too, so they could send it to a lab to make sure there were no cancer cells the doctors couldn't see growing in that. If there had been, it would have meant they would have cut a bit more skin out to try and get rid of all of them. There weren't any, so that was good. I didn't have to have chemotherapy or anything, because it hadn't spread below the skin. I'll just need to go to hospital every few months for the next few years so they can look at my skin to make sure no more globs of cancer are popping up.

"But anyway, when I went to the hospital to have it cut out, the procedure wasn't too bad, but they gave me this local anaesthetic injection, and only about a minute later they wanted to start cutting it out! I said the injection might take longer than that to work! I told them that it seemed anaesthetics take longer to work on me than on most people, since once, I'd had a general anaesthetic, and a nurse gave me an injection in the hand, and said, 'Count back from five to zero, and by the time you have, you'll be unconscious'.

"So I counted, five, four, three, two, one, zero, minus one, minus two – right into minus figures, and then the nurse said the anaesthetic couldn't be working, so they gave me gas instead – you know, the kind of gas I think dentists sometimes give people to make them go unconscious instead of giving them an injection to numb the pain in a tooth they want to work on.

"But anyway, when I was having my skin cancer cut out, and I told the doctors and nurses that the anaesthetic might take longer to work on me than on most people, one of them reassured me that they could massage the area so the anaesthetic would move around to all of it, and then they'd prick the area to see if I could still feel anything, so they'd know to wait a bit longer if I could. They massaged it and then pricked the area, and I could still feel it! So they gave me another anaesthetic injection. I could still feel pain there after that, so they gave me another one, that didn't quite work either, and then another one; and then they told me they'd given me the maximum amount they were allowed to give.

"Then they started the procedure. It still hurt a bit. Not much; it just felt like having several little injections. It would probably have hurt a lot more if the anaesthetic hadn't worked at all. But I kept saying, 'Ouch!'

"At first, they said things like, 'Maybe you're finding it hard to distinguish between pressure and pain', and, 'You've probably got all kinds of horrible things going on in your imagination'. But I said, 'No, this is definitely pain!' I wished they wouldn't keep thinking the pain might not be real.

"They told me to relax, thinking it wouldn't hurt so much then. But I was pretty sure it would.

"After a while though, the doctor cutting the cancer and extra skin out said, 'It seems there's a bit at the top that hasn't been numbed properly'. That was probably because I said ouch when she was working on some bits but not others.

"Then they were working on a bit that had been numbed well, and I managed to relax because it wasn't hurting. One of the nurses said, 'See, now you're relaxing, you're not feeling any pain.'

"I said, 'No, it's the other way around; it's because it isn't hurting at the moment that I can relax.'

"They were nice caring nurses though.

"And I was pretty much alright really. Like I said, it only hurt like a series of little injections when they were working on the bit that hadn't been properly numbed. I don't suppose I felt everything they were doing. Well, I can't have done, because I didn't feel them take the cancer out. I had another skin cancer taken out a couple of years before, and it was interesting, because the anaesthetic did work properly for that, although it did take longer than they expected to work, and they did have to give me another anaesthetic injection after the first one, but then it worked; and when the doctor took the cancer out, it felt like it feels when someone pulls a bit of plaster off their skin. Not a bit of skin with little hairs on it, but a bit you can pull plaster off without it hurting.

"But anyway, when I came back from the hospital after they didn't quite manage to make the anaesthetic work that time a couple of years ago, I had a look on the Internet because of something I'd heard, and I found out that some research has been done into whether anaesthetics don't work so well on people with red hair. An article I read said that scientists are only in the early stages of research, so they can't really be sure of anything; but there seem to be some findings that some anaesthetic drugs are more effective than other ones for people with red hair, because of some kind of genetic mutation they reckon we've got that makes the blocking of the body's pain signalling less effective or something, so pain signals still reach the brain when they wouldn't for other people.

"They haven't studied many people yet, so I don't think anyone's certain about any of the findings, since they can't be sure at the moment whether they would apply to everyone, or just to a small minority of people, for some reason they haven't found out about yet. But it'll be interesting to read more about what they find out when they've done more research!"

Becky agreed that it would be interesting.

She told Diana that she still might enjoy the programme about how much pain might be to do with a psychological effect though.

Becky Has More Thoughts About the Television Programme she Plans to Watch About the Mind and Pain

She eagerly sat down to watch it herself. She was doubtful about the claims it seemed to be going to make. But she thought that if it was true that some people are more confident in the power of painkillers with well-known brand names than in the power of others, then maybe it would be because they'd heard about them working for people they knew, or because they assumed they must have a good reputation because they would have heard about them often being used, or because they'd seen adverts for them that praised their benefits, so they might expect them to work more than they expected the others to work, that they hadn't heard of.

She thought that if things like that really happened, then maybe one reason why people's extra confidence in them helped them work better than the other ones might be because some of the people taking them would become less tense and stressed when they took them, because of their relief that they'd probably begin working soon, which might itself help ease their pain, because at least the pain from any very tense muscles they had would be diminishing; so it would be as if that was helping the painkillers to work.

286

Becky Talks to Diana About how Stress can Sometimes Cause Pain

She'd read something about how pain can sometimes be made worse by stress, and partly eased by relaxation not long before, and had told her auntie Diana about it, hoping it would help her, because Diana had been interested in psychology for years, and was thinking about one day working to try to help people with severe anxiety problems like panic attacks and phobias, as well as some other problems, so Becky thought it might be useful for her to know that pain reduction could be one of the possible benefits some people might get from learning to calm their anxious thoughts and feelings, or from getting themselves out of circumstances that kept stressing them out, especially if some people told her that part of the reason they were so anxious was because they were in pain, and they didn't know how long it was going to last or how bad it was going to get or anything – Becky thought that instead of thinking there must be hardly anything she could do about it in that case, her auntie Diana might be able to encourage them by saying that if they did things that made life less stressful for them, some of their pain might get quite a bit better, depending on what was causing it.

She did think Diana would be well-advised to recommend that they went to see a doctor too though, in case there was something physically wrong that would need sorting out. Not that Diana would have needed telling to do that.

Becky had enthusiastically gone to Diana to tell her what she'd learned, and said, "If you ever get to work with people with anxiety problems, like you're thinking of doing, I've found out about some things you could say that might help some of them, if they've got certain kinds of pain: I've read that if people can relax their muscles, it can help some pain subside a bit, because pain can feel worse when a person's muscles are tense. A couple of books I've looked at say that stress can even make some pain come on in the first place, and that de-stressing can make some pain even go away, for a few reasons:

"One is that stress can cause tension in the muscles that can lead to people tensing their bodies into awkward postures that aren't good for them, and muscles in awkward positions can begin to hurt. The longer a person stays in an awkward position for, which they might do without even realising they're in one, the more the body parts around their tensed muscles might hurt. Changing the posture, relaxing, having aching body parts massaged, and things like that, can relieve the tension, so the muscles and the body parts around them can stop hurting.

"Sometimes a person might have to do things to relax or to change the position they're in time and time again over days and weeks and months to keep the pain away for good, or to make it less bad, along with changing their lifestyle to make life less stressful, since habits of tensing up while they're stressed might be hard to break, since it's the natural thing to do.

"And when part of a person's body hurts, anxiety about hurting it some more can make their muscles tense up, including the muscles around the painful area, especially when the person will be risking feeling pain whenever they move it; so it might be unconsciously held in an awkward position to keep it as still as possible, and moved in a tense

288

way, and that might make it hurt more over time. I mean, I know that sometimes it's very important to keep a body part still when it's been injured, such as when a bone's been broken and it needs to be kept still so the body can fuse the bits together again; but I think there are times when part of a person's body's in pain, and they hold it in a tense way unconsciously because they're worrying about it hurting more if they move it, but the muscle tension that causes itself can make it hurt more after some time, and it wouldn't hurt as much as they're worried it would if they moved it.

"And I read that anxiety and stress about other things, such as not being able to work because of the problem, can make the muscles even more tense, so the part of the body around a painful area might hurt even more than it would otherwise after a while. So relaxation, or doing something enjoyable or distracting, can cause the tension to ease, so the part might start hurting less.

"People can get into the habit of moving and holding parts of their bodies in awkward positions over time if they're in pain, I think, so even when the pain that was caused by the thing that caused it in the first place goes away, they can still be tensing them up in those positions; and that in itself can lead to pain.

"One thing that might help is if people who know they get tense muscles sometimes at work, or when they're sitting concentrating on something else for a long time, can stop for a minute, perhaps every hour or so if they can, and also after every stressful experience they have, say if the boss has just yelled at them before going back to his office or something, and think about whether any parts of them feel tense, or might be tense; and if they think they are, they can make a conscious effort to let them go limp for a minute or two, so they relax a bit. There are probably some good exercises on the Internet to release tension too that they could look up.

"And then I think it can help if people make a conscious effort to get into a better posture, so they'll be less likely to just go back to being in one where they might be putting a strain on some of their muscles and joints, and tensing up."

Diana instinctively sat up straighter at the thought that her posture ought to be better. Then she thought her body felt more tense in that position, so she slouched down a bit again.

Becky noticed that and smiled. Then she said, "I told my mum about how it can help to change your position to help your muscles relax and things when I first read about it, but I didn't say the thing about how the kind of people who might find doing that the most useful are people who've been sitting in the same position for a while; and she said, 'That can only apply in certain situations. When you were very little, you wanted me to help you learn to walk, before you could even stand up. I held you up while you tried for ages. My muscles began to hurt after a while, but if I'd changed my position and let them relax, you'd have fallen over. I don't think you'd have liked that very much, somehow! Mind you, I did make sure we stopped for a rest every time they got painful!'

"I said, 'Oh Mum! I'm not saying people ought to change their position no matter what, so things could happen such as that someone could be carrying a heavy box at work, and the boss could yell at them, and they'd think, "Oh dear, all this noise he's making might stress me out, and I'm already putting a strain on my muscles, so I'd better change my position and relax them quick before they start hurting," so they'd drop the box, and all its contents might go rolling over the boss's feet! Somehow I think he'd be even more annoyed with them then, and then they'd be even more stressed! I'm sure people can tell when it's a good idea to change their position and when it isn't!' "

Diana laughed, and then said, "Maybe your mum knew what you meant really. Actually, I can understand how the advice you've been talking about might sometimes come in useful. I started changing my position sometimes not long ago, after I started waking up in the morning on some days with a numb right hand. I had to wiggle my fingers around for quite a few seconds to get the blood circulating in it better so I could use it properly when it happened. I wondered if there might be something seriously wrong, since I've heard that people get numbness on one side if they're having a stroke, so I wondered if my hand being numb meant I might be at risk of having one, although I wouldn't expect to be at risk of it until I'm older.

"But I looked on the Internet, and I found out that there are quite a few possible causes of it, and one of them is doing things that often put your wrists or hands in an awkward position where the nerves are being pressed on. I would have gone to the doctor about it if it had been any worse, or happened more often, but I thought I'd just wait a little while to see if it stopped happening. I realised I was leaning the heels of my hands hard on my desk sometimes when I was at my computer. I wondered if doing that might be pressing on a nerve that goes through the wrist into my hand, and then I might be lying on my hands in my sleep for a while too, so that would mean the nerves got pressed on even more. So every time I realised I was pressing the heels of my hands down from then on, I moved my hands to a different position. And I haven't woken up with a numb hand since. I can't say for sure that that was what was causing the problem; but I'll wait and see, and if it doesn't happen again, then I'll think it probably was that."

Becky said, "That's interesting. I hope it was only that that was causing the problem. Anyway, I've been thinking that the things I've been learning about trying to make sure your muscles aren't tense might help you give advice to some people who've got problems with anxiety one day. Another thing is that I've heard that the more people can de-stress at work, or the less stress they get lumbered with in the first place there, the less likely they'll often be to end up taking time off sick. That might not be just because they sometimes take time off sick because of the mental effects of stress; it might sometimes be because it causes physical pain in the end that people can decide they need time to recover from.

"I suppose I can't be sure it's true, but I read on a website that stress that gets worse and worse can result in the body making the blood vessels in places like the back narrower till the stress dies down, so not so much blood will flow around them; it does that because the body will want to send more of its blood to the muscles in the arms and legs to give them more strength, in case the stress is being caused by something the person needs to fight off or run away from. The part of the brain that controls that kind of response won't know enough about what the cause is to be able to make a distinction between the kind of problem that can be solved by fighting or running away and the kind that can't.

"The only way the part of the brain that knows what's really going on in the person's life can stop the part of it that's doing that from getting the body ready to fight or run away is by calming down; it can't do it by just telling it to stop doing it, like by reassuring it that it isn't as if there's a monster in the room or something; the other part of the brain's actions are just automatic, so it can't order it around . . . Well, it might help if it tries and that makes the person less stressed, because they find it amusing or something; but the part of the brain we're conscious that we're thinking with won't even know another part of the brain's just set off that kind of reaction, unless the person recognises the signs of it, like feeling a lot more anxious."

Diana said, "That sounds a bit strange: One part of the brain not knowing what another part's doing? And how one part of the brain could try to order another part of it around? What?"

Becky said, "Well I know it sounds weird, but it makes sense if you think about it; I mean, just think of the number of chemical reactions and other things that must be going on in your brain all the time; you know, your brain communicates with all your nerves so it can receive an instant signal if you hurt yourself, and it's processing everything you hear so you can understand what it is, and releasing chemicals that change your mood if you hear something sad or funny or whatever, and doing all kinds of other things.

"Well just imagine if you were conscious of your brain doing all those things. How would you ever be able to think of anything that required the least bit of concentration, when all the time, you were thinking things like, 'Chocolate! I like that, so I must release a dash of dopamine into my system to make the body I'm in feel good for eating it!' 'This room's getting cold! It's time I made my body shiver!' 'I'll just think about how to move my body and what to move when so I can get up and shut the window.' 'Now I'm going to work out how much of what I ate today to turn into fat.' Or whatever. How would you ever be able to concentrate on anything? So it's a good thing that some parts of the brain just go about their business quietly, without the part of the brain you concentrate with knowing what they're doing."

Diana said, "I suppose so. That's interesting."

Becky said, "When you think about it, you might realise the brain's amazing really . . . And one part of it can think about how amazing the rest of it is without the rest of it getting big-headed! . . . Probably anyway. But just think: When you want to get up in the morning, you don't have to try to remember how best to do it – you know, thinking through what parts of your body to move in what order, and how to move them, and that kind of thing; you just decide you want to get up, and your brain just knows what to do. And that happens with loads of other things you do during the day too . . . Well, it doesn't just happen with you, personally, obviously; it's the same for everyone, of course.

"If someone asked you to write down what order you move the parts of your body in and how you move them when you're getting up, or doing any number of other things, you might only have a vague idea of what order you do things in, and you might have to really really think about it, because the part of your brain that takes care of those things just does it without the part you think with even having to plan it through.

"Most of the time, that system works well. There are just a few things that part of the brain does without you wanting it to, like falling asleep, say in the middle of your favourite television programme, or like me in the middle of a class, which ends up with me being told off by a teacher, who must think I've just decided to use the classroom as my bedroom and the lesson as my bedtime, when I didn't drop off to sleep deliberately! Mind you, that's only happened a few times.

"Anyway, I was telling you about one reason why things like back pain can come on, according to what it said on this website I was browsing – you know, that if a person's stressed, and part of the brain sends more blood than normal to the muscles in the arms and legs in case the stress is being caused by something the person needs to fight off, the back might not have quite as much blood flow as it really needs till the person calms down again, because the body will be using some of the blood it would have sent there to give the arm and leg muscles a bit more strength. It seems from what this website I read was saying that a lack of blood can increase the pain a person feels.

"It said that if the mind doesn't calm down, the fact that there's less blood flowing around the back will mean that the back won't be getting such a rich supply of nutrients, especially oxygen, which the blood contains a bit of, surprisingly, and it helps the body make energy – not just energy for getting up and doing things, but energy to fuel all the things the body does quietly without us thinking about it, like digesting food . . . Well, sometimes it does that a bit less quietly than other times.

"But anyway, if there's less blood flowing about the place, the waste products that are always being made when the body does things like turning food into nutrients that are in a form it can use won't be carried away to where they can be processed and then flushed out when the person next goes for a wee so efficiently, because less energy made from the lesser amount of oxygen there because of less blood being there will mean the body's processes won't be working so well in places like the stomach and back, so the waste products will hang around in the system for longer, possibly causing problems.

"I don't think it's just back pain that can be brought on or made worse by stress; I think all kinds of chronic pain can be.

"The problem is that if the stress goes on for some time, the things the body does so it's all ready to fight off this person it somehow thinks exists, like diverting blood flow to the arm and leg muscles so they get more energy, which will mean that at the same time, there'll be less blood to flow around areas like the back and the digestive system – that process might cause a build-up of the body's waste products in places like that, which could eventually cause muscle spasms that can be really bad like cramps; and the stress will cause muscle tension too, and those things can cause back pain or some other pain. Strange really, since then the person will be in no fit state to fight this imaginary person the body thinks must exist off at all!

"That's what this website said anyway . . . Well, I don't mean the thing about imaginary people, but the thing about what the body does. It said de-stressing will reverse the process, although it often isn't easy, because once pain has set in for a while, people might often worry about what's going wrong, and whether they're going to be prevented by the pain from doing all the things they enjoy doing, as well as from making a living by working, so their stress might actually get worse, and that could make their pain worse, because even more blood might be flowing to the muscles in the arms and legs instead of going to their back, because something in their body won't realise it's just worry making them stressed, but it'll behave as if it might be someone threatening them who they might need to fight or run away from.

"And the frustration of having had to give up doing quite a few things because of the pain, and also all the extra worrying people might have time to do because of the spare time they might have during the times they used to do the things they had to give up, could lead to tension that could make the pain caused by the muscle tension that was already there worse."

The Subject of Back Pain and Vitamin D Levels Comes Up

Diana looked thoughtful, and said, "You know, this is all interesting. But I don't think I'm going to be able to say it all to people I might one day help with anxiety problems; I mean, I can just imagine if I was working on a helpline for people with bad anxiety, and someone phoned up, and an hour later, I'd finished telling them all the things you're telling me, only to have them start sobbing down the phone, saying, 'And all I wanted when I phoned up was to tell someone about my problems and get a sympathetic ear!'

"Really, there are probably lots of things that cause back pain that have nothing to do with stress at all; so I'd have no way of knowing whether any person's back pain had anything to do with stress or not. You know – heavy lifting can cause back pain, and probably a number of other things can too. Things like slipped disks can cause hellish back pain, and they're best treated by a doctor.

"But one thing I did hear was that a study found that a lot of people with back pain have been found to have low levels of vitamin D. I don't know how often that might be anything to do with the cause though, since different things cause back pain."

Becky said, "Yes. It's probably worth investigating; but until they find out more, it'll be impossible to know whether it can sometimes be something to do with the cause, or whether it's really just a coincidence, since the same people who might be most likely to have low vitamin D levels will sometimes be the same people who are most likely to get back pain, because older people are probably most likely to get it, and also older people are among the people most likely to have low vitamin D levels, because the body finds it harder to absorb vitamin D into the system in old age.

"Or it's possible that the back pain came first, and the low vitamin D levels came afterwards, because people with bad back pain are probably less likely to be able to get out into the sunshine than a lot of other people are.

"Still, it'll be worth people with low vitamin D levels trying to improve them, even if it doesn't help with any pain they've got."

Diana said, "I expect you're right. I can't be sure if vitamin D levels really have anything to do with back pain. Anyway, I reckon you'd make a good lecturer when you grow up . . . or even before! Maybe even now!"

Diana and Becky Tease Each Other a Bit

She joked, "It's surprising you know so much at your age. Maybe you've got a strange rare disease called reverse ageing or something, where you have a mental age that's quite grown-up when you're really young, and then you regress to having the mental age of a baby when you're physically grown-up; so in theory you could get a job as a university lecturer now, and be lecturing for years, and then one day, all the students could come in expecting a weighty lecture on the latest research about anxiety symptoms or something, and instead, you'd come into the room, look around, and suddenly scream, 'Where's my dummy!' And then you'd start bawling your eyes out.

"... Sorry, that's not very nice, is it."

Diana wasn't always the most tactful of people.

Becky protested, "No it isn't! Stop teasing me! I'm trying to be serious!"

Diana said, "Sorry. What you're saying's interesting really. But I probably won't remember it all. I don't know how you can! You're like a walking encyclopaedia."

Then she half joked, "You know, sometimes, I wonder whether you're really a human at all, or maybe you're a robot that's been developed using the latest technology, and it's been sent to us as an experiment to see if it's good enough to fool everyone into believing it's human. Maybe the baby your mum really had was swapped for you at birth! Goodness knows where the poor thing must be now."

Becky protested, "Don't be horrible!"

Diana said, "Sorry, I don't mean it. Anyway, Robot Face, maybe it'll be best if you send me an email with links to this information, so I can browse it every so often to remind myself of it, and so I can find out whether it's thought of as actual fact by scientists, or whether it's just someone's theory, or something that's being studied but that doctors aren't quite sure about yet. Mind you, you can carry on telling me about it now too if you like. I might remember at least some of it. And thinking about it, even if some of it's still only a theory, or not quite right, I don't suppose it can do anyone any harm to reduce their stress levels. So I could say to anyone who tells me they've got back pain but that doctors haven't been able to help them that some people think that doing things to reduce stress can sometimes help. I wouldn't have to go into great detail about the reasons why, unless someone wanted me to.

"Anyway Robot Face, carry on."

Diana's nickname for Becky was Robot Face from then on. Becky didn't seem to mind.

She was just about to carry on, when Diana smiled and said, "Actually, thinking about it, I'll just go and make a cup of coffee before I listen to the rest of what you've got to say. I think I need some caffeine to build up my stamina for concentration. Maybe I'm just a bit of a wimp!"

Becky followed Diana into the kitchen, and then when she was about to make her coffee, grinned mischievously and said, "Why not put loads of coffee in the cup? If you put a heaped tablespoonful of coffee in there instead of a teaspoon-ful, do you think you'd have enough stamina to drink it? Would you dare?"

Diana giggled and made a face, and said, "No way! That would be way way too strong for me!"

Becky and Diana Talk About How Sleep and Exercise Can Affect Some Kinds of Pain

When she'd made her coffee, they went back in the other room, and after Diana had taken a big swig of it, she told Becky to carry on telling her what she'd been telling her before.

Becky said, "Alright then. Another thing is that I found out that another way stress can make pain worse is by making it more difficult to sleep, because if a person has worries going around and around in their minds, it might keep them awake, or they won't be able to sleep so restfully and deeply, and it's in the deep sleep that the body mostly repairs body tissues from tiny bits of wear and tear they get during the day, according to something I read. It said that if someone isn't getting much deep sleep, their body won't be able to do that so much, and the accumulation of little bits of wear and tear will start to cause pain. De-stressing before bedtime, so as to increase the chances that sleep will be more restful, might help ease the pain, because a better sleep will make it easier for the body to do repair work on itself. That makes sense, doesn't it.

"And I read that not doing much exercise could make pain feel worse, because the muscles will get out of condition, so they'll get tired and start aching more easily. So even if a person can only manage to do a bit of exercise, it will often be better than nothing, especially since it can make blood, which is full of nutrients, circulate faster round the body, so a better flow of nutrients will get to the parts that need healing, so the body might be able to do whatever it can do to try to heal them more quickly than it might do otherwise. The actual part that hurts won't need to be exercised for that to happen; so, for instance, someone who found walking too painful to do much of it might still be able to do rowing, and so on.

"Sometimes, a person might need to rest altogether for a while so as not to aggravate any injury they've got. And if someone starts exercising and they begin to feel pain somewhere, it's probably best if they have a bit of a break, for anything between seconds and weeks or even months, in case it's their body giving them a warning that they'll damage something if they're not careful. Still, their body might sometimes be just letting them know they need to do a bit of warming up slowly before they put all their energy into what they're doing in case they strain something. But I've heard that some people have found that exercise can help ease the pain that's caused by some problems for a while, like some arthritis pain. I don't know if it always works, because I think arthritis can be caused by different things; and I think people who've got it have to be careful about which exercises they do, so as not to put much strain on the actual joints with arthritis in them; but I think there are exercises that can be good for some people who've got it."

Becky thought it was quite possible that sometimes, beginning to exercise very gently and working up to exercising at a faster pace over the space of several minutes might help, partly because her auntie Diana had told her she'd bought an exercise bike some time before, and she'd found that her knees hurt when she first tried to use it, as if the sudden stress on the joints or the muscles around them, or on something else in the area, wasn't good for them. But she'd found that when she slowed down to a point where she could cycle without her knees hurting, and then had gradually gone faster and faster over the space of several minutes, she could eventually cycle at the speed she'd tried to at first, without her knees hurting at all. So she'd decided she'd just need to warm up like that every time she went on the bike from then on, thinking that then things would likely be alright.

She'd found she had to discipline herself to keep cycling slowly for a while at first though, and to remember to do it every time. But she'd found that soon, she didn't need to cycle slowly for as long as she had at first before she could cycle faster without her knees hurting.

She'd told Becky she'd made sure the seat was at a decent height though, since she'd had experience of cycling on an exercise bike where the seat was low, and that had hurt her knees. Then she'd read that that was a common experience for people who had their saddles too low on exercise bikes, as well as for people who had them too high. So she'd realised it must be important to adjust them to the right level.

Becky had decided to try and remember that, so she could tell people she met who said they were thinking of using an exercise bike about the importance of having the saddle at the right height for them.

But when Diana told her that her knees had hurt when she'd first used her exercise bike, Becky said, "Do you think you might have a bit of arthritis in your knees?"

Diana said, "I hope not! I'm probably too young for that. Mind you, I have heard of young people getting arthritis. But I've bashed my knees a few times over the years, so maybe they weren't in the best of health before I went on the bike, so it didn't take as much for them to hurt as it would've done otherwise. I don't know."

Becky said, "I wonder if people are more likely to get arthritis in joints they've injured in the past."

Her auntie Diana replied, "I hope not! I've never injured them that badly though."

Becky Talks About Things That can Ease Some Arthritis Pain, and Healthy Eating

Becky said, "I've been reading a bit about arthritis on the Internet. One thing I read is that heat, like from a warm bath or a hot water bottle, can help ease the pain for a while, and so can ice, or something just as cold like a packet of frozen vegetables, maybe ones that have passed their sell-by date, so it doesn't matter if they defrost, because the person using them might not have wanted to eat them anyway by then. Why they would have bought them in the first place if they were so unenthusiastic about eating them they let them pass their sell-by date, I don't know. But still."

Diana giggled and said, "Yes, but I'm not sure anyone's going to want a pile of mushy dripping vegetables on their knees or another part of them when they defrost! Actually though, I sprained my ankle once, and a doctor advised me to keep my weight off it for a couple of weeks, and to maybe put my ankle on a bag of frozen peas that was wrapped in a towel, so the cold would help get the swelling down. I did that for a while. Not till they defrosted and went all mushy though."

Becky giggled, and then said, "Just in case you've got a bit of arthritis in your knees though, I read that some people say there are foods that can make arthritis worse, and foods that can make it less likely to come on, or less bad . . . I mean foods that are eaten, not foods that are draped around people in packets from out of the freezer and things like that. It might not work for everyone, but some people say that giving up oranges and tomatoes and plums and some other acidic foods has made their arthritis pain go away; and some people say giving up potatoes and bread helps them. And I read some advice that said it's best to cut down quite a bit on sugary and salty foods, and fried foods, and processed foods like ready meals and convenience foods that you just put in the oven or microwave and eat when they come out."

Diana said, "That's a shame! The time when a person's most in pain will be the time when they'll find ready meals and things like that most useful, because moving around or standing up for some time preparing food might make their pain worse! And it's a pity all advice on healthy eating says we need to cut down on sugary foods! I tried eating a Brussels sprout once while I was trying to imagine it was something sweet and sugary, just out of curiosity, to see if that kind of thing works, after something I read recommended doing things like that. It didn't work! Not for me anyway."

Becky grinned, and said, "Yes, it does seem a shame that it seems it's best to cut out convenience foods and sugary things. Mind you, what you say reminds me of something I heard on telly. I think Mum enjoyed it! It was about how parents can entice kids to eat more vegetables. It said children can be a lot happier to eat them if they're chopped up and mixed with other things. They even chopped up some raw Brussels sprouts and mixed them into some yoghurt, and gave them to some kids to eat as a pudding, and they enjoyed them! Mum's never tried giving me vegetables for pudding though . . . at least not that I know about!"

Diana laughed.

Then Becky said, "Anyway, about what you said about it being a shame about what it says on the Internet about ready meals not being as good for people with arthritis as vegetables and some fruit, because when you're in pain you want something convenient to eat, you can at least get some prepared vegetables from supermarkets, like carrots and onions that have already been peeled and washed and chopped up, and bits of cauliflower and broccoli that have been washed and broken into small bits, and mixtures of chopped-up melon and mango and things, and bits of apple all cut up, and other things.

"I read some advice on the Internet that said that arthritis can sometimes be made better if people with it eat a lot of vegetables, and fruits that aren't that acidic, and nuts and seeds – I think especially sunflower and pumpkin and chia seeds, and also flax seeds, which I think are also called linseeds – after the chia seeds and flax seeds have been soaked to soften them up so the body can digest them more easily than it can when they're in their normal state, where they're too hard for the body to do a good job of it. But then, nuts and seeds are high in calories, so it's best not to eat loads in one go. Another thing I read is that oily fish like sardines can help with arthritis too.

"Well, I don't know if all those things help with every kind of arthritis, and I don't know how much they can help; but from what I've read, it seems they can at least help with some kinds, so they'll be worth trying.

"That might be especially because I think part of the reason why lots of vegetables can help is because they're low-calorie – at least I think most of them are – so if people with arthritis are eating those instead of fattening things with a lot of salt or sugar in them, or other things that aren't healthy, they can lose weight more easily, or keep themselves slim so they don't start putting on lots of weight, and that can help, because the more weight a person puts on, the more pressure it puts on their joints; and the more pressure that gets put on them from weight bearing down on them, the more they'll hurt if they've got arthritis . . . I mean, obviously it's best to go to the doctor to find out what's really going on; but I think all these things can help.

"Have you held one of those bags of sugar that weighs a kilogram, or a litre bottle of drink? If you have, you know it's quite heavy; so imagine holding about six of them at once! It might make your arms ache after a while. Well, it would mine anyway! And it would be about a stone in weight. So if a person's got that amount of weight on their stomach from fat, and their knees have got to carry it, plus lots of other stones in weight, quite a lot of them from fat, maybe that's part of what makes them hurt when they've got arthritis sometimes.

"And it's not just because fat's heavy when there's a lot of it that it can cause problems; I read that when there's a lot of fat around a person, it releases chemicals that cause inflammation in the body, and that can make arthritis worse even in parts of the body that haven't got any pressure of weight on them, like the hands . . . So if you've got arthritis in your knees, you'd better make sure you don't get fatter than you already are, or it might get worse!"

Diana chuckled and said sarcastically, "Thanks for warning me about my podge levels!"

Becky's Embarrassing Attempt to Help a Woman in Church

Becky wondered if exercise could help ease some other kinds of pain by helping people lose weight, along with them being careful about the kinds of foods they ate. She'd suspected for a while that carrying a lot of weight around could put stresses on the muscles and joints, because of some of the things she'd read. She'd recently spoken to someone at the church her mum took her to who was over twenty stone, who'd said she was often in pain, especially in her back. Becky had said, "I'm not surprised, since when you think about it, you must be carrying around the equivalent of the weight of another grown adult in fat. Imagine carrying around, say, someone who used to be one of your friends at school, if you met them now. Imagine how much you'd ache if you tried carrying them around all day, or even just after a couple of minutes! Maybe your body gets just as tired carrying around their weight in fat!"

The person she was talking to was sensitive about her weight, and wasn't amused, especially since she wondered if some people nearby might have heard what Becky said! Later, she did wonder if Becky might have a point though. But she thought it would be wise to go to the doctor and get a second opinion about the cause of her pain.

Meanwhile, after they'd got home from church, Becky's mum told her off for making the comments she had about the woman's weight, saying that for all she knew, the woman might have had the pain first, and put on weight because it meant she'd found it harder to exercise, and because it had made her want to comfort eat. Becky admitted that her mum might have a point, but said the woman could have told her that if it was true, but hadn't.

The incident had been embarrassing for Becky's mum. She often found the things Becky said embarrassing; she thought it was something she'd probably just have to get used to, though it wasn't easy.

Becky had said to the woman, trying her best to be helpful, "Maybe changing your sleeping position would help a bit. If you normally lie on your back, that might make things worse, because the small of your back probably won't be resting on the bed, because people's bodies don't go straight down, because the bottom sticks out, and the bigger and fatter your bottom is, the more it'll stick out. Yours sticks out quite a long way. So there'll be a gap between the small of your back and the bed; so the bottom of your spine won't have anything to rest on; and imagine the stones and stones of flab in your big belly weighing down on that poor little spine of yours; it won't be any wonder if it finds it hard to cope! Maybe you could try putting something underneath the small of your back in the gap, like a little towel, so it's got something to rest on; and I've read that bending the knees up helps too, because the gap between the back and the bed gets smaller then; or you could try sleeping on your side or your stomach or something, instead of on your back.

"Mind you, if you sleep on your side, I suppose all your belly flab might flop down a bit and pull down on the muscles at the side of your stomach and chest, and put too much strain on them, so they might start hurting. And sleeping on your stomach might hurt your back too if it gets bent into an awkward position. Maybe you just need to experiment to find out what works. And think about whether your mattress is comfortable too, since if it isn't, lying on that all night might make the pain worse."

Becky's mum and the podgy woman had both been embarrassed. Becky's mum had blushed and said sternly, "Rebecca, don't be so rude!"

Becky had said indignantly, "I'm trying to help her! What would you prefer, that I didn't say anything, and if I can say something that helps her, I don't get to say it, and she carries on being in as much pain as she is now?"

Becky's mum, still blushing, had said, "Well just try to say whatever you want to say politely!"

Becky had responded, still feeling indignant, "How am I supposed to do that? How is it possible to say what I want to say and still be polite?"

Her mum hadn't been sure, and had said, "Well you could at least say it privately, instead of in front of a whole load of people!"

Becky had said crossly, "We never see her anywhere private! We only ever see her here! So how could I!"

Becky's mum hadn't been sure what to say to that, since it was true that they only saw the woman in church, and she didn't think it would be appropriate to advise Becky that she should have told the woman to go somewhere private with her so she could give her some advice about her belly flab. So she just hoped Becky didn't have much more embarrassing advice for the woman so they could go home. To her relief, it seemed that Becky had just about finished what she wanted to say, so they did so not long afterwards, after her mum had apologised to the woman for any embarrassment Becky might have caused.

Becky Tells a Story About a Man Whose Back Pain Eased a Lot When his Stress Levels Went Down

It was not long after that that Becky had read about how stress might sometimes make pain worse. Another thing she told her auntie Diana was that she'd read in a psychology book about a man who'd gone to a doctor with back ache, after having been off work with it for nearly a year. The doctor had examined him to see if there was anything seriously wrong with his bones or nerves, or anything like that; but he had found it was mostly a muscle tension problem.

Becky said, "The man told the doctor he'd been under a lot of stress for a while, partly because he'd tragically lost a daughter and grandchild not long before, so he'd been grieving. He said he'd been advised by other doctors and other people to give up activities he'd once enjoyed like meeting his friends to play snooker, in case it aggravated his back some more; but he said being inactive at home was another thing that was stressing him out, because he got really bored. He'd also been advised to give up work, because other doctors had assumed it was the demands of his job that were damaging his back; but not doing anything, and not seeing his friends any more, made him miserable. I think it was in the days before the Internet, so he couldn't make a group of friends online and chat to those a lot, and get absorbed in conversations on Internet forums and things. He'd actually enjoyed his job, partly because he liked being with the friends he had at work.

"The doctor he told about how stressed he was advised him to gradually ease himself into getting more active again, walking a little way the first day, a bit further the next, further the next, and so on, since walking can help with some kinds of back pain. He also advised him to begin to do what he enjoyed again, starting to spend time out with his friends again, building up to spending as much time with them as he had before.

"He also arranged it so the man could speak to a health professional at his work, who could advise him on gradually getting back into going to work again, such as by just going for one day the first week, then a day and a half the next week, two the week after, and so on.

"And he recommended things that would help him get better sleep, such as not smoking in the evening, because he said nicotine could keep him awake, and not drinking coffee or tea after about 5 PM, because of the caffeine in them that would stimulate his system. And he recommended that if he woke up during the night, he should try to bore himself back to sleep, by reading something dreary.

"When the man came back to see him five weeks later, he was back to work full-time, although on lighter duties, and he was going out with his friends again, enjoying himself more, and feeling quite a bit less stressed. He said his back still ached a bit, but he was carrying on anyway, and it was at least a lot better than it had been before. The doctor was surprised at the difference in him.

"The doctor said he'd had quite a lot of patients who'd got quite a bit better when they started doing things to make their lives less stressful, although he often did things to relieve their immediate tension first, like massaging parts of them in certain ways. And he taught them ways of protecting their backs from strain, such as by bending their knees and keeping their backs as straight as possible when they were reaching down to lift heavy things off the floor, rather than just bending the back, which people shouldn't really do, because it means they'll be letting it take a lot more of the strain of the weight of the things than it will if they bend their knees so they're nearer the ground so they don't have to reach down so far to lift the things up.

"But he said he'd even come to believe that back pain that comes on at work is more often caused mostly by the stress of having to put up with an awkward boss or not liking work, or having something else that's upsetting going on in life, than with the physical demands of the work; so he felt sure that if the stress could be reduced at work, it could reduce the pain, and so reduce the absenteeism; and he said that if people have the courage to say no to doing things at work that are over and above the call of duty if they're stressful, and make sure they have enough spare time, and give time to doing things in their spare time that they'd enjoy, he thought they'll be able to start experiencing less muscle tension, because their work will stress them out less, and they'll be relaxing more, so they'll have less pain."

Becky's Uncomplimentary Verdict on the Television Programme About Pain

Having read and talked about all that, Becky was interested to find out if the programme she was planning to watch on television about the experiment with painkillers could prove that the mind could have even more effect on pain than she'd thought, because she was curious to learn more. But she was disappointed.

The presenters got some rugby players to each put one of their arms in icy water to see how long they could keep them there for. First they gave them the trusted brand of painkiller, and they kept their arms in the water for about fifteen minutes, having reduced pain because of the tablets. Then they gave them the much less well-known brand, and got them to put one of their arms in icy water again, without letting them know that the tablets had exactly the same ingredients as the ones in the well-known variety, and most didn't keep them in it for as long. The presenters said that was proof that the well-known brand of painkiller worked better, saying it must be simply because people had more confidence in it working, so the pain didn't seem to feel so bad. But Becky yelled at the screen:

"What if it's proof of something different entirely? That's not a good experiment at all! What if the reason they didn't want to keep their arms in icy water for so long the second time was because they knew how much it was going to hurt from their experience of it the first time, and that was putting them off having them there? The experiment would have been better if some had been given the unknown brand first to see if they still took their arms out quicker the second time! It might have been better still if some didn't take any painkillers at all, and put their arms in the icy water twice to see how long they could keep them there, and to see whether they took them out more quickly one time than the other; and if they kept them in for as long as the others did, it might mean the painkillers weren't helping any of them to brave the freezing water at all!"

Becky's mum came in at the commotion Becky was making by shouting, and asked sarcastically, "Do you think that if you shout loud enough, they'll hear you in the studio?"

Becky said indignantly, "No!"

Becky Criticises Another Science Experiment

There were other times when Becky spoke to the television too. There was a science documentary Becky usually enjoyed watching, but one evening it was about the mistakes people make, and she thought she found a big mistake in it! Near the end, it showed a woman who'd trained some monkeys to do certain things, who claimed to be able to demonstrate that when they were given a certain choice, they kept making decisions that weren't sensible, saying that proved that people are just doomed to make certain mistakes in their thinking over and over again, because humans evolved from monkeys, so if monkeys make the same mistakes as humans tend to, it will mean humans are in the habit of making them because their brains are evolved from monkey brains, so they've got some of the same faults.

The programme had said, and demonstrated, that people often make the mistake of doing things because their instincts quickly tell them they'll lose out if they don't, when in reality they aren't likely to lose out at all, but their impulses are just making them think they will.

It gave an example of one way that could work in practice, saying advertisers or retailers will often use their knowledge of the human tendency to act hastily if they think they'll otherwise miss out on something to manipulate people into buying the products they're trying to sell, for instance by putting something on special offer or putting a sale on, but announcing that offers will end soon, which will mean people will have to be quite quick in deciding whether to buy something if they want it at the cheaper rate, so they might make up their minds to get it without thinking as carefully as they should, because their emotions could be urging them to hurry so as not to risk missing out, so they might end up buying things they realise later aren't as good as they thought, when they'd have found that out if they'd taken time to examine them more closely before; or they might buy what's in the sale, even though other brands are cheaper even though they aren't on special offer, and they'd have discovered that if they'd just taken a bit of time to look around.

The monkeys on the programme had been trained to in effect buy grapes with tokens from a man and a woman who were each selling them to them, after they were taught that they could swap a token for a grape. First they were trained to expect one grape per token, but then they must have been pleasantly surprised when the woman started giving them two. The man started giving them three per token, but then he stopped and only gave them two. The monkeys preferred to get their grapes from the woman from then on, even though she and the man were both offering the same number of grapes.

The programme presenter said that was a mistake in their reasoning that proved that humans were doomed to make similar ones, because the fact that the monkeys made the same ones must mean humans must have inherited the tendency from monkeys, so it must be just hardwired into the brains of humans; and the reason it was a mistake was because the monkeys hadn't reasoned through that they were getting the same number of grapes from both people, even though the man was giving them fewer than he had before, so it didn't actually matter which person they went to; they were obviously just hastily deciding not to go to the man, because he'd started giving them fewer so they thought they were getting a worse deal, without thinking things through. But Becky said to the television,

"Oh really! What if it means something completely different? If someone offers something, but then starts giving less than they seemed to be going to, people's sense of fair play will be hurt, and monkeys probably have one too, so they might be going to the woman because they're annoyed with the man because they think he's been unfair, so they want to protest or show their disapproval. That's even though he isn't necessarily being unfair in reality, because the extra grapes could have been a special bonus, not the usual deal, for all they knew. But they still might be put in a bit of a bad mood by getting fewer, like some people would be, I suppose, if someone offered cake around, and then gave some people bigger bits than others; some people might feel deprived, even though they were actually getting more than they would have done if no one had been offered any cake. Actually, I'd probably feel like that, thinking about it.

"Mind you, that would be partly to do with the meaning people might think it has if someone gives them less cake than they give the others – they might think it must mean the person doesn't like them as much, and that might be part of what makes them feel a bit upset. So what if the monkeys thought that when the man gave them fewer grapes, it must have meant he'd decided he didn't like them as much as he had before, so they went to the woman instead, because they didn't want to keep being reminded of that? How do you know monkeys don't think like that?

"Or more likely than the fair play thing, maybe, the monkeys are disappointed every time they only get two grapes from the man, because their hopes have been got up that they'll get three; and the disappointment puts them in a bad mood, and the prospect of being put in a bad mood by that is bothering enough for them to weigh it up in their decision about who to go to in order to get the grapes, and that's why they go to the woman. Feelings matter, you know! If someone knows they're going to get feelings they don't like if they do a certain thing, they're not making a mistake if they avoid it! Why hasn't the person doing the experiment thought of this? Doesn't she believe monkeys have feelings or something?"

Becky hadn't finished there, but continued saying to the programme,

"And as for this stuff about the monkey experiment showing that humans are doomed to make mistakes because monkeys do, maybe we are, but I think there's something wrong with your logic here: Why should humans be doomed to do what monkeys do? Some government leaders might be, but that doesn't mean the rest of us are. For instance, some monkeys can quickly get aggressive with each other, but that doesn't mean humans are doomed to do that and there's nothing that can be done to change human behaviour; everyone knows that good parents can train their children not to get violent that easily, except where they've got some kind of disorder. So it's not sensible to say you're proving that if monkeys have evolved to do something, it'll mean humans will do it too because it's just a part of human nature and that's that!"

Becky's mum came in as she was speaking, and said, "Talking to yourself are you? Whatever! Get to bed Becky, it's getting late."

Becky became interested in the way programmes and films are made, and when she heard it's possible to do media studies at university, she immediately decided she'd like to do it. She wanted to do a psychology degree too, so she applied to do two degrees at once. She knew it might be difficult to persuade universities that someone as young as her could do not just one but two degrees at once, but her school reports were so glowing she felt sure she and the school could persuade them.

It turned out she was right. Her local university accepted her to do the courses she wanted.

Acknowledgements

In addition to my own ideas, in creating this book I am indebted to numerous authors whose writings on therapy, self-help, psychology, and avoiding deception and fraud have informed some of Becky's advice on various topics. However, I am especially indebted to the following:

Chapter one (coping with teasing): *Easing the Teasing: Helping Your Child Cope with Name-Calling, Ridicule, and Verbal Bullying* by Judy S. Freedman, M.S.W., L.C.S.W.

Chapter two (anti-bullying strategy): *Schools Where Everyone Belongs: Practical Strategies For Reducing Bullying* by Stan Davis.

Chapter four (the HALT technique, bulimia and other eating disorders): *Anorexia Nervosa: The Wish To Change* by A. H. Crisp, Neil Joughin, Christine Halek & Carol Bowyer.

Chapter five (giving up smoking): *Freedom From Addiction: the Secret Behind Successful Addiction Busting* by Joe Griffin & Ivan Tyrrell with Denise Winn.

Chapter seven (dealing with anxiety, the rewind technique /fast phobia cure): *How to Master Anxiety* by Joe Griffin & Ivan Tyrrell with Denise Winn; (systematic desensitisation): *Freedom from Agoraphobia* by Mark Eisenstadt.

Chapter ten (getting over depression): *How to Lift Depression ... Fast* by Joe Griffin & Ivan Tyrrell with Denise Winn.

About the Author

Diana Holbourn has written self-help articles and is the author of *The Early Life of Becky Bexley the Child Genius* and other books about the same character. Taking short psychology courses, working on a helpline and reading psychology books has prepared her for writing the self-help information that appears as part of the story in the Becky Bexley series. Diana lives and works on the south coast of England, where the sun shines . . . sometimes.

For more about the author and her books, visit:
www.DianaHolbourn.com

Other books in this series So Far ...

Becky Bexley, Book Two

Becky Bexley the child genius goes to university at a much younger age than most people do. She copes with the coursework, but has a few unexpected difficulties. Things begin well, as she makes friends she has fun with, and finds herself giving one of her psychology tutors some psychological help. She has a laugh working on a local community radio station with other students, and interviews the brother of a founder member of the pop group Fleetwood Mac. The paranormal comes up for discussion after a student tells the others about scary night-time experiences he's been having.

However, at a Christmas party in the psychology department, a succession of stressful events begins involving tutors behaving badly that makes Becky worry she risks being thrown out of university.

Becky's advice is based on genuine therapy techniques and psychological research, and the books in this series combine humour with handy information.

Becky Bexley, Book Three

Child genius Becky Bexley entices a group of her fellow university students to play a rowdy game in class for fun one day that has worried tutors coming to investigate what's going on.

On another day, she and a group of other students have a long long discussion where they talk about such things as world leaders taking foolish risks, false rumours, and interviews with transsexuals, and they tell stories about scams and broken friendships.

The discussion often becomes humorous though, as they tell each other funny news stories, make up jokes, and think up wacky ideas for fun.

More Stories About Becky

There are more stories about the experiences of Becky Bexley the child genius at university and afterwards that can be read online here:

www.broadcaster.org.uk/beckycontents.html

Printed in Great Britain
by Amazon

23725132R00189